With Love, Thea

MADI J. ANDERSON

ISBN 979-8-9930136-1-9

Ebook ISBN 979-8-9930136-0-2

Cover by Jason Kowallis

Illustrations by Jason Kowallis

1st edition 2025

Playlist

Call Your Mom — Noah Kahan

Dan — Noah Kahan

Pink Skies — Zach Bryan

Falling Slowly — Glen Hansard and Markéta Irglová

Fix You — Cody Fry

All My Love — Noah Kahan

She Used To Be Mine — Sarah Bareilles

Northern Attitude — Noah Kahan

The Scientist — Coldplay

I miss you, I'm sorry — Gracie Abrams

Wings — Birdy

doomsday — Lizzy McAlpine

Till Forever Falls Apart — Ashe, FINNEAS

loml — Taylor Swift

You're Gonna Go Far — Noah Kahan

healing hurts — BLÜ EYES

ceilings — Lizzy McAlpine

Content Warning

Your mental health is extremely important to me. *With Love, Thea* contains content/themes that may not be suitable for all readers, including death, suicide, self-harm, alcohol abuse, scenes of intimacy, and mental health issues. Please read at your own discretion.

And if you or anyone you know is struggling with suicidal thoughts, please reach out.

Suicide Hotline: 988

Disclaimer: This book takes creative liberties with certain legal processes, especially regarding inheritance. In real life, inheriting property like a cabin usually involves probate and other legal steps. For the sake of storytelling, the characters in this novel bypass those requirements. Please don't consider anything in these pages a guide to actual law or inheritance procedures.

For Dan. Thanks for believing in me.
And for anyone who has made the choice to stay, even when it feels like the hardest thing in the world. I'm glad you're here.

Chapter One

How the hell do I do this?

That's all I can think as I sit in the car, staring at the funeral home, hands numb on the steering wheel. I know I'm supposed to go inside and—what, exactly? Grieve? Comfort my parents? The steps are all tangled in my head. I used to be great at figuring things out. Give me a math problem, a spreadsheet full of errors, my parents arguing, and I could always find the pattern, the answer that would smooth everything over. I was the smart one, the calm one. I liked that about myself. Now, I'm not so sure.

I watch my hands, willing myself to move. If I don't, maybe none of this is real. Maybe Beck will call and ask why I'm late, or I'll see him waving from the steps. But there's no reset button. It's my brother in there, not a stranger, and I can't make that not true.

Eventually, I force myself out of the car. The air outside is hotter than it should be, and it's just one more thing that feels wrong. Beck hates being hot. And he would hate this even more—the whole production, the flowers, the people. He never wanted a funeral. He said it once, offhand, like he didn't think anyone was listening. But I was.

Twenty-seven years, and it ends with a room full of people whispering about how tragic it all is. I can almost hear them now, saying his name, and my stomach twists tight.

Just get through this. Get through today, and you can go home, get out of these clothes, and be alone in the quiet.

I push through the doors and walk into a hush that's somehow more suffocating than the silence of my car. A man in a dark suit with a sorrowful smile is waiting for me. He steps forward before I can even look around.

"Ms. Miller?" he asks with a gentle voice. "I'm Tom, the funeral director. I just wanted to say that I'm so sorry for your loss."

I don't have a response, so I give him a smile that feels borrowed from someone else. A version of me that might have existed last week.

"Please let me know if there's anything you may need." Then he gives my shoulder a squeeze and steps aside. I walk in, the black high heels I bought in the middle of the night two days ago clicking on the tile floor.

The room for Beck's service looks nothing like it did when I was here for some distant uncle years ago. This time, it's much more personal. There are flowers everywhere, and tall vases and wreaths stuffed into every corner. Along one wall, there's a table draped in white, covered in photos of Beck. Him as a baby with cake smeared across his cheeks. At a track meet, standing next to our proud parents. At prom in Dad's old suit. My fingers hover just above the glass, tracing the outline of his smile. Each photo is a punch to the gut. He was real. This was his life. How can he just be gone?

A picture in the back catches my eye. It's Beck and me as teenagers at the beach. One of the last memories I have of him before things started to shift. I remember spending that whole trip reading. Beck had to practically beg me to go out into the ocean with him. Now, I wish more than anything I had just gone into the stupid water.

I peel my eyes from the photo and turn away.

Near the back of the room, my mother stands with her handkerchief, her face bare and raw, eyes bloodshot. She's not speaking, just sobbing, shoulders shaking, her grief loud and messy, impossible to ignore. Her screams from the night she called echo in my mind. There's something almost beautiful about how she lets herself fall apart. I wish I could. But I just keep standing here, feeling nothing and everything, not sure I even know how.

I take in the rest of the room, eyes landing on the thing I'm most afraid of. The casket is closed—thank God—but that doesn't matter. He's in there. Or what's left of him is. I can't picture him that way. In my head, Beck's still alive, still laughing, still making fun of my hair or stealing fries off my plate. I stand rigid, fists clenched, waiting for the reality to hit, for the tears to finally come. But nothing happens. I'm numb.

I wander from table to table, pretending to study the little shrine to Beck's life. Medals. Graduation caps. Birthday cards. His life reduced to a handful of objects. I try to remember the moments tied to each thing, try to hear his laugh. But it's already slipping away.

When all this is over, I'm going to yell at him. Not just for leaving, but for making me do all this without him.

I swallow my anger, my resentment, my grief, and stand up straighter.

Suddenly, there's a woman in front of me. I don't recognize her, but her eyes are wet with tears. "Oh, you poor dear," she says, then hugs me. My body goes stiff. I can't hug her back. I just stand there with my hands hovering, wishing it would end. She finally lets go. "How are you holding up?"

I stare at her.

That question.

I hate that question.

I finally settle on, "I'm doing okay, thank you."

She gives me a look full of pity. "So tragic. And so young. He was such a good kid. Just . . . troubled is all. At least he's in a better place."

A better place.

It sure doesn't feel like a better place. And if it is, why did he even have to come here at all? Why do any of us come here? Just to die and leave everyone else fucking miserable.

Before I can say anything, Lucy, my best friend, materializes at my side. Her yellow dress makes her stand out, but it brings a real smile to my face. Beck bought her the dress. Technically speaking, he lost an arm-wrestling match and had to. But she never let him forget it. He'd be cracking up right now.

She puts herself right between me and the woman. "Hi, I'm so sorry to interrupt, but I just need to steal Thea for a second," she says, grabbing my arm.

"Of course," the woman responds.

"Thank you so much for coming," Lucy tells her as she gracefully guides me away.

When we're out of earshot, Lucy pulls me into a hug. The tightness in my chest loosens.

"Thank you," I whisper.

She smiles. "Of course." She tucks her hair behind her ear. "Sorry I'm late. Juniper's hearing aids didn't charge, and Riggins has been messing with them all morning, but they should be here soon—"

A fresh wave of guilt hits me as she talks about her daughter. It's been years since I've seen either of them in person. Since I left for an attempt at a new life in New York. We still reach out to each other, but not as much as we should. Not as much as I should.

"Lucy," I interrupt, grabbing her hand. Her eyes meet mine. "I don't even know what to say."

"Good," she says, gently but firmly, squeezing my fingers. "Because whatever you want to say can wait. Nothing matters right now except being here with you." Her soft smile parts a little more of the fog, reminding me I'm not alone. My eyes start to sting, and I almost let go. But then I hear my mother's sobbing, and I blink the tears away, slipping my hand from Lucy's, and keep moving. Lucy doesn't go far; she lets me borrow her steadiness, just like she always has for the twenty years we've known each other.

We stand together in the last quiet minutes before the funeral home fills. The emptiness presses in, my mind already spinning with the thought of faces I barely know, hands I don't want touching me, everyone whispering about Beck. My chest tightens.

Then the doors open, and people start to filter in. Old neighbors, distant cousins, a few of Beck's friends I barely recognize now. Some keep their heads down as they sign the guest book; others glance over and offer me a sympathetic, heavy-lidded look, as if they're not sure whether to say something or just nod and move on. I stand off to the side with Lucy, letting her presence anchor me while the world gets noisier and smaller by the minute. She keeps glancing at me, asking with her eyes if I need rescuing again, but after a while, even she runs out of small talk.

The room is filling up, and the air is thick with too many flowers and too much perfume. The stories about Beck start to blur at the edges. I lose track of time, just listening, just breathing, my feet starting to ache in these dumb heels I'll never wear again.

Finally, it gets to be too much. The walls feel closer than they should, and I need out, even if it's just for a second.

"I'm going to get some air," I whisper to Lucy.

"I'll come with you," she says without missing a beat.

I shake my head. "No, it's okay. I just really need a few minutes alone."

She hesitates but eventually nods, squeezing my hand one last time before letting it go.

I slip out into the foyer and push through the doors, desperate for something that feels different. But I'm not the only one with that plan. My dad is also out here. Standing off to the side with his hands shoved deep in his coat pockets, staring out at the parking lot like he's waiting for something that isn't coming. I didn't even notice he'd come out here.

I consider turning back inside. I'm not sure I have the strength to talk to him right now, but he looks up and sees me, and that's that.

Without saying a word, we both migrate to an empty bench and have a seat. Dad just stares straight ahead, his jaw clenched. After a while, he lets out a long, shaky breath. Dad is like me. Quiet. Reserved. It was always us against the big personalities of my mother and Beck.

For a long time, neither of us moves. I count the breaths between us. People come and go behind the glass doors, the world keeps spinning, and still, we just sit there.

Finally, Dad shifts. He reaches into his coat and pulls out an envelope. He turns it in his hands, as if he's still deciding what to do, and then finally holds it out to me. His voice is rough as he speaks. "I've been carrying this around for days," he says. "I kept telling myself there'd be a better time, but there isn't. Beck left this for you. He wanted you to have it. I just . . . I couldn't do it until now."

I stare at the envelope. "What is it?"

He doesn't answer, just gives me a look that says I should open it. With shaky hands, I take it. My name is written on the front in handwriting I would know anywhere. Beck's slanted, half-messy font. My breath catches in my throat. Is this—No. I'm not opening this. I'm not doing this. I shove the letter back into my father's hands. "No." Is all I say.

He sighs, then pulls a single folded sheet of paper out of the envelope. I brace, nearly getting up to run, when I see the words "Last Will and Testament" written across the front. It's not a note explaining all this, it's . . . his will. I grab the document from my father's hand and read.

I, Beckett Miller, being of sound mind, not acting under duress or undue influence, and fully understanding the nature and extent of all my property and of this disposition thereof, hereby make, publish, and declare this document to be my Last Will and Testament.

My eyes skip down.

I devise and bequeath my property located at 435 Wondering Lane, South Creek, Colorado, together with all furnishings, fixtures, and any land associated with said property, to my sister, Thea Christine Miller, and my best friend, Hansen Reed, to be theirs absolutely and forever.

I blink, not understanding. My heart thuds hard in my chest.

Hansen Reed.

I stop reading. Then I read it again. The words blur. I read them again and again, but they don't make sense. The cabin—Beck's cabin, the one our grandfather left him. Beck's giving it to me and . . . Hansen. A man I haven't seen in seven years.

I feel dizzy.

"I don't understand," I whisper, staring at the paper. "Why would he leave me the cabin? Why would he leave it to me and Hansen?" I want to scream. "He knows I hated that place. He knows Hansen and I—" I can't finish the sentence.

"I don't know, Thea." My dad sounds tired, so tired. "He just gave me this envelope and said to make sure you got it if something ever happened to him. Maybe it was all he had to give, and he wanted you both to have something."

I look at him, a new form of desperation clinging to me. "So, you knew? You knew he was going to . . . do this?"

He shakes his head. There are tears forming in his eyes. "No. He gave this to me years ago. People do things like this sometimes. It doesn't always mean what you think."

I fold the will back up and shove it deep into my dress pocket. I don't want it. I don't want the cabin, or the memories, or the responsibility. I want Beck to walk out of the funeral home and tell me that this is all a bad joke, that he's fine, that I don't have to think about all the ways I failed him.

Dad stands, straightening his tie. "I'm sorry to drop this on you now. He had very clear instructions that you should have it as soon as possible if he were to ever pass away." He stops, like there is so much more he wants to say, but he doesn't. "I'd better go inside with your mother." Then he leans down to offer a kiss on the top of my head before walking away. I watch him go, the will burning in my pocket, my chest cracked open.

For a long minute, I just sit there, stunned. The wind smells faintly of earth and pine, and suddenly I'm ten again, sitting on the cabin steps, waiting for Beck to come back from wherever he'd wandered off to. I hated that place. I hated how lonely it felt, how every creak and groan sounded like a ghost in the walls. I don't want to go back. I don't want any of this.

My heart hammers as I stand. My hands shake. My whole body feels like it's shutting down. The only thing that exists is the overwhelming feeling of how wrong everything is.

All I can think about is Beck. I miss him so much it feels like I might split open. I wish I could cry, but the tears refuse to come.

In my mind, I hear Beck's voice: *Breathe, Thea.*

But it doesn't help. It's too much.

"Thea." My name, flat and dry, cuts through the noise. I look up and wonder if I'm imagining things. Or maybe the universe thinks I haven't been tortured enough the last few days.

Hansen Reed stands in front of me wearing a black suit, white shirt, and blue tie. His hair is slicked back, except for one stubborn strand. He looks almost exactly the same as he did back when he and Beck were inseparable, and I hate that it's good. Too good. Like he's stepped out of some magazine spread for grief, while Beck is in there, dead and gone. The unfairness of it makes something ugly twist in my chest.

His name's been mentioned over the years, but we haven't spoken in seven. He met Beck at fourteen, and the rest was history. Both were sprint stars. Both had those dumb bleached blond tips. Both fixtures in my life. Hansen spent so many nights at our house, sometimes I forgot he had a home of his own.

My mind instantly goes to the will. To the cabin. Does he somehow know? Is that why he's here?

But I can't find the words to ask. Instead, we just stare at each other. Every single memory, every single conversation, they all come rushing back like a dam that's been overflowing for years finally allowed to break. Tears prick the back of my eyes.

Keep it together. You can't break—not now, not in front of him.

"Please don't ask how I'm holding up," I finally say, hoping that my voice sounds much stronger than it feels.

He lets out a breath. His brown eyes stare so sharply into mine. There were so many times I used to look into those eyes. So many times, in the last seven years, I wished I could see them again.

"Okay. I won't," he says.

I try to move past, but pain grips me so tight I can barely breathe.

"Thea," he says again, his voice raw now. "I'm so sorry about Beck."

In my head, I want to scream at him until he tells me where it all went wrong, why this happened. Why his name is included in the last thing I'll ever get from my brother. But on the outside, for the first time in a week, tears actually come.

"Did you know?" I ask.

He blinks. "Know what?"

"Did you know that he was going to do this? That he didn't want to be here anymore?"

His chest heaves with a breath. "Thea . . ." His voice shakes.

"Forget it," I say, trying to pass him again, but he grabs my arm. It's gentle, and I hate how much I missed his touch. Our eyes lock, and I'm reminded of how much I used to crave his attention. Now, I'm just furious.

"Can we talk? Please?" he begs.

"Talk?" I let out a bitter laugh. "You want to talk? About what?" My words come out cruel. "How you walked away from my brother when he needed you?"

How you walked away from me?

"No, you don't get to show up at my brother's funeral and ask to talk," I say.

He drops my arm. "Thea, I—"

I cut him off, tears spilling over. "You failed him, Hansen. You walked away." My finger jabs at his chest. "He's gone because of you."

He's unmoving. And it pisses me off even more. I want him to scream at me. To tell me I'm wrong. That it's not his fault my brother is gone. That it's mine.

But he doesn't. So, I continue. "It doesn't matter what either of us has to say now."

I reach into my pocket, pull out the will, and shove it at his chest. "Here," I say, voice shaking. "It's Beck's will. He left us the cabin. Both of us." I laugh, but it's devoid of all humor. "I don't want it. I don't want any of it. You take it. You take all of it."

He looks stunned, glancing down at the paper, then back up at me.

"I have to go," I say, wiping the tears from my face and turning away before he can say anything else.

All week, I've wished to feel something. But now, with Hansen ripping that door open, I realize that feeling won't bring Beck back. Maybe it's better that I feel nothing at all.

You just have to get through the rest of your life, Thea. That's all.

Chapter Two

Leaving South Creek feels off, like I'm forgetting something important but can't put my finger on what. I have all these memories stacked up—some good, some I'd rather not touch—but I didn't realize how much I missed it until I came back. The hardest part is saying goodbye to Lucy. She's always been the one thing that makes sense here, and seeing her again just reminds me how much I need her. How much I still feel alone, even with her right there. But there's work and New York and this idea that if I just hold on a little longer, I'll be able to come back when life feels less upside-down.

I only took a week off for the funeral. Even that felt risky. My boss, Albert Peterson, has this way of looking at you like you're wasting his time, which is rich for a guy with cufflinks that probably cost more than my rent. When I told him why I needed the time, he barely looked up from his laptop. I guess empathy isn't really a thing at Peterson & Weston.

When I get back to New York, the city just keeps moving. The trees outside my window still claw at the glass. My neighbor's dog still loses his mind at every person who passes. Sunlight still finds a way to wake me up way too early, same as always. Nothing has changed, except now there's a grinding ache inside me.

I go through the motions. I walk home from work the long way, past the bakery where I used to get coffee, the yoga studio I stopped going to after Beck got really sick. Sometimes I wonder if I'm just floating through my own life, invisible. The city is loud and busy and full of people, but I feel like I might just fade into the background if I stand still too long. I lie awake at night, counting cracks in my ceiling, tired but wired, like my brain won't give me a break.

The ache in my chest doesn't go away. Grief isn't dramatic, it turns out. It's slow and stubborn. It's just there, always, like a bruise I keep hidden. Some days it's all I can think about. Most days, I just try to keep moving.

A few days slip by. Then a week. Then two. I keep showing up for work, answering emails, nodding along in meetings. Eventually, my coworkers stop giving me that look that's half sympathy, half awkwardness, like they weren't sure if I'd start crying or just combust. I think I'm getting better at pretending to be normal, but honestly, nothing has changed. Every day feels like a copy of the last one. I do the same numb routine with the same dull ache under everything.

A month passes. Four weeks since the funeral, five since Beck. Time feels like it's barely moved, but also like everything that mattered happened a hundred years ago.

It's Monday morning, and the office is already buzzing at 9:10 a.m. The phones are ringing, the printers howling. Someone is laughing like it's Friday instead of Monday. I nod at a few people without really seeing them and duck into my cubicle. The spreadsheet on my screen is just a blur of numbers. I keep hoping routine will dull the edge of this pain, but numbers can't fix this.

The truth is, I never even wanted this job. Right after college, I didn't have a plan, just a friend with an apartment in New York and a promise that he could get me in at Peterson & Weston. I wasn't sure. Part of me wanted to go back to South Creek, but that felt like admitting I'd made a mistake by leaving in the first place. So I took the job, moved to the city, and years later, I'm still here. Stuck in a job I never really wanted, too scared to make a move, and not sure where I'd even go if I did.

I make it through the whole day mostly unnoticed. At some point, I must have eaten lunch. I must have answered at least a dozen emails. I'm pretty sure I even went to a meeting.

It's a few minutes before five when Mary from HR stops by my desk, clutching her cartoon cat mug. "Hey, Thea. Did you get that compliance training email? They need everyone to click through by Friday." Her tone is bright and practiced.

I blink, trying to process the question. "Yeah. I saw it."

"Great. Just making sure." And then she's gone, weaving through the office with her mug, on to the next box to check.

Is this really my life now? Going to a job I've never liked? Talking to people I hardly know? Clicking through compliance emails by Friday?

I shut down my computer, gather my things, and work on convincing myself I've made it through another day.

I'm halfway to the subway when my phone starts ringing. It's an unknown number. I almost ignore it, but something makes me answer.

"Hello?"

"Thea?" The voice on the other end is hesitant but familiar. And I'd recognize it anywhere.

It's Hansen.

Just hearing him say my name makes my stomach drop. I pause on the crowded sidewalk, letting people stream around me, suddenly unsteady.

He says something, and I think he's asking me if I'm still there, but I can barely hear him over the city noise and the static in my own head. There's no way I can talk to Hansen. Not here. Not now. I pull the phone away from my ear, quickly hang up, and shove it into my bag. Then I stand frozen for a minute, heart pounding.

By the time I finally make it back to my apartment, my face is wet, and I'm not even sure when I started crying.

I sink onto the floor, staring at my bag like it might explode. Then, like a bad dream, my phone starts ringing again.

I don't move as the muffled ringtone plays itself out. When it's over, I reach into my bag and pull out the phone. This time, there's a voicemail. My first instinct is to delete it and pretend none of this is happening. But that's exactly what I've been doing for weeks, and so far, it hasn't worked out.

As much as it would be easier, I can't run from Hansen. Not anymore. Not with Beck gone.

So, I press play.

Hansen's voice is raw. "Uh, hey. It's me again. I'm sorry about earlier. I shouldn't have called you out of the blue like that. I just . . . I wasn't really sure what else to do." He clears his throat. "I went to the cabin the other day. You wouldn't even recognize it now. It's still standing, but it needs a lot of work. I want you to know, Thea, I can take care of it. Whatever that means." His voice cracks, and then he says, "I just hope we can talk. About this. About everything. Just . . . call me back. If you want." There's a pause. Then, "Take your time."

The line goes dead. I listen again and again, like the words might change. But they never do.

I wander my apartment, opening drawers, desperate for something to anchor me. At the bottom of my nightstand, I find it: Beck's letter. The only one he ever sent. It was years ago during one of his better stretches at the inpatient facility. At the end of the letter, there's a drawing. It's a simple one of his dream of the cabin. All lush green, and a wraparound porch and two chairs by a firepit. There are a few words written under it:

I'll make it a place we actually want to be, Thea just wait.

I did wait. Fifteen years of waiting. For Beck to get better, to keep a promise, and to take his illness seriously. I stopped believing he ever would. The last time he'd called about the cabin, he needed cash for repairs. I told him no. I was tired, and I didn't trust him not to waste it. I thought if I cut him off, maybe he'd finally hit rock bottom and crawl back up. But what if that was the last straw? What if I pushed him too hard?

Now all that's left is guilt and this empty ache. And the cabin he always dreamed would save him.

I slam the drawer shut, but there's no shutting Beck out. I hear his voice in my head: *You owe me this.*

I try to pull myself together. For a while, I stand at the window, watching the city drag itself toward evening. I keep thinking about Hansen's message, about Beck's drawing, about how easily everything slips away. Maybe I could just ignore it. Let Hansen deal with the mess, let the cabin rot. But then what? The last piece of Beck would just fade away. I can't let that happen. Not because I think I can fix anything, but because I can't stand the idea of losing even the ghost of him.

Thinking some air might help my racing thoughts, I grab my keys and let myself out, walking slowly, letting the city noise replace the chaos in my head. I'm not sure how long I wander, but it's long enough for the sun to duck behind the buildings, long enough for my thoughts to go quiet for once.

When I come back, my landlord is fussing with the mail in the foyer. "Oh, Taylor. Good to see you," she says.

I almost laugh. "It's Thea, Mrs. Smith."

"Right. Thea." She peers over her glasses. "You all right? You look like you've seen a ghost."

Yeah, it feels that way, too. "I'm fine. Just tired."

She sighs. "Maybe you should take a vacation. That's what I do whenever I'm feeling tired."

A vacation. I scoff, but there's something in her idea. Maybe that's what I do. Take one last trip to the place where Beck tried to build something good. But as I stand there, the word *vacation* starts to unravel. I picture myself packing a bag, buying a plane ticket, but I know I wouldn't just go for a weekend and come back. The thought of returning, of picking up where I left off, of walking back into the office, into this apartment, makes my stomach turn.

What would it mean to actually leave? Not just visit, but let go of this city, this job, this version of myself that's been stuck for so long? The idea terrifies me. But there's a glimmer of relief in it too, like the first deep breath after being underwater.

I realize I'm still standing with Mrs. Smith at the bottom of the stairs, keys in my hand. She's watching me, waiting for something. "Well, you take care—" she begins to say.

"Hey, actually, do you have a second to talk about my lease?" I interrupt, and even as the words leave my mouth, I can't believe I'm saying them. But for the first time in months, maybe years, I feel the tiniest spark of something like hope. Or at least, motion.

I'm going back home.

Chapter Three

FIFTEEN YEARS AGO

On a scale of one to a million, my dread for gym class was off the charts. But something I dreaded even more? The first track day in gym class. There was something so humiliating about being forced to run in circles under the hot August sun, sweat sticking my shirt to my back, while the rest of my classmates made it all look easy. I always felt like the universe had designed gym class specifically to remind me I was built for the library, not for sports.

I stood at the edge of the field, arms crossed, eyeing the faded white lines that ran endless loops around the football field. Our gym teacher barked instructions, but I was too busy calculating how slowly I could jog without getting yelled at. It felt like a special kind of torture to have us do this the first week of school. I just wanted to get through it without doing anything embarrassing.

When the whistle blew, I started off at a reluctant jog with my head down, just trying to blend in. I was in dead last place rounding the curve by the bleachers when a blur of motion shot past me. Someone's arm clipped mine hard, and before I could even react, my foot caught on the uneven track, and I went down. My palms and knees landed roughly on the hot asphalt. The sting shot up my arms, while heat radiated from the ground to my skin.

For a second, I didn't move. I was positive my classmates had just witnessed the embarrassing fall. There was no way I could get up and brush it off like it never happened.

Maybe if I stayed still long enough, the earth would just swallow me whole.

Then a shadow fell across me.

"Oh my God, I'm so sorry," the voice of the shadow said. He dropped down beside me, his hands hovering awkwardly like he wanted to help but didn't know how. "Are you okay?"

I looked up. I recognized the boy from class, but we hadn't met yet. He was tall and too skinny for his height, with sun-bleached hair sticking up in wild directions, and cheeks flushed from running and panic. He was cute. Annoyingly so.

"I'm fine," I mumbled, still making zero attempt to get up. "It's not the first time I've been invisible."

His brow furrowed. "No, you weren't—I did see you. I just couldn't stop myself in time. I swear I'm not usually this much of a disaster." He reached out to offer his hand.

I took it, realizing I couldn't hide in the middle of the track forever. As he gently pulled me up, a dozen eyes burned into my back. My cheeks burned red. I waited for him to laugh, or maybe toss out some snarky comment so that everyone would laugh. Instead, he just looked worried. I wanted to walk away and pretend I didn't care, but for some reason I couldn't. Because he wasn't making fun of me. He was apologizing.

"Really, I'm so sorry," he said. "I just started here, and I guess I got carried away trying to show off to the Coach Warren."

"It's okay," I said, softer this time. "Seriously. Gym class is hazardous anyway."

He finally managed a shaky laugh. "Still, I owe you—uh, what's your name?"

"Thea," I said, dusting off my hands.

He grinned. "I thought so. I'm Hansen." He stuck his hand out, like we were supposed to shake on it. I hesitated but ultimately shook it. His palm was sweaty, but somehow that made him seem even more real.

"How did you know who I was?"

He looked embarrassed as he glanced down at his sneakers. "I, uh, joined the track team this week. Your brother, Beck, he introduced himself right away, told me all about the team, and mentioned his sister was in my grade."

I rolled my eyes. "Yeah, Beck likes to talk."

Hansen smiled. "He said you guys both have the same eyes. So, I just guessed."

I almost smiled back. "That's some next-level detective work."

He laughed, the tension finally easing from his shoulders. "Only when eye color is involved, apparently. Sorry again for running into you."

"It's fine."

His face softened, and I noticed how deep his brown eyes were. I looked away before he could catch me staring.

"Well, I better get back to it." He started to jog backward, still grinning, and a single piece of hair fell onto his forehead. "See you around, Thea."

For the rest of class, every time Hansen sprinted past with that easy, loping stride, I felt his eyes on me. And that night, when Beck mentioned a new boy on the track team, and how fast he was, and how he might break the school record, I didn't say anything. I just sat there, letting their conversation swirl around me, and remembering a pair of brown eyes.

❧❧❧❧❧ ❦❦❦❦❦

The next evening, I was curled up in the old wingback chair by the window, knees tucked tight to my chest while writing. It was my favorite spot in the house, the only place I could fade into the background and let the noise of my family become something distant.

But the quiet didn't last long. The front door slammed open, and Beck's voice filled the house. "Mom! I'm home! And I brought someone!"

I heard my mother's footsteps as she entered the kitchen. "Oh, how wonderful. You must be Hansen. Beck's told us so much about you."

My stomach dropped. *Hansen*. As in the guy who ran me over yesterday. As in the cute guy who ran me over yesterday. As in the cute guy who ran me over and noticed my eye color yesterday.

Shit.

A laugh drifted into the room. The same laugh that filled my head last night as I tried to sleep. The words on my page started to blur. I didn't look up. I didn't want to see him again, not when I was already in my safe place, not when I still felt foolish about how flustered he'd made me. I pressed my pencil so hard to the page it nearly tore.

Beck's voice boomed again. "Told you he was taller in real life."

Then my mother called out, that gentle warning in her tone. "Come say hello to your brother's friend, Thea."

I froze, pretending to scribble something in my notebook, hoping she'd forget about me. But a few minutes later, Beck and Hansen rounded the corner and spilled into the living room. Beck spotted me instantly, his grin widening.

"There she is," he said, as if I'd been hiding. (Which I absolutely was). "She's always in her chair."

Hansen looked even taller inside our cramped living room. His hair was as messy as yesterday, and he looked just as cute as I remembered. His dark eyes found mine, and he smiled.

"Hey, you," he said.

Beck's eyes swung my way. Instead of answering, I tried to shrink farther into the chair.

"Oh yeah, that's right. You two are in gym class together," Beck said. "Small world." Then, without a second thought, he grabbed my notebook straight out of my hand.

"Beck," I groaned.

He ignored me, of course. "She's always writing something in his notebook. You'll get used to it."

I reached out and took the notebook back. Beck just laughed.

"I think it's cool," Hansen said quietly, as if it were a secret just for me. I didn't know what to say to that, so I just looked away, hoping he wouldn't see how red my cheeks were.

Dinner was a whirlwind of Beck and Hansen trading stories, my father actually chuckling at their jokes, my mother bombarding Hansen with questions and beaming at every answer. Beck had always been great at making friends. His larger-than-life personality was one that drew people to him. What was hard for him was keeping the friends.

I wasn't optimistic that Hansen would last long.

After dinner, when the plates were cleared and the dishwasher started, I retreated to my chair. I tried to write, but the words wouldn't come. I could hear Beck and Hansen laughing in the hallway as their voices bounced off the walls.

It wasn't long before footsteps creaked across the living room floor. Someone lingered in the doorway, but I kept my eyes down on my notebook.

Then a pair of battered sneakers entered my field of vision. "Hey," Hansen said, voice lower now, not quite as cocky as earlier. "Can I sit?"

I shrugged, not trusting myself to look at him. He dropped onto the ottoman across from me. He didn't say anything for a while, and I was aware of every inch of space between us. I could hear the faint clatter of dishes in the kitchen. The house felt unusually still.

"You're a bit of a mystery, you know that?" he said after a minute. Not in a teasing way, more curious.

I looked up. "Not really."

"You hardly said two words at dinner."

"Probably because I didn't have anything to say."

He smirked. "Liar."

That caught me off guard. "Excuse me?"

"I saw your notebook. You've got pages and pages in there. Nobody with that much to write has nothing to say."

I stared at him, really annoyed that he was right. "Maybe I just like writing better than talking."

He gave that some thought. "Maybe. Or maybe you're just careful with who you talk to."

"No offense, but you don't know me."

Hansen leaned back, stretching his arms over his head before letting them drop to his knees. "You're right. I don't. So why don't you tell me something then."

I closed my notebook and hugged it to my chest, trying to look casual. This was a silly game, but I didn't want him to leave. So, I'd play.

"I have brown hair," I said.

He snorted a real laugh. "How about something a little less obvious?"

"I like to write."

His lips twitched. "Oh, she's got jokes."

I tried to hide my smile, but there was no way he didn't see it.

"Beck says you're annoyingly smart. Is that true?" he asked.

Heat crept up my neck. "You'll learn quickly that Beck exaggerates."

"I have a feeling he's not exaggerating on this one." Hansen said it like it was the simplest thing in the world, like it was obvious. He leaned forward, and his knees nearly brushed mine. "You should own it."

"Being annoyingly smart?"

He bumped my knee with his own. "Yes."

The touch jolted me. I tried to play it off by rolling my eyes, but I'm not certain I was successful.

"It's not exactly something people like about me," I said. "Most of the time, it just makes things harder."

He grinned, sitting back but not looking away. "I like it," he said. And not quietly. "I like that you're not trying to impress anyone."

I snorted out a laugh, glancing at him. "Oh, I am. It's just not working."

Why the hell did I just admit that to him?

And why did it feel so easy?

He searched my face. "Maybe you're hanging out with the wrong people."

"Maybe."

He was quiet for a minute before asking, "What are you writing in there, anyway?" He eyed the notebook in my lap.

I looked down. "Oh. Nothing really. Just my thoughts."

He nodded slowly, a little smile dancing at the corner of his mouth. "I think that's pretty cool. Putting your thoughts down like that."

"I think the cool thing is probably talking about them out loud."

"I don't really think it matters," he said. "As long as you're getting the stuff out before it eats you alive."

"You sound like you speak from experience."

He hesitated. His hands fidgeted with the laces of his sneakers. For the first time since he ran into me on the track, he wouldn't meet my eyes. Then he rubbed a hand over his face. "My dad died recently," he admitted. "Car accident."

My stomach dropped at his confession. "I'm so sorry, Hansen."

He shrugged. "That's why we moved to South Creek. My mom wanted me to have a fresh start. Said there were too many painful memories at our old place."

"Did you want to move?"

He looked up, startled, like the question had caught him off guard.

"No," he said finally. "I didn't want to move."

I really didn't know what to say, so I chose not to say anything at all. Instead, I just sat with him in the moment. When he spoke again, his words were smaller, like he was afraid of them. "My mom was really struggling, though, so I get it. It feels like she blames me sometimes. He was picking me up from school when the accident happened."

In his words, I felt his sadness and guilt. "Hansen," I said softly, "it's not your fault. You know that, right?"

He nodded, but I could tell he didn't believe me.

"I can't imagine how hard that must have been for you," I said. "For both of you."

He let out a shaky breath. "Yeah. It just gets stuck in my head sometimes."

"Maybe you should write about it," I suggested.

Hansen looked at me and smiled. "Maybe I will." He rubbed the back of his neck as he let out a breath. "Sorry—I have no idea why I just trauma-dumped all that on you. I don't usually talk like this." He shook his head and looked so embarrassed it was adorable. "I guess you're just . . . easy to talk to, or something."

"Don't worry. That feeling will pass."

He laughed. "Again with the jokes."

Just then, Beck's voice echoed down the hallway, breaking whatever thing had started to build between us. Hansen stood and gave me that crooked grin one last time. "I think you and I are going to be great friends, Thea Miller."

I felt my lips twitch with the start of a real smile.

He disappeared down the hall, and I watched him go, my heart fluttering in my chest, annoyed at myself for caring but unable to stop.

Chapter Four

Now

The drive up to the cabin takes longer than I remember. The road winds through what used to be nothing but pines and quiet, but now the trees are thinner, the silence broken by the hum of construction and the occasional golf cart zipping down the shoulder. Every so often, my phone vibrates in the passenger seat with another email I won't answer, another reminder of the life I left behind.

I quit my job with no notice, just a blunt email and a box of desk junk left for the cleaning crew. Maybe it was reckless. Maybe I'll regret it tomorrow, or next week. But right now, I can't find the energy to care. I'm a great accountant, but I was never going to bleed for a place that would forget about me by Monday. If my savings run out, so be it. I want to feel like I'm choosing something, even if it's just leaving.

By the grace of God, Mrs. Smith let me break my apartment lease. So, I shoved all I owned into the trunk of my car and started driving. I figured if I was going to do this, if I was going to go back to South Creek, I might as well fully commit.

Nobody knows I'm here. Not my parents, not Lucy, not Hansen.

The turnoff to the cabin is exactly where it's always been, but the driveway feels smaller, choked by weeds and the kind of wildflowers that grow wherever they please. The cabin itself sits at the end with its faded brown paint that's peeling in long strips. The roof is sagging in places, the shingles are curling like old leaves, and the windows are streaked with years of dirt. One of them is cracked from the inside. There are weeds where the flower beds used to be, so dense they almost cover the path to the steps. The place looks fragile, like one hard wind would knock it down for good.

I tell myself I'm ready for this. That I didn't torch my whole life in New York just to sit here paralyzed in the driveway. But my hands are shaking on the steering wheel, and for a second, I almost turn the car around. Who am I kidding? I don't feel ready. I feel hollow and scared and so far out of my depth I might drown. But doing nothing feels worse. So, I get out, gravel crunching under my boots, and force myself toward the porch.

There are remnants of what looks like someone trying to repair the deck. Piles of wood stacked near the front door, and a hammer. Beck must have come here. When, I don't really know. Toward the end of his life, we didn't really talk much.

The first step of the porch gives under my weight with a sickening crack, and my leg plunges through halfway up my shin. For a moment, I just stay there, heart pounding, until I pull myself out, jeans streaked with dirt and splinters. "Seems like a fitting start," I mutter, brushing off my hands.

There's a collection of business cards wedged in the crack between the door and the wall. Different logos, same desperate message: SELL NOW, FAST CASH, PRIME LOCATION. One has a handwritten note—*Call me! Buyers waiting!*—with a smiley face at the end.

I shove them in my pocket. They want the land, not the cabin. Nobody wants the cabin. Nobody but Beck.

Under the beat-up doormat, the spare key Beck hid is still there. I nearly laugh. Then I unlock the door. It creaks open like it's been waiting for years. The smell of it hits me first. It's a swirl of damp wood, mold, rust, and rot. Inside, the living room is a mess of broken glass and food wrappers. The old couch is slumped in the center, with bits of drywall from the ceiling scattered on top of it and across the floor.

The worst part is the silence that's so thick, I swear I can almost see it.

But I swallow my dread and step inside. As I walk around, a breeze moves through the cracked walls, carrying the scent of pine and something sweet. And I swear I hear Beck's laugh, muffled and far away.

My hand trails along the dusty walls, fingers catching on splinters. I open every drawer, every cabinet. All I find are empty bottles and dead flies. In the kitchen, I peek under the rug, yank open the fridge (which is a mistake, since there's been no power for who knows how long), and slam it shut again, gagging at the smell.

Then I head to the stairs, taking two at a time.

The second floor is in better shape than the main level. There are two bedrooms, one bathroom, and a short hallway full of dust. I head to the room Beck and I used to share and yank open the door. Sunlight slants through the cracked window, and my eyes land on a stack of boxes and large black garbage bags in the corner, thrown together like someone meant to come back for them and never did.

My heart pounds so loud, I'm certain it's vibrating off the walls.

I want to walk out. Leave all this for someone else to deal with. But I also can't bring myself to leave. This room is the last place he tried to make his own, the last scraps of him that haven't been boxed up or thrown away.

Beck didn't have many things to his name when he died. He was living with my parents the last four months of his life, and anything he left behind is untouched in that room. I didn't go in it during the week of the funeral. Every time I walked by, it was like I'd catch on fire if I dared to look inside.

My father went in once, briefly, to look for any type of note or explanation. He never found anything.

But now, these things are here, right in front of me. And I'm not on fire.

I grab the bags first, ripping them open to find only clothes. Beck's clothes. And they smell just like him. Emotion grips me with fierce strength. I pull out a few pieces, trying to remember if I'd ever seen him wear it, letting myself get lost in the memories.

After taking my time folding them and placing them gently in piles, I move to the boxes. The first one is full of unopened bills, most stamped with a red PAST DUE. Electricity, water, credit cards. The numbers get worse with every envelope, the threats more urgent. Some are months old. Others, years. My heart drops as I flip through them. I know Beck had issues with money; that is no surprise. But seeing it on paper just makes it all the more real.

I toss the bills aside, the pain in my heart growing stronger. I open the next box. Bottles. Again. Just like in the kitchen. Vodka, whiskey, gin. All empty or with just a few swigs left. My hands shake as I lift one, and all I can see is the last year. How he lied about drinking again. How we learned that he hadn't been taking his medication.

Something hot and wild breaks loose inside me, and I hurl the bottle against the wall with no hesitation. It shatters, glass spraying across the floor. I grab another, and another, throwing them hard enough that my arm aches, until the closet is empty and my breath is ragged. Each crash is a question he'll never answer.

My vision starts to blur, and I realize I'm crying. I slump against the wall, surrounded by broken glass and the stink of old booze. I reach for one last bottle, but my hand slips. The glass breaks wrong, and I feel it before I see it—a sharp sting across my palm. The blood appears fast. I gasp, clutching my hand and swearing under my breath. The pain is hot, making the room tilt and blur.

I'm on the floor, knees drawn up, trying to press my hand against my shirt to stop the bleeding, when I hear the grind of tires on gravel out front. Then a car door slams, and footsteps crunch up the path. Panic rises in me, but before I can move, the front door creaks open.

"Hello?" The voice echoes up the stairs.

You've got to be kidding me.

The footsteps make their way up slowly. I wish the floor would swallow me whole, or maybe that the stairs would collapse, and he'd have no way up. But when he steps into view, I know neither wish is coming true.

Hansen takes one look at me, at the blood, the glass, the mess, and his whole face tightens. "Thea?"

I honestly can't find any words to explain the situation I've found myself in.

He blinks, then his dark eyes drop to my hand. "What the hell happened?"

"It's nothing," I snap, sharper than I mean to. I can't help it. Everything feels like glass in my chest.

"It doesn't look like nothing."

"I was trying to clean up the bottles and accidentally cut myself on one." I know my story makes absolutely zero sense given the amount of broken glass in the room, but it's the one I'm going with.

Thankfully, he doesn't push. Just steps closer, his face softening. "Let me see your hand."

"I said I'm fine."

"You're not. You probably need stitches—"

"Hansen, just stop. You don't have to pretend to care."

He sighs, but there's a gentleness in it, and it makes my throat tighten. "I'm not pretending. Just let me help, Thea." He doesn't wait for my protest again. Instead, he kneels beside me and tears a strip of fabric from his shirt. He moves slowly, like if he goes too fast, I'll bolt.

"Let me see your hand."

Against my better judgment, I let him. Because even beneath all the guilt and anger, there's a version of me that once felt comforted by him. That version is still here, bruised but not dead.

His fingers are warm and careful as he wraps the cloth around my palm. I look away, my jaw clenched so tight it aches. It's more than just the pain. It's being touched by Hansen after all these years. It's been so long, it's nearly as painful as the cut.

When he's finished, he releases my hand and moves away.

"I still think you need stitches," he says.

"I'll take that into consideration."

Just a whisper of a smile appears on his face. "When did you get here?"

"About an hour ago."

He lets out a breath. "And how long are you staying?"

My eyes move to his. "I don't know."

He gives a gentle nod. Silence stretches between us. Then he speaks low. "What do you want to do here, Thea?"

What do I want? What a loaded question. What I want is to wake up somewhere else, someone else. But every time I close my eyes, I see Beck. I see my guilt. I see all the unanswered calls. I see it all.

"You first," I say, voice barely above a whisper. I want him to decide so I don't have to.

"We could sell it as is," he says. "Let someone else deal with the mess and the hassle."

"And they'll just tear it down and build a cookie-cutter vacation home."

"Most likely. But I've been researching, and we'd get a lot for it."

I won't lie. The money is tempting. My parents have already paid off all of Beck's debts, and I have no job. I've always wanted to go back to school. Get my doctoral degree. And college is expensive. It could help. But the idea twists inside me. Selling it would be the easiest way out, but it would also be the final betrayal. Knowing that someone else was here, tearing down all the memories, all the things Beck cared about. Just another way I would be failing him.

"Is that what you want? To sell it?" I ask.

"I don't know. I can't help but feel that I would be betraying Beck if I did."

"Yeah, I know what you mean."

He takes a beat. "We could fix it up first. Do all the things Beck wanted to do. That way, we would have control over it. *Then* we could sell it. Unless, of course, you want to live here—"

"No," I quickly interject. "I don't want to live here. I just—I can't just let them tear it down."

Hansen stands, a newly found pep in his step. "Okay. So, I fix it up and sell it. We can split whatever we get fifty-fifty. I can come here on my days off and do most of the work. You wouldn't even have to do anything. You could go back to your life."

I let out a sound that's too close to a laugh. *What life?* I think, but I don't have the courage to say it out loud.

"Seriously, Thea. Beck left this place to both of us, not just you. If you want out, just say the word. I'll handle it. It's the least I can do."

I look around at the wreckage. At the bottles, the bills, the broken things nobody bothered to fix. The anger drains out of me, leaving only this raw emptiness. I want to tell Hansen to handle it himself, to just let me disappear again. But I can't. If I leave now, I'll just keep running, from Beck, from this place, from myself. And I'm so tired of running.

"You didn't tell anyone you were coming back, did you?" Hansen asks in a gentle voice, like he already knows the answer.

"No," I admit, and I hate that he can still see right through me.

Hansen's brown eyes are so deep, I can understand why I once lost myself in them. He looks as worn out as I feel.

The cabin is Beck's mess, but it's mine too. Or maybe this is the only thing I still know how to do: stay and try to make things right, because that's what Beck would have wanted.

"I'm staying," I whisper. "I have to make this right."

Hansen's brow furrows. "You're staying?"

I nod. "To help fix it up and sell it."

He looks genuinely stunned. "I can do it, Thea."

"I know you can do it," I bite back. "Believe me, I know how capable you are. But I want to do it too. So, I'm staying."

"What about New York? Your job?"

"There is no job, and there is no New York," I say, matter of fact. "So, I'm staying."

Something much stronger than just surprise flashes across his face. I don't want him to question me, so I keep going. "I don't know why this had to happen," I say, trying not to cry again. "But it's happening, so I'm going to see it through. For Beck."

Hansen watches me, and I can feel all the things we're not saying crowding the space between us. Any questions I have for him now are too tangled up with my own guilt.

Then he surprises me by asking, "So, partners, then?"

I freeze. Something about that feels personal, and so fucking scary. I haven't thought much about what staying means for Hansen and me. How close we'll have to be. How much we'll have to see each other.

"We don't have to be friends, Thea," he continues, sensing my discomfort. "When this is done, we can go back to never talking again, okay?"

My mind is screaming at me to run as far as I can. Get back in my car and drive until I hit the ocean. But I also know I have nowhere else to go.

"Okay," I say. Not because I've forgiven him. But because, for now, I can't bear to do this alone. "And we'll split the cost of the renovation." I leave no room for him to argue.

He nods. "Deal." He gestures toward the door. "Come on, I'll take you to the hospital for your hand."

I'm about to say I'm fine when I glance down and see the blood soaked through the fabric, and all the pain I've been trying to ignore pulses through my hand. So, I agree.

Chapter Five

Turns out Hansen was right. I needed stitches. According to Dr. Williams at South Creek Memorial, it "could've been a lot worse," and I "should be grateful it didn't cut a major artery." After some quick dissolvable stitches and a wrap, he sent me on my way.

I now sit in the hard plastic chair, cradling my bandaged hand, trying to ignore the steady throb pulsing under the gauze. The stitches itch already, and I keep glancing at the automatic doors, half-hoping Lucy won't actually come, even though I'm the one who called her.

When she bursts in, she looks like she came straight from her office. Working as the marketing manager for her dad's company, she wears a white blouse and her hair pulled back in a perfect slicked-back bun. She clutches her keys in one hand and phone in the other. When she spots me, she hurries over, and the worry is etched so deep in her face it makes me feel guilty.

"Oh my God, Thea. What happened?" She drops her bag at my feet and kneels down, reaching for my good hand as if she needs to check that I'm real. "Are you okay?"

"I'm fine," I manage, though my voice comes out small. "Just some stitches."

She sits back, eyeing me. "You call me out of the blue, tell me you're back in South Creek, and then drop the little detail that you're at the hospital? What the hell, Thea?"

I sigh, my guilt only growing. "I'm sorry. Things got messy. I didn't know how to explain."

Lucy shakes her head, her exasperation melting into concern. "You always say that. Now, let me see." She inspects my bad hand with a gentle touch. "Looks like you lost a fight with something."

"A glass bottle," I mutter. "It was my fault. Wasn't paying attention."

"Don't scare me like that again, okay?"

"I won't." It's a lie and she knows it, but she lets it slide.

Lucy stands. "Come on. You're coming home with me. I'm not letting you bleed out in some hotel. Or even worse, your parents' house."

"Actually," I say as I stand. "I was hoping I could stay with you and Juniper for a while."

She softens instantly. "Really?"

"I'm staying in South Creek for a bit. Just while I deal with the cabin."

She pulls me into a hug. "Of course, Thea. Stay as long as you need. Juniper will be thrilled."

That makes me smile.

Outside, the sky is slate gray, the air hinting at rain. Lucy unlocks her car, glancing at me sideways. "So, you do know you have to tell me what happened and why you're here, right?"

"I promise I'll explain it all."

We both hop in the car. But before she starts it, she turns to me. "You might want to start with why I saw Hansen Reed sitting in his car when I got here."

❧❧❧❧❧ ❧❧❧❧❧

Lucy's house isn't far from the hospital. It's a cute white place with a crooked porch and handmade wind chimes jingling in the breeze. It's in a good neighborhood. One where you would feel safe keeping your front door unlocked. She and her ex-husband, Riggins, bought it when Juniper was a few years old. After they divorced two years ago, he insisted she stay here.

She parks out front, and we head inside. It smells faintly of cinnamon, Lucy's favorite scent of candles. I've always said you can tell a lot about a person by what candle scent they enjoy. My mother was always jasmine or fresh linens. Lucy, anything having to do with baked goods. Beck loved all things pine. He didn't care if it was the middle of summer, he wanted to burn a Christmas tree candle.

Before the door can shut behind us, Juniper comes running into the room, her smile a sight for sore eyes. She's so much like her mom with her dark curly hair pulled into a messy bun and an oversized hoodie swallowing her small frame. Even though I just saw her at Beck's funeral, I swear she's grown three inches. "Aunt Thea," she signs.

"Hi, Junie."

When Juniper was born early, it was devastating. There was a good chunk of time where doctors weren't sure if she was going to make it. I remember so vividly visiting Lucy at home. She was only sixteen, just a child herself, and dealing with her daughter being in the NICU. The doctors were amazing, and ultimately, Juniper was okay. But they found pretty early on that she had profound hearing loss. Enough that she needed hearing aids, and the doctors urged Lucy and Riggins to learn sign language.

They didn't skip a beat. Before she was even home from the NICU, the two signed up for classes. By the time Juniper was four, all three were speaking it fluently.

I also took lessons. Not as much as Lucy, but I tried my best. I hate that my time in New York has caused me to forget quite a large chunk of it.

Juniper pulls me in for a quick hug. Then she notices my bandaged hand. "Are you okay? Mom said you were at the hospital," she says, using her hands and voice. She doesn't always speak out loud, but when she's around people who don't know ASL very well, she usually does.

"Yeah. I'm okay. Just clumsy."

She grins, and I vow to spend any spare time I have brushing up on my signing.

"Mom also said you're staying with us."

I smile. "I am."

That has her beaming. "Well, you're in luck then, because I just made some lemonade. You want some?"

"More than you know." Then, remembering, I add the sign for *thank you*.

Juniper keeps the smile on her face and hugs me again before darting off to the kitchen.

"She's really excited to have you here," Lucy says while walking me to the guest room.

"She'll learn pretty quickly that all I really have to offer are my math skills."

Lucy scoffs. "That could be good for her. She needs all the extra help she can get in that department."

I put the one suitcase I brought with me in the corner of the guest room. The room is smaller than I'm used to, and yet I feel totally comfortable. Like I've been away from home for so long, and I'm finally back and can take a deep breath. "I just feel bad that my sign language is not what it used to be," I admit.

Lucy faces me with a comforting smile. "We can work on it." Then she gestures toward the room. "Well, make yourself at home. Juniper's got play practice in an hour, but we'll be back for dinner. I'm making spaghetti."

It may sound plain, but Lucy is a goddess in the kitchen. Even her spaghetti is worthy of writing home about.

"Thank you, Lucy. For the room. For dinner. For everything."

Her emerald eyes meet mine, and there's nothing but love in them.

"Just no snooping in my bedroom drawers," she says. "Unless you want to see some very disturbing things that, frankly, I'm not sure you're mature enough to handle."

I laugh. "Deal."

When they leave for play practice, I let myself collapse onto the bed. Then, I open my laptop to watch endless videos on cabin renovations. I find everything from cost estimates to before-and-after photos to lists of mistakes to avoid. There are so many things I don't know how to do, and the weight of it presses in. Occasionally, I look around at the mismatched furniture, the faded family photos on the wall, the evidence of a real, lived-in home. I wonder if it's possible to build something like that from scratch, or if it just grows around you when you're not paying attention.

I'm halfway through a YouTube tutorial on refinishing hardwood floors when the front door opens and slams shut.

"Thea?" My mother's voice carries down the hall, sharp with worry.

My body goes still. What the hell is she doing here? More importantly, how the hell did she even know I was here?

"Thea? Are you here?"

"I'm in here, Mom," I finally call back, shutting my laptop and pushing it aside.

She sweeps into the room, looking impossibly put together in a pink sundress and her old jean jacket. Her hair is perfect, her makeup flawless, but her eyes are wild. She sees my bandaged hand, and her mouth tightens.

"Oh, sweetheart." She crosses the room in three strides and enfolds me in a hug. The out-of-nowhere contact from her feels foreign to me, but I don't stop her. "I was hoping it wasn't true."

I'm not sure what to say, so I choose nothing. For a second, I wonder if she's hugging me or just holding on to what's left. Beck's gone, after all.

My relationship with her has always been tangled. After I was born, she was given the news that it was dangerous for her to have more children. I think that broke something in her, but it didn't stop her. A short ten months after I arrived, Beck did too. And, somehow, it was decided—by fate or family lore—that he would be the favorite. Even as kids, it was obvious: I'd spend my afternoons helping Mom in the kitchen or Dad out in the yard while Beck was off getting into trouble, making everyone worry. Yet he always got the bigger slice of her attention.

Maybe that's why I spent years keeping my head down, letting everything with Beck slide. It never mattered how much I accomplished. They wanted the golden son. The one who brought home trophies, the one who filled the house with friends and noise. When I got into the math program at Berkeley, I secretly hoped they'd be upset, beg me to stay, act like they'd all fall apart without me. They didn't. They congratulated me and carried on like it was a regular Tuesday. When I left, it took them three weeks before they called.

It's not that I wasn't loved. I just wasn't . . . seen. I thought I was holding the family together, but it turns out they never really needed me at all.

She surveys the chaos of the room. Mismatched posters line the wall, thrifted knickknacks on the shelves that have no rhyme or reason, a dresser lined with Juniper's art projects. She picks up a rainbow pillow from the bed, arching an eyebrow. "This room is quite . . . unique, isn't it?"

"It's Lucy," I say.

She smiles. "That it is." She sits beside me, smoothing her dress. "Now, care to explain why I had to hear from Mrs. Larsen that my own daughter was in town and that she was at the hospital? I nearly had a heart attack."

I sigh. *Ah, Mrs. Larsen. South Creek's very own PI.* I'm not sure how, but that woman is everywhere.

"I'm sorry, Mom. I didn't mean not to tell you. I just needed a little time to figure things out. Lucy had space, and I didn't want to worry you and Dad."

She gives me a tight smile. "I'm not upset that you showed up without telling us. I'm upset you went to that cabin. That *death trap*." She says the words like she's spitting out poison.

"It's not that bad," I say weakly.

She shakes her head. "Thea—" She stops, looking lost for a second. "I wish you'd think about yourself for once. Not about Beck or what he left behind."

I look at her, more confused than ever. My mother used to never care what I did with my life or my time. I could have joined a cult and moved to the middle of nowhere with a guy named Gluten, and she wouldn't have bat an eyelash. It was always Beck who pulled her attention, Beck who needed her. Now she's watching me like she's afraid I'll disappear too.

"I am thinking about myself, Mom," I say quietly.

She gives me a tired, uneven smile. "Why not let Hansen handle this whole thing? That's what his mother and I think. You don't need to drag yourself through this."

My face falls. "You talked to Hansen's mom?"

"Just briefly. She agrees with me on this." That I highly doubt. Winnie Reed never agreed with my mother. On anything.

"Mom, if Beck left me the cabin, I have to believe he had a reason. I'm doing this for him, but also for myself." *For my guilt*, I don't say.

She must not like my answer, because she stands and grabs her purse. "Don't give me that look, Thea. This isn't a good idea, and you know it. Your life isn't here anymore. Don't let this place pull you under, too."

There's a scream pushing at my throat, but I can't find any words. I'm fifteen again, choking on everything I want to say to her.

"So, that's it? You just quit your job and pack one suitcase and what? Play fixer-upper with your brother's best friend? You need money, Thea. Renovations aren't cheap."

"I have it covered."

Red begins to appear just above her collarbone, a sure sign my mother isn't happy. "Well, you seem to have it all figured out."

"I do," I lie.

She studies me, and there's something soft and sad that settles into her expression. "I can't support you on this."

Her words hit harder than I expect them to. I don't trust myself to say anything else, so I don't.

"Please call me when you've come to your senses." And with that, she leaves. But her words stay, sticking to the air around me like heavy smoke.

This is not how I wanted things to go.

I close my eyes and let out a shaky breath. My hand throbs in time with my pulse, but I swing my legs off the bed anyway.

I'm doing this. Even if it's a mistake. Even if it kills me. And whether she approves or not.

Chapter Six

T hat night, my phone buzzes on the nightstand.

> I'll meet you at the cabin tomorrow morning at 6 a.m.

So much for wishful thinking. Any hope that I dreamed our conversation the other day dissolves the instant I read his name. My stomach turns with a mix of dread and anxiety.

I barely sleep, and by four, I'm wide awake. I shower, pull on some old jeans and a hoodie, and tie my hair up, trying to convince myself that I'm ready for this. When I step into the kitchen, expecting total darkness and a silent house, I freeze. Lucy's already there, standing behind the counter.

"Lucy?"

She glances up and smiles, and I see something gentle in her eyes. "Good morning. There's coffee in the pot, and your eggs will be ready in just a sec."

I can't help but smile back. The tightness in my chest loosens just a little. "You didn't have to get up with me, you know."

Lucy waves me off, like I'm being ridiculous. "Please. Juniper went to Riggins's, and I never sleep when she's not here anyway. I might as well put my insomnia to use. Now sit."

I don't argue. I never win anyway. I slide onto a stool, and Lucy's right behind me, setting a plate in front of me. There are eggs, toast, and strawberries cut up just the way I like. She's got her own plate across from me, but she watches in anticipation until I take a bite.

"And?"

"It's really good, Lucy."

She shrugs with fake nonchalance, but I can tell she's pleased. "You know what I always say. If you're gonna have a hard day, you might as well start it with something delicious."

I lean forward, catching her eye so she knows I mean it. "Thank you. Really."

"Eat before it gets cold," she says, and I don't need to be told twice.

Lucy's always been incredible at taking care of the people around her. I think that's what drew me to her in the first place. Making food has always been her go-to. It's how she shows her love. Sometimes in ways you don't even notice until you're sitting in front of a plate you didn't know you needed. When I left South Creek, she was the hardest part to leave behind. I never realized, until now, how much that must've hurt her. Or how much I'd missed this, missed her, and our mornings like this that feel like home.

Lucy's the first to break the quiet. "So, you nervous about today?"

I let out a breath. "No. Yes. I don't know. It's just hard to know what to expect. I've never renovated a cabin."

Lucy pours herself more coffee, then slides the pot toward me. "What's the worst that can happen? Hansen's a jerk, the place is unfixable, you both get tetanus, and you come home and make pancakes with me and Juniper. Honestly, that's not too bad."

"You think that's the worst that could happen?" I used to think a lot of things were the worst thing that could happen. Now everything feels small compared to Beck.

"I'm choosing to remain optimistic."

I poke at my eggs. "I just . . . I wish I knew what I was walking into, you know?" I swallow hard. "Especially when it comes to being alone with Hansen. A part of me still hates him." I whisper the last part.

"Good. I think you should."

My eyes shoot to hers in surprise. She simply shrugs. "You don't have to have it all figured out, Thea. You just have to show up."

I smile, but it feels shaky. "That's what scares me."

She grins. "You're braver than you think." Then she smacks the table, startling me. "Now, just give me a few minutes to get dressed."

I blink. "Why?"

"So I can come with you, obviously."

"No, Luce, you don't have to—"

She cuts me off with a look. "Of course I do. I'm not letting you face this alone."

"What about work?"

She waves me off. "I already told my dad I'm not coming in today."

The gesture may seem small to others, but to me, it's huge.

"Give me five minutes."

Before I can protest, she's already halfway down the hall, and I'm left sitting in the warm kitchen, weirdly grateful, and just a little bit less afraid of whatever the rest of the day holds.

❧❧❧❧❧ ❦❦❦❦❦

By the time we pull up, the sky's just starting to lighten, soft blue bleeding into the treetops. I don't expect him to be there since it's still a few minutes before six, but Hansen's truck is already parked out front, his silhouette backlit by the sunrise. He's standing there, sleeves shoved up, hair wild, hammer in hand, looking like he's been awake for hours.

"I thought you said you were meeting at six," Lucy says, putting the car in park.

"We were." I'm already peeling off my seatbelt.

"Seems someone wanted a head start."

Gravel crunches under my boots as I climb out. Hansen glances up, swiping sweat from his brow, and for a split second, we just stare at each other. Two people who were never supposed to meet again like this. He looks good, which is no surprise. There has never been a time when Hansen Reed hasn't looked good to me. He could be covered in dirt wearing a garbage bag, and my body would still have a reaction to him. I was hoping that through the years, the wanting would dwindle, and I think in my mind, it had. But now, standing in front of him yet again, having him look the way he does, I realize my body hasn't gotten over him in the slightest.

"Hey," he calls, voice rough but in that Hansen way that always sounds kind.

"Hey," I manage, and it doesn't sound nearly as steady.

"How's the hand?"

I hold it up, showing off the bandage. "I'll live to see another day."

Lucy interrupts us by slamming the car door. Hansen's eyes dart to her, and a smile breaks across his face. "Is that Lucy Hayes?"

She folds her arms, giving him a look I've seen break lesser men. "As you live and breathe, Hansen Reed. Bet you weren't expecting to see me."

He steps off the porch, grinning. "Honestly, I'd be disappointed if you didn't show."

Lucy narrows her eyes, suspicious but amused. "We brought coffee, but I think maybe water might be more beneficial judging by how much sweat is on your shirt."

Hansen laughs, shaking his head. "So, you here for a grand tour or to work?"

Lucy glances at me. "Definitely a yes on the tour. The work part is undecided."

I roll my eyes, but I'm smiling. It's amazing how much better I feel having Lucy here.

"Well, come on in. Just try not to fall through a floorboard on your way up."

I try not to take that personally.

We follow him up, and I avoid the hole where my feet went clean through. The wood still creaks under my weight but holds.

I step inside, boots sinking into the outdated green carpet. Lucy wrinkles her nose at the smell that can only be described as musty, but she doesn't say a word.

Hansen rubs the back of his neck, searching for the best place to start. "So, first we've got to get all the damaged stuff out. Carpet, baseboards, cabinets. As you can see, I've already started on the living room carpet. I've also got a dumpster scheduled to get delivered soon so we can start throwing it all in there."

I look at the sections of carpet left and feel completely overwhelmed. This isn't just a mess, it's a disaster. I have no idea where to start. I don't know how to fix things. Not here, not anywhere.

Lucy must see something on my face, because she grabs my hand for comfort. "Hey. I know it looks like a lot, but you'll take it one step at a time."

I nod, swallowing hard. My eyes drift to Hansen, and I realize how much he's already done. The old carpet is half-pulled up, heavy and dark with years of water damage. He moves through the space like he was born to do this.

He continues, "I brought some tools that I already had. Utility knives, crowbars, gloves. There's a bunch more in my truck. We can finish the living room and then once that's out, we'll see what we're dealing with underneath and go from there."

Lucy eyes the room. "You sure sound like you know what you're doing."

"Don't you remember that Hansen did construction work for years before becoming a firefighter?" I say without even realizing I'm saying it.

Lucy gives an understanding nod, while Hansen doesn't.

"We'll have to cut the carpet into strips so we can haul it," he says. "Otherwise, it'll be too heavy to move."

"What about an electrician so we can get the power back on?" I ask. "If the wiring's shot—"

"It is," Hansen says, not looking up.

Lucy chimes in. "Feel free to soften the blows, Hansen."

"I'm sorry," he says. "I've already called an electrician. He's coming out by the end of the week. That way we can know better what we're dealing with since it's not really my specialty."

I nod. "Okay."

He grabs a pair of gloves from the counter and hands them to me. "Here. Want to make the first cut?"

I hesitate. "So, that's it? We're just diving in?"

"That's the plan."

I look at Lucy, who simply shrugs. I'm not sure what I thought was going to happen, but somehow, me actually doing some of the renovation work seemed far-fetched.

"You know I'm an accountant, right? I've never done this before," I say to him.

The very corner of his mouth turns up. "Yes, Thea. I know you've never done this before, but I promise, it's a lot easier than you think."

Fair enough. I'm a capable woman.

Without allowing myself to overthink any more than I already am, I kneel and guide my blade as it slides through the carpet like butter.

And for the next several hours, that's what we do. We cut strips, roll them up, and shove them in bags. The work is messy, and smells, and I hate it. Lucy helps as much as she can, keeping things light in what could be an otherwise very tense situation. It's not until she announces she's going to grab lunch that I notice just how much her presence was helping.

Moments after she leaves, silence settles over the half-stripped living room. Hansen keeps busy hauling the last rolled-up carpet to the porch. He moves like a machine. I, on the other hand, can't calm my anxious body.

Everything is too much. The mess, the smell of rot, the sight of Hansen in the cabin.

Finally, I can't take it anymore. I lean against the wall, arms crossed, and blurt out, "You know, it's kind of funny when you think about it."

Hansen stops in the doorway, setting the carpet down so he can look at me. "What is?"

"This whole thing. We all know the strange connection my brother had to this place, but he also knew how much I dreaded ever coming here. While he got the fun memories with Grandpa and the lake and long summer nights, I got yelled at and found mice in my things and had nights where I was so hot I literally contemplated sleeping in the freezer."

Hansen chuckles under his breath.

"I'm just not sure why he did it. And on top of that, why bring us both into this? Why not just leave it to me, or just to you? Why both of us? Was it some kind of joke?" I try to laugh, but it comes out sharp and bitter. "Like, 'Hey, Sis, you know that cabin you hate so much? Well here, now it's yours, and guess what? I'm also going to make it my ex-best friend's. The guy that you can't even stand to be around. Wouldn't that be so much fun? What a twisted way to make sure you never get to move on!'"

Hansen wipes his hands on his jeans, eyes steady on mine, and he finally speaks. "I don't know, Thea. Beck did a lot of things that didn't make sense."

I look away, throat tight. "What really gets me is the fact that even after everything you two went through," I point a finger straight at him, "he still wanted you to be here."

He's quiet for a long time, and I know what I'm saying is hurting him. But I don't care. I want him to hurt. I want him to feel just a fraction of the pain that I do.

After a minute, he says softly, "You think I wanted this, either? I didn't ask for any of it, Thea. I didn't ask to be brought back to the most painful memories of my life."

I let out a harsh laugh. "Then why not say no? Why not just ignore it and move on? It's not like he's here to make sure we're following his wishes."

"Maybe because I'm trying to make up for all the shit that happened." Hansen's voice is raised but still oddly calm. "Did that ever occur to you? That I feel guilt that's so fucking heavy it physically makes me sick? I walked away that night. I left him. I left you. And no matter what I do, I can't take any of that back."

I stop, my anger suddenly taking a back seat.

Guilt is something I can understand.

He takes a deep breath, running a hand over his face. "I'll never be able to change the things that happened. But this, being here with you and doing this, I can do that. I don't know what he was thinking. I really fucking don't. Maybe it was a joke. Or maybe he just thought we'd be better at this together."

I sink down onto the floor, suddenly exhausted. I don't know what to do with any of these feelings. The guilt I have for what happened with Beck. My resentment toward Hansen for being the one I have to share it with. The confusion about what any of it is supposed to mean for my life now.

"You want to tell me the truth behind what happened with all the glass upstairs?" he asks, softly.

I laugh, then look at my bandaged hand. "No."

He sighs. "Fair enough."

A silence settles over us, but he quickly breaks it. "We'll need to check the subfloor," Hansen says, like the last few minutes of conversation never happened, and we're back to just being coworkers in this mess. "If it's warped or moldy, we replace it. After that, we move on to tearing out the baseboards and checking for rot along the walls. We'll probably have to replace some drywall, maybe even some studs if water ever got deep enough."

I can't decide whether to laugh or cry. So, I settle on neither. "You know, when I learned that you were leaving construction to be a firefighter, I was honestly surprised."

Hansen leans against the wall across from me. "Was it really so hard to believe?"

"Sort of. You spent years fixing stuff for my family. My mother used to wait by the door just to hand you a list of chores. I guess I never knew you wanted to do anything else."

"Sometimes you do things because you're good at them. Sometimes you do things because you love them."

"So, you're saying you hate this and you're a bad firefighter?"

His lip twitches upward. "Pretty much."

My eyes wander the room, taking in how much work is ahead of us.

"Let's get back to work," I say, but I don't move. Not yet. Something in Hansen's face—maybe that he looks almost as tired as I feel, or the way his jaw flexes when he's trying not to say something—makes me pause.

"Are you in this, Hansen?" I ask, my voice low. "Because I can't do this if you're just going to walk away again."

Maybe it's not a fair question, but I can't resist asking. The last time I said goodbye to him nearly killed me. I can't go through that again.

He looks at me, his expression serious. "I'm not walking away," he says. I nod.

"Are *you* in this?" Hansen then asks me.

I sigh. "Beck always told me what this place could be," I say, not meeting his eyes. "I always thought it was just another one of his big ideas, you know? He'd get on a kick and then . . . lose it. Just when things would start to come together, he'd stop answering my calls. Or he'd blow all his money on something stupid, or just disappear for weeks. I wish I'd seen how hard he was trying. I wish I'd helped him, even a little. I wish I'd believed him."

I hear my voice crack, and that's when I realize I'm crying. I swipe at my face, embarrassed, but Hansen doesn't flinch. "So, yes. To answer your question, I'm here to stay. I'm not letting him down this time."

There's a silence that stretches, thick with everything neither of us has ever said. And in that silence, something shifts in me. I look at him and see the tired eyes, the hands that have always known how to fix broken things. I remember, suddenly, being seventeen and watching him mow our lawn, sweat-damp hair, arms tanned from the sun, and thinking he was the bravest, kindest person I'd ever known. That crush, the one I swore I'd buried, flares up like an old sprain in bad weather. I hate it. I hate that I still want him to look at me the way he used to. I hate that a small, ridiculous part of me wishes he'd reach out, just once, and touch my hand, and not because I was bleeding.

But I see now—he's just as lost as I am.

I let out a shaky breath. "I don't want to be mad at you, Hansen. And I'm not. I just . . . don't know how to do this with you."

He nods, swallowing, and his voice is rough when he says, "Me either. But I'm here, and we'll figure it out."

And for the first time, I almost believe him.

We stand in that wrecked room, both worn out and weighed down by everything we can't say. Something shifts in me—a little less anger, a little more space to breathe. It isn't forgiveness, not yet. But maybe it's the beginning.

"Okay," I say. "Then let's get back to work."

And for the rest of the day, we do just that.

Chapter Seven

FOURTEEN YEARS AGO

T he fight started small, like they always did. Beck was in the kitchen with music blasting from his phone, the same song on repeat for an hour. He said he was baking, if you could call tearing through bags of flour baking. White dust covered the counters, and there was a burnt smell coming from the oven.

I hovered near the doorway, clutching a half-finished math worksheet, trying to work up the nerve to ask him to turn the volume down. My head was pounding. Beck's laugh was too loud, everything about him just a little too much.

"Can you just—" I started, but he spun around, eyes wild and bright, pupils too big under the kitchen light.

"What?" he snapped, but there was still a smile on his face. "You have a problem with what I'm doing?"

I hesitated, already feeling like I'd lost. "Can you turn it down? Please? I have homework."

He stared at me, and for a second, something mean flickered across his face. "You always have homework," he said, mocking. "Do you ever do anything else? You know this is your one life, Thea."

I tried to laugh it off, but his words stung. He'd been like this for two weeks now. I should have been used to it, but I wasn't. "I just need to concentrate, Beck."

Beck's mood flipped so fast it made my head spin. The grin collapsed. Now he looked tired. "Yeah, well, sorry if I'm not perfect like you."

I hated when he did that—twisted everything I said to make it about him. "I didn't say that."

He slammed a pan down. "Of course not. You never say anything. You just look at me like I'm broken, like you're waiting for me to mess up again. Is that it?"

"Beck, please—"

"Stop telling me what to do!" he shouted, and there were tears in his eyes now. "You think you're so much better than me, don't you? Just because you're quiet and everyone thinks you're so fucking smart. Well, guess what, Thea? You're nobody. Nobody cares. Nobody even notices you unless I'm around to make shit interesting."

Something inside me snapped. "Why do you always do this? Why do you have to hurt me just because you're hurting?"

He laughed. "Because you're here. Because you never leave. Because you think you can save me. Newsflash . . . you can't."

Those words hit me like a slap, knocking the air out of my lungs. I couldn't trust my face not to crumple, so I turned and bolted. When I reached the hallway, I nearly ran into Hansen. I had no idea he was even there. He looked at me with wide eyes, but I couldn't stop. I pushed past him, out the back door, and into the night.

I pressed myself against the side of the house, the cold seeping through my shirt. My breath came in ragged bursts. I felt stupid for crying, stupid for not fighting back, stupid for thinking maybe this time would be different.

Then the screen door creaked behind me, and I flinched, swiping the tears away from my face.

Hansen's footsteps were quieter than I expected. He didn't call my name, just rounded the corner and crouched down a few feet away, not too close, not too far. Now that I wasn't running, I could get a better look at him. He was in an old T-shirt and jeans, and his hair was falling in his eyes as usual. He waited a moment, like he was giving me a chance to send him away.

I didn't.

"Want some company?" he asked.

I shrugged, not trusting my voice just yet.

He sat, pulling his knees up, mirroring me. We didn't speak for probably two minutes. But the silence between us wasn't heavy or awkward. It was just there, and comfortable. Like it always was with him.

Finally, Hansen broke it with a low voice. "I'm sorry about Beck."

I let out a shaky breath. "It's okay."

He looked quickly in my direction with concern etched on his face. "You want to talk about it?"

Hansen had known my brother for a year now, and the most surprising part was that he was still around. Even through all the bullshit, he still kept coming back. Any time this happened, any time things got too big, too hard, he was there. It did not help the massive crush I had on him.

I shook my head, then nodded, then shook my head again. I felt so stupid, crying like this.

"What about one word?"

I look at him, confused. "What?"

He smiled. "Start by telling me just one word that describes how you feel. Sometimes, it's easier to start slow, then build on it."

The idea was strange, silly even. But the way Hansen's eyes were looking at me, I found myself saying, "Invisible." Hansen's smile grew, and I continued. "It's just always been hard with him," I admitted, my voice barely more than a whisper. "He's my brother, but it's like . . . he's always pulling me in and then pushing me away. Sometimes I think he likes hurting me, just to see if I'll break."

Hansen was quiet for a long time. "I know what you mean. He does that to everyone, in his own way. But you—" He paused. "You're stronger than he thinks."

I huffed, once again trying to wipe away the tears. "Doesn't feel like it tonight."

He leaned closer. "I know it's hard. I know it hurts. But you don't have to go through it alone, okay? Not when I'm here. We're friends, Thea. That's what friends do."

His words hit somewhere deep, somewhere I'd been trying to cover up for years. Nobody ever said things like that to me. People looked past me, or through me, or saw only Beck's sister, the quiet one who was good at math. Sure, I had Lucy and I loved her, but she had Riggins and a baby on the way. Her life was big and hard enough without me adding my problems to it.

But Hansen was looking right at me, and it made my chest ache in a new, confusing way.

I swallowed. "Sometimes it's like nobody even notices I'm here unless Beck's around to make a scene."

"You aren't invisible, Thea. And the right people will see that," he said.

I was quiet. The tears had mostly stopped, but the ache was still there. Something shameful and dark twisted inside me.

"Sometimes I hate him," I said suddenly. The words just slipped out, and I was instantly terrified I couldn't take them back. But it also felt so good to let them go. "Sometimes I want to scream, and then run away and never see him again. And then I feel awful, because he's my brother and I'm supposed to love him, right? And I do. But sometimes . . . sometimes I just want to disappear. Or I want him to disappear. What kind of person does that make me?"

Hansen was quiet, like he was really thinking about it. Then he shrugged. "I think just a normal one."

I stared at him. The relief I felt was so sudden, it almost made me dizzy.

He nudged my shoe with his. "C'mon. Wanna do something?"

"Like what?"

With a cocky smirk, he pushed himself to his feet. "Like a race."

I made a face. "A race? Why?"

"Because," he said, stretching his arms over his head like he was preparing to run a mile. "Running helps when I'm upset. Clears my head."

I snorted. "I assure you, running has the opposite effect on me. It usually just makes me want to lie down and die."

He grinned wider. "You're just scared you'll lose."

I rolled my eyes. "No, I'm scared I'll puke."

"You're stalling," he said, and then, before I could protest, he took off across the yard.

"Hey!" I shouted, scrambling up. I didn't want to run. I hated running. But I also didn't want to give Hansen the satisfaction of winning without me even trying.

I pushed off the house and sprinted after him. My legs felt like lead at first, but after a few strides, something loosened. Hansen was fast, but he kept glancing back, laughing, and letting me catch up. My lungs burned as we ran down the road, but it was a good kind. Briefly, it felt like I was just a kid chasing another kid through the dark, and nothing else mattered. Not Beck, not school, not the ache in my chest.

I almost caught up to him just as he slowed to a stop at the end of the road. I skidded to a halt beside him, breathing hard. Hansen bent over and placed his hands on his knees. He looked up and smiled at me.

"How do you feel now?" he asked, still a little out of breath.

I surprised myself by smiling. For the first time all night, I felt lighter. "Better," I said, and I loved that it was the truth.

Chapter Eight

NOW

The thing about small towns at night is how empty they feel. How the quiet has a weight, pressing you back into your memories whether you want them or not.

It's late. Late enough that the only lights on Main Street are the flickering ones above the pharmacy sign and the twenty-four-hour diner. I couldn't sleep, not even close, so I slip out and start walking, letting the warm June air wrap around me. I take the long route, letting my mind wander through the events of the day.

I turn the corner by the post office and almost miss him—a runner, just a shape in the distance, head down, pounding the pavement like he's being chased. I almost keep going. But then he cuts under the yellow pool of the pharmacy sign, and I stop. It's Hansen. Same broad shoulders, same determined stride. Only this time, there's something unfamiliar about the way he moves. It's urgent and almost desperate, nothing like the guy I remember from high school, running just to burn off energy or impress someone in the stands.

I think about turning away and heading home so he can have this moment. But something stops me. Maybe it's because I've spent so long pretending I don't care about his life, that it doesn't affect me. But tonight, I want to see—really see—who he is now. What seven years of silence and guilt have done to him.

He speeds up as he passes the diner, sweat darkening the back of his shirt, his breathing ragged and uneven. There's nothing graceful about it. He looks like he's running from something he can't outpace. I watch him make a hard turn toward the old ice cream shop, and before I know what I'm doing, I cross the street, following at a distance.

He slows as he nears the edge of town, glancing over his shoulder as if expecting headlights, or maybe ghosts. There's nobody here but us. Him, running from his own ghosts, and me, chasing mine.

He finally stops at the bench outside the post office, folds over at his waist, and braces his hands on his knees. I duck behind the awning of the antique store, giving him space but unable to look away. He stays doubled over for a long time, then sits and stares at the ground. From here, I can't see the details, but I know the shape of that kind of exhaustion. The kind that comes from inside, that no amount of sleep or running can fix.

A part of me wants to disappear before he notices me. Let him have his pain alone, the way he clearly wants it. But another part, one I haven't listened to in years, makes me stay. Not out of morbid curiosity, but because I know what it's like to hurt in public and still feel invisible. I want to give him privacy, but I also want to witness. I want to know what's real.

It hits me, there in the dark, that I have no idea what Hansen's life has looked like since the fallout. I left South Creek and told myself, for years, that it was just easier not to know. Lucy would try to update me as best she could. "Hansen's still at the station," or, "He's working too much again," but I always changed the subject. Pretended his world stopped when mine did. But it didn't. He's had seven years to build a life that I refused to see, and I wonder now how much of it has been shaped by the same guilt and grief that keep me up at night.

And not just about Beck, either, but with his dad. It was in the quietest moments of our friendship that he would admit the guilt he felt about his death. I used to think he'd grow out of that guilt, let it fade with time, but now, watching him alone like this, I wonder if it just settled deeper, the same way mine did.

He drags a hand over his face, and I think he might be crying. His shoulders jerk, once, twice, and I feel a sharp ache in my chest. I think of Beck and how often I let him disappear into his own darkness, how I'd wait for him to make the first move, to call or text or show up at my door. I told myself I was giving him space, but really, I was just afraid. Afraid of saying the wrong thing. Afraid of admitting I couldn't fix him. And now he's gone, and all I have left are the things I never said.

I don't want to make that mistake again.

But the distance between Hansen and me feels like a canyon.

He leans back on the bench and tilts his head to the sky. When he shuts his eyes, he looks so young. I'm startled by the urge to comfort him.

I take a step forward, then stop. What would I even say? *"Sorry I've been blaming you for everything wrong in my brother's life? Sorry I left when I couldn't take being his sister anymore? Sorry I have no idea how to talk to you without getting angry?"*

Eventually, his breathing slows. He wipes a hand across his face, and in the glow of the streetlight, I see the shine of tears before he brushes them away. I look down, giving him a moment of privacy he'll never know I offered. I don't know how long I stand there, hidden by the awning, watching him. Long enough for the heat to fade from the night, for the world to settle back into quiet.

It's not strange, seeing him like this. When we were younger, everyone thought Hansen was made of steel. Beck used to tease him for it, but I always knew better. I saw the way he looked at people, the way he looked at me when he thought I wasn't paying attention. I saw the cracks, even if I pretended not to.

When I look up again, Hansen stands and stretches his arms above him. He looks exhausted, but better than a few moments ago, like he's gathered some of his strength back. I watch as he starts running again. He's slow at first, then he picks up speed until he disappears into the dark.

I stay for a moment longer, letting the emptiness of the street settle around me, feeling every bit of the distance between us, but also, for the first time in years, the possibility of something else. I don't know what to do with that feeling yet. But I know I can't go back to pretending. Not with Hansen. Not with anyone.

Chapter Nine

Mornings in South Creek are never as quiet as the nights. The birds are in full volume mode, and there's more than one dog somewhere down the block howling at nothing. And I'm not sure how many lawns in South Creek there are, but it seems every single one of them needs to be mowed this morning. But all of it washes over me and becomes just background static as I stand in front of the bathroom mirror. My toothbrush hangs from my hand, and toothpaste foams at the corners of my mouth, but I make no move to finish. I keep my eyes fixed on the tile beneath my bare feet, refusing to meet the look on my own face. I already know what I'll see: the same wide-eyed shock that's been haunting me since last night.

Every time I blink, I see him again. Hansen, backlit by the streetlights, running. The quiet violence of grief radiating off him in waves. My chest aches with guilt.

I finish brushing my teeth and splash water on my face hard enough to sting, hoping the cold will startle the ache away.

It doesn't.

I almost call Lucy, desperate for her to come home and talk me off the ledge, but her dad's already on the warpath after she missed work to help me at the cabin. I can't ask her to take another day off just because I don't know how to be alone with myself.

Downstairs, the kitchen is empty, and the house feels eerily quiet with just me in it. I make myself some coffee and toast as I stare at the clock on the microwave. I have to leave now if I want to meet Hansen at the cabin on time.

But seeing him now feels entirely too vulnerable.

I can always just check in on him, make sure there's nothing urgent that needs my attention, then bail if I need to.

Yeah. That'll work. It will be fine.

Everything will be fine.

The drive is short, but my hands are tight on the wheel the whole way. Hansen's truck is already there, parked at a crooked angle in the grass like he gave up halfway through straightening it.

How is he always here so early?

I sit in the car for a second, listening to my heart thumping, then I force myself out of the car.

The front door of the cabin is half-open. Inside, the living room looks even worse than the last time I was here. It's a battlefield of ripped up carpet, plywood, and tools.

Somewhere in the kitchen, there's a crash, followed by a muttered curse that echoes down the hall.

"Hansen?" I say out loud.

There's no answer. Just another thud, louder this time. My pulse kicks up. For a split second, I imagine walking in on something bad. Blood, a broken arm . . . worse. I run to the noise, and there he is: on his knees by the fridge with one hand braced against the wall for balance. The other is clutching a cabinet door that's completely unhinged. There's a mess of broken wood at his feet, and a thin red line of blood snakes from his palm down his arm.

"Jesus, are you okay?" I drop to my knees beside him, reaching for his hand before my brain can catch up. He flinches just slightly but lets me take it.

"I'm fine," he mutters, and he's not meeting my eyes.

"You're bleeding."

"It's nothing." He holds up the useless cabinet door by way of explanation. "This thing just decided to give me a run for my money."

I take a look at the cut across Hansen's palm. It's deep, but not enough that he needs stitches. "I think you'll live," I say, then gently let his hand go. "Maybe we should both be wearing gloves at all times. Or, I don't know, bubble wrap."

The corner of his mouth twitches, but the smile dies before it reaches his eyes. "Yeah. At this rate, neither one of us will have any limbs left."

"Here." I get up and grab one of the towels we have lying around. "Wrap it up."

He takes the cloth and wraps it around his hand. As he does, I notice his eyes. They're so distant and empty. So different from the Hansen I thought I knew. Did something happen before his run last night? Or has that pain always been there and I'm just now seeing it?

"You sure you're good?" I ask, softer.

He finally meets my gaze. "I've had worse."

Do I bring up last night? How would I even admit it? *Hey, saw you running in the middle of the night. You looked like you might have been crying. Want to talk about it even though I've been nothing but cold toward you?*

No. Definitely not like that.

He clears his throat. "I thought we could start on the kitchen floor today. It's tougher than the carpet, so it might be a little bit more of a fight."

"Harder than the carpet? Perfect," I say with all the sarcasm I can muster. "Are you sure you're up for it? We can always call it and come back tomorrow refreshed."

"I'm fine, Thea."

"Are you sure? Because—"

"Thea." He doesn't yell my name, but it's not quiet either. I instantly swallow any other words I have. Not because I'm scared of him—I'm never scared of Hansen—but because of the hurt in his eyes. I don't want to push him. Not today.

Hansen closes his eyes and lets out a deep sigh. "I'm sorry."

I try to smile. "It's fine."

He steps closer, and he looks unbalanced. "It's not. I just . . . I had a long night."

I know.

"It's okay, Hansen, really. If you're okay, then we can get back to work."

Hansen doesn't flinch as he spends the next thirty minutes teaching me how to peel up linoleum. I'm not good at it, since it's literally the opposite of doing math at a cubicle, but I keep at it. The only positive is how loud everything is. It drowns out my brain. My thoughts. There's just work. And the sweat pouring down my forehead.

Hansen and I barely speak. He helps when I need him, but otherwise, we just work in silence. Every so often, one of us glances over, like we have something to say, but the words stay locked away for both of us. I'm grateful, honestly. Talking feels impossible. Especially after what happened earlier.

An hour passes, maybe two, and then I lose track of time. The sun climbs higher outside the kitchen window, and it paints the whole cabin in gold. I don't realize how deep I am in the work until Hansen nudges me with his boot.

"Thea." His voice is gentle, but it cuts through the haze. "You've been working that same piece of floor for five minutes."

I blink, coming back into my body. My hands are trembling, and I hadn't even noticed. I pull off my goggles. "Sorry. I didn't even realize I had zoned out."

"It's easy to do with this kind of work. Sometimes, that's the best part about it."

"Is that why you like it?"

He stops, his brown eyes thinking deeply about my simple question. "I think so."

I nod. My shoulders are tense, and I have no doubt that I'll be needing to use Lucy's massage chair tonight.

"Come on," Hansen says. "Let's take a break. Get you some water." He doesn't wait for me to argue, just heads for the front door. I follow, honestly grateful for the excuse to breathe air that isn't thick with dust.

Outside, I drop onto the front steps and stretch my legs out in front of me. The water he hands me is cold enough to hurt my teeth, but I drink half the bottle in one go, letting it wash the taste of dust from my mouth. Hansen stands a few feet away, leaning against his truck, his face turned up to the sun.

The air smells like freshly cut grass. It stirs up the memories of Beck mowing the lawn first thing in the morning in the summer. I can see his grumpy face as my father made him do it. In the distance, I hear the faint clink of someone hitting golf balls. There's a new calmness here. One that never existed when I was younger.

"I hate to admit how peaceful it is up here," I say.

Hansen glances over, a smile tugging at his mouth. "Did it not feel that way when you were a kid?"

I snort. "About as far from it as you can get. All I could think about was how many wild animals were out there in those trees waiting to eat me."

He raises an eyebrow. "And you don't think about that now?"

"Oh, I do. I'm just much more accepting of my fate these days."

He laughs, and it feels so real. "It's incredible how much has changed. I only came up here a couple times with Beck, but it's like a different place now."

"My grandfather would be rolling over in his grave if he knew what it has become. If he could roll. He was a big guy."

"You never really talked about your grandfather."

"That's because he was a misogynistic asshole," I say it flatly, with no apology. "He hated my grandmother. When she died in childbirth with my mom, he just . . . transferred that hatred over to her. Tried to pawn my mom off on his sisters more than once, but it never stuck. I used to wonder what my mom would've been like if she'd had a better father. It couldn't have been easy being raised by him.

"When he bought this place," I continue, "I thought maybe he'd change. Maybe he'd want to be a grandfather. But I learned pretty quick it was all for Beck. He wanted a grandson, and he was willing to overlook everything else. When I showed up, I was just an inconvenience. I begged my mom to let me stay home, but she never did. 'He's my father, Thea,' was all she'd say."

Hansen is quiet, and I can tell I've surprised him. "Sorry," I say, "that was probably way more than you wanted to know."

"No," he says quickly, "I'm glad you told me. Beck always made your grandfather sound like a saint."

"Yeah, that tracks. Beck never saw the worst of it. I could've told him, but . . . I don't know. I didn't see the point."

"I wish you would have said something back then." Hansen meets my gaze. "I would have listened."

"I know you would have," I say, and I mean it.

There's a new tension in the air. I look at the cut on Hansen's palm, still wrapped in a makeshift bandage. The image of him running flashes in my mind again, and the words I've had in my throat all day spill out.

"I'm sorry for what I said at the funeral," I blurt out. "That you were the reason Beck is gone."

Hansen opens his mouth to stop me from continuing, but I stand and stop him in his tracks. "I don't believe you're the reason he's gone. Because even if you hadn't left that night, Beck would've found another excuse to push you away later. I think you probably did what was right for you."

He shakes his head. "You don't have to apologize."

"I know. But I want to. This entire thing has been so incredibly hard to navigate, and I think I was just looking for someone to blame and you were the easy target. But that wasn't fair to you. So, I'm sorry."

"Thank you," he says, so quietly I almost miss it.

He lets the words hang, then: "You know it's not your fault either, right?"

I wish more than anything I could say yes. Let myself off the hook. But I can't quite get there. "I don't know," I admit. "Toward the end, we barely talked. I kept thinking if I just tried harder, if I found the right meds, paid for another rehab, gave him more time, more money, more forgiveness, maybe he'd turn a corner. Maybe he'd stay alive, just for me. Every time it didn't work, I'd tell myself that the next time would be different. I let him crash with me when he was already three days drunk. I lied to my boss, to his landlords. I let him yell, and then I let him cry, and then I let him promise and break it all over again."

Hansen doesn't say anything. He just sits with it, like he knows nothing he says will fix it, but he's not going anywhere.

"When I first got the call, when I heard Beck was gone—" My throat closes up, but I force it open. "I was relieved. Just for a second. Because he'd struggled his whole life, and I thought, maybe he was finally free. And . . . I didn't have to worry about him anymore. I didn't have to keep waiting for that phone call, the one that finally came."

My face burns. I can't swallow the shame. "As soon as I thought it, I hated myself."

"You loved him, Thea. It's okay to have two feelings about something. Even if they don't make sense together."

I nod. "Yeah. Maybe you're right."

He smiles. "I usually am."

I let out a shaky laugh, grateful that he's lightening the mood. "All right, don't let it go to your head, big boy."

After one last drink of water, I slap my knees and stand. "We should get back to work before I get way too comfortable sitting down."

But Hansen hesitates. "Are we okay?"

There are a thousand things I could ask him. About that night, about everything since. But the words tangle in my throat. So, I give him what I can.

"Yeah. We're okay."

Chapter Ten

When I first landed in New York, everything seemed lit up from the inside. For once, it was just me against the world. There was no safety net, no parents, no brother's shadow. I believed I could carve out a space where I actually belonged, somewhere I'd feel safe. Like I mattered. That glow faded faster than I'd expected, and no matter how hard I tried, I couldn't make the city feel like home.

Honestly, I'm not sure I've ever really even known what "home" feels like. People talk about it like it's this obvious thing: you walk in the door, and the tension in your shoulders drops, and you look forward to coming back at the end of the day. There's someone there, waiting for you. Whether it's a familiar smell, or the right kind of noise, every little detail is a kind of relief. If the world falls apart, at least you have that.

I've spent years chasing that feeling, coming up empty every time. Until now. Until Lucy let me crash in her tiny guest room, with the pillows that don't match and carpet that should have been replaced decades ago. But when I walk in after a long day of ripping out floors and being reminded of some of the worst things, something shifts. The smell, the quiet, the way the light falls across the bed. It all feels right. It feels like comfort.

I wander into her kitchen, following the sound of clattering pans and Lucy's soft humming. She's at the stove, stirring something that smells amazing.

"Hey," I say. "Can I help with dinner?"

Lucy doesn't look up from her concentration, just gestures to a bag of carrots on the counter. "Chop those for me?"

"Of course." I grab a knife and get to work, ignoring the dull ache in my muscles from the day.

After a minute, when she can peel her eyes away from the pot, Lucy glances over. "How was your day?"

"It was good," I say. "We ripped up the kitchen floor."

She grins. "Sounds like a party. I'm devastated I missed it."

I snort. "It was certainly something. What about you? How's work?"

Lucy's face darkens, the light leaving her green eyes. "Ugh. Don't even start. My dad has me working on a big new client. A dating app, because God knows the world needs more of those."

I raise an eyebrow. "Is it at least a good opportunity?"

She scoffs. "It's a 'hope you don't disappoint me' opportunity." She drops her spoon and leans her hip against the counter. "I've been at the company for years and still, every time I take on something new, it's like he's waiting for me to screw up. I've landed some of our biggest clients. I singlehandedly got Emery Drinks to switch, and now they're number one in the world. But he still talks to me like I'm going to let him down."

Lucy's parents are the opposite of my own. While mine can't give two shits about what I'm doing, Lucy's are always in her business. Always watching.

"What about quitting? I know you've wanted to."

She sighs. "I've thought about it. But honestly, what else would I do? If I left my dad's, I'd never do marketing again, that's for sure. Which means I'd be a single mom who never finished college and has only worked one job since she was eighteen. Who's going to hire that?"

"Lucy, you're so much more than that."

"You have to say that."

I shake my head. "No, I really don't."

She resumes her stirring, and the kitchen starts to fill with the sound of bubbling sauce. "What about ice skating?" I ask, careful to keep my tone gentle. Lucy started skating before she could properly run. She was on track for the Olympics until Juniper came along, and ever since then, it's been a sore subject. "I know you still think about it. Don't even try to deny it."

Her jaw tightens, as expected. "I'm thirty, Thea. There's no life for me in skating. Not anymore."

"You could teach. Coach, maybe."

She doesn't look at me, but I see her mind working as she chews it over. "Just . . . think about it, okay? I hate seeing you so miserable."

She points her spoon at me. "And what about you, Missy? You quit your big New York job. What's next for Thea Miller?"

I roll my eyes. "Thea Miller is just trying to survive the week."

Lucy nods, understanding in her eyes. "A noble goal."

I chop a few more carrots before speaking again. "I have always wanted to go back to school. That was the plan in New York, but then Beck needed me, and I was so busy, and had to spend all my money on his rehabs. More student loan debt on top of that didn't seem the smartest."

Lucy slaps the counter with gusto, and I nearly hit the ceiling. "You going back to school is a great idea! I can totally see it now. Dr. Thea Miller. That's hot."

I laugh. "Glad to have your approval."

She grabs my shoulders, forcing me to look at her. "I want you to know, if you need to stay here, or just want to, you can. As long as you want. You don't have to figure it all out right now. But you have a home here, Thea. Always."

A knot of anxiety I didn't even realize I had in my chest loosens. "I'm not sure what incredible deed I did in my past life to deserve you, but it must have been something truly incredible."

Lucy beams. "You owned a rescue pet center."

I raise an eyebrow. "Really?"

"Yes. You saved thousands of animals' lives. So, yes, you're quite deserving of my incredible friendship."

I don't bother holding my smile back.

Lucy puts her spoon down with a little flourish, slaps the lid onto the pot, and leans in conspiratorially. "Now, tell me . . . how was Hansen? After the whole midnight runner incident?"

I didn't plan on telling Lucy I saw Hansen running, but she was waiting for me the second I walked in the door that night like I was a teenage kid that had just been caught sneaking out. The rest is history.

"He was fine," I say.

She narrows her eyes. "Don't bullshit a bullshitter."

I cave in less than three seconds. "Okay, well, I didn't exactly bring it up."

She gapes. "What do you mean you didn't bring it up?"

"What was I supposed to say? 'Hey, I lurked in the shadows while you had a breakdown'?"

She shrugs. "Honestly, yeah. I'm sure that would have worked. If anything, it would have been a good icebreaker."

I roll my eyes. "I wasn't going to say that." I play with a misshapen carrot. "But we did talk," I offer, and her eyebrows jump.

"Okay, that's something. Unless it was bad. Was it bad? Did you fight? Throw pieces of the kitchen floor at each other?"

"No one threw anything. He asked about my grandfather, and I told him."

Lucy's eyes go wide. "You never talk about your grandfather."

I nod. "And then I apologized for what I said at the funeral. About Beck and it being his fault that he's gone."

Lucy just stares at me, then smacks my arm. "Way to bury the lead, woman!"

I wince, but I'm smiling. "Sorry. It just . . . there's a lot of hurt there still. I think maybe there always will be. But blaming Hansen wasn't making anything better."

Lucy wraps her arms around me. "That must have been really hard. I'm proud of you, Thea."

I squeeze her back. "Thank you."

We linger in the hug, letting it be a comfort for both of our long days. When she pulls away, there are tears in her eyes. "Lucy," I say, wiping a tear. "Why are you crying?"

"It's nothing. I just really missed you, is all. I'm not sure if I ever really said how much, but it was a lot. Like, embarrassingly a lot. I know you needed space, and I wanted to respect that, but it was like . . . part of me was gone."

I swallow hard, feeling my own emotions come to the surface. "I missed you, too. Even more embarrassingly. New York sucked without you. Everything sucked without you. I suck for leaving you."

A tear tracks down Lucy's cheek. "Great, now this is turning into a cryfest."

I laugh, my own voice wobbly. "I'm sorry."

We hug again, and before we can pull apart, the front door bangs open, and Juniper comes flying through. She doesn't look at either of us, just barrels straight up the stairs, her bedroom door slamming behind her so hard the pictures on the wall rattle.

Lucy's face morphs into concern, then tightens as Riggins steps through the door behind Juniper. He's changed so much since we were kids. Gone is the lanky boy, replaced by a broad-shouldered man, with hair a little darker and features a little sharper.

He closes the door with a soft click, then glances between us. Lucy's arms are already crossed.

"Lucy." His voice is careful, and then he nods at me. "And Thea."

"Hey, Rigs," I say, the nickname slipping out before I can stop it. There was a time when he was just as much a friend to me as Lucy. Then he broke her heart. I can't forgive him for that. Correction, I won't be forgiving him for that.

Lucy steps forward, eyes flashing. "What the hell was that?"

Riggins sighs and runs a hand over his face. "She's fine."

"She didn't look fine."

"It was just a long day. She needs some space to cool off."

"Don't downplay this, Riggins. Not to me."

"I'm not, Luce. She's fourteen. Everything's the end of the world."

Lucy lets out an incredulous laugh. "Oh, you did not just say that."

I edge toward the hall. "Maybe I should let you two talk in private."

Lucy whips her head around. "Don't you dare leave, Thea!"

I freeze, caught between them like always. Riggins laughs, but there's no real humor in it. "Luce, you have to calm down. Junie's fine."

Oh, no. He did not just tell her to calm down.

I put my hands on her shoulders, hoping to stop her before she grabs a knife from the counter and drives it right through her ex-husband. "Hey. Why don't I go talk to Juniper? A little aunt-niece debrief." I shoot a look at Riggins. "And I think you should leave. You've done enough."

Lucy takes a shaky breath. Riggins looks at me, and the big, brave face he put on slips ever so slightly. The old Riggins, the one who was actually good for her, is poking through.

He nods. "Yeah. You're right. I'm sorry." His eyes go to Lucy's. "Just tell her I love her, okay? She can call me before bed to talk if she wants."

He heads out, letting the door swing shut behind him. Lucy closes her eyes and rubs her temples. "God, he gets under my skin. How did I stay married to him for twelve years?"

I squeeze her arm, not even wanting to touch that question tonight. "Go finish dinner. I'll go talk to Juniper."

"You sure?"

I nod, and she gives me a grateful smile.

Upstairs, I stop in front of Junie's door. There's a flashing doorbell outside her room. The kind that lights up the ceiling so she knows someone's there. I press it and wait. No answer. I grab a notepad and pen from Lucy's office and scribble "It's Thea," then slide it under the door and ring the bell again.

There's a shuffling sound before the door cracks open just enough for me to see Juniper's red, tear-streaked face.

"Hey," I say softly. "Can I come in?"

She nods, and the door opens. Her room is classic Juniper. Musical posters, overflowing closet, makeup scattered across her vanity. She flops onto her bed. She's clutching the orange bunny Lucy bought when she was pregnant with her.

"Is Mom mad at me for slamming the door?" she asks, signing while speaking.

I shake my head, sitting on the plastic pink chair by her vanity. "No. Your mom's not mad. She just wants to make sure you're okay."

She sniffles, wiping her nose on her sleeve. "I hate crying. It's so embarrassing."

"I used to think that too when I was your age. Honestly, sometimes I still do. But it doesn't mean you're weak, Junie. It just means you care. That you're human."

She picks at one of the ears on the bunny.

"Do you want to tell me what's going on?" I ask.

She sighs and says, "I hate my dad."

I blink, not expecting that at all. "That's a big thing to feel. Want to tell me why?"

"He's the reason my parents aren't married anymore. He just . . . gave up. On us. On Mom. He didn't even try to fix things."

Well, shit. I'm not even sure where to start with that.

I lean forward. "Junie, divorce is . . . it's messy. It's almost never just one person's fault."

She cuts me off. "I'm not stupid. They think I didn't know what was going on back then, but they're wrong. I saw it. I saw how he treated her."

My heart breaks for her, and I wish more than anything I could take her pain away.

"I'm sorry you had to see all that," I say. "But I promise it's a lot more complicated than that. And your parents, both of them, they love you. Even if it doesn't always seem that way."

Juniper's eyes are wet again. "I'm just so mad at him. I don't want to see him. I don't want to talk to him. I don't care if he loves me. He just acts like everything is fine. With me. With my mom. Like nothing has changed."

I reach out and rest my hand on her knee. "You get to be mad. You can be angry as you need to be—at him, at the whole situation. It's okay to feel that way, Junie. You don't have to push it down or pretend you're fine."

She wipes her nose again, then looks up. "Do you think Mom is okay?"

God, that hurts. The way she's trying to be brave for Lucy, even now. I give her the most honest answer I have. "Your mom is the strongest person I know. She's going to be okay. And you will too. But it's okay if it doesn't feel like that right now."

She nods, but I can see the uncertainty in her face.

"You should talk to them about this," I say. "I think they would want to know how you're feeling."

She hesitates, then signs, "Yeah. Maybe."

"If you need any help, or backup, or you just want to talk, I'm here, Juniper."

She smiles at me, and I think the conversation might be over, but then she glances up at me, her eyes serious in a way that makes her seem older than fourteen.

"I've wanted to say that I'm sorry about your brother," she continues, "I know I already said it at his funeral, but I've been thinking about it a lot lately. I obviously don't have a sibling, but I can't imagine how hard that must have been for you to lose him."

I smile, and it's small and a little bit shaky, but it's there. "Thank you, Juniper. That means a lot."

We sit in the hush for a moment, and I realize just how much I've missed talking to her. How much I've missed being her aunt.

"Hey, Junie," I say, signing as I speak. "I've been working on my signing since getting back, but I was hoping you could give me some refreshers. If you want to, of course."

Her face lights up. "Yeah. Definitely."

I smile, the weight in my chest a little lighter. "Thank you."

Chapter Eleven

THIRTEEN YEARS AGO

Beck got his license three weeks ago. And he hadn't stopped begging me to go out driving with him since. Most of the time, I turned him down. I had homework, or a headache, or I just didn't feel like playing passenger to my little brother's new obsession. But that afternoon, I said yes. Maybe it was the way he stood in the kitchen, bouncing on his toes, jingling the car keys. Or maybe I just felt guilty for how distant we'd been lately.

"Come on, Thea," he said, nearly vibrating with excitement. "Let's just go somewhere. Anywhere. Please?"

I pretended to sigh, but the truth was, I was already caving. "Fine. But I'm picking the music."

Beck grinned triumphantly and tossed me the aux cord as we headed out to Mom's old Civic. I slid into the passenger seat and plugged in my phone.

"No sad-girl playlists," Beck warned, already buckling his seatbelt.

"No promises," I shot back, but I scrolled for something lighter anyway. I landed on a Broadway song I always sang when we were kids. Beck started the engine, glanced over to make sure I was ready, and pulled out of the driveway with a little too much flair.

"Easy there, Hot Rod," I said, bracing myself as we swung around the corner.

He laughed, flicking on the turn signal even though no one was around. "I'm a natural. I could drive across the country right now."

"Let's stick to the speed limit first."

It felt good to tease him, to slip back into our easy rhythm. For a while, we just drove with the windows down and the late spring air whipping through the car. Beck drummed his fingers on the wheel, humming to the music, and I caught myself smiling, really smiling, for the first time in a while.

We sang along to every song. Beck was always louder, always a little off-key, making up harmonies and beats that didn't exist. When my favorite sad-girl song came on, he made an exaggerated face, but by the chorus, he was shouting the lyrics out the window, not caring who heard.

We passed the edge of town and wound down the two-lane highway, past fields going green again and the old quarry where we used to sneak out with flashlights. With the sun shining and the music up, it was almost possible to forget how quickly time was moving.

At a red light, Beck glanced over at me. "You know what I've been thinking about?"

"Hopefully how to drive a car."

He ignored me. "I want to travel. Not just to, like, Florida or New York. I mean really travel. I want to backpack through Europe. Maybe work somewhere weird, learn to surf, even hike in Switzerland. Just . . . do something big."

I looked at him, at all his energy. When Beck was up, he was up, and you could feel it in the air, like standing close to a power line. I loved seeing him like this, but I always worried about how fast he could fall.

"That sounds amazing," I said. "But you hate hiking."

He grinned. "Only here. If it's Switzerland, I'm sure I'd love it. Everyone loves hiking in Switzerland. And surfing . . . I mean, how hard could it be?"

I laughed. "You'd get eaten by a shark on day one."

"Then at least you'd have a cool story to tell."

The light turned green, and Beck started forward. "You should come with me," he said. "You're the smart one. You'd actually keep us alive."

I snorted. "I'd spend the whole trip keeping you out of trouble."

"Exactly. That's what older sisters are for."

He said it lightly, but something in his voice made me pause. "I haven't been a very good one lately."

Beck shrugged. "We're fine. I just wish . . ." He trailed off, then tried again. "I wish we were closer, sometimes. Like those siblings you see in movies, you know?"

I looked out the window right as a crow dove over a field. "Nobody's actually like that, Beck. Life isn't a sitcom."

He laughed, but it sounded a little forced. "Yeah. Still. I think it'd be nice sometimes."

I felt a pang of guilt. I knew what he meant. I'd always wished for a stronger bond with Beck. But we'd always been two very different people, with two very different personalities that didn't always mix. "How are your new meds?" I asked, hoping to change the subject.

He groaned. "I don't want to talk about my meds."

"But I do. And you just said you wanted us to be closer. Being closer means talking about personal stuff, like meds."

His fingers tightened on the steering wheel. "They're fine." His words may have said one thing, but his tone told me a completely different story.

"No new side effects?"

"Nope."

"And you're sleeping okay?"

He let out a laugh. "Jesus, Thea. I'm fine, okay? I'm taking the meds, I'm writing down all my side effects for the doctors, and I'm keeping a daily log of how I feel, okay? Happy?"

I smiled. "Happy."

Beck looked over at me, then rolled his eyes. "Sorry, I didn't mean to snap at you. I just get it all day from Mom and Dad, and sometimes I just don't want to think about meds and doctors and all that shit that's messed up in my head."

"Okay," I said. "I understand."

He drove on, and the town started to shrink behind us, leaving nothing but open road. The music changed, and Beck started singing again, louder and more ridiculous than before, making faces until all thoughts I had about his meds were long gone.

He took us out to the overlook, a spot we hadn't visited in years. From there, you could see the whole valley. The rooftops, the river, the patchwork of fields. Beck parked and instantly turned to me. "So. In the spirit of being closer, why don't you tell me about you and Hansen?"

I groaned, tipping my head back. "Seriously? That's what you want to talk about?"

He was relentless. "Just tell me that you like him. Then I'll leave it alone."

"I don't want to talk about it."

"Nice try."

I rolled my eyes, but my cheeks burned. "I don't like him. We're just friends."

He looked at me, skeptical. "He likes you, Thea. You know that, right?"

"You're wrong. He doesn't."

"He does. He gets all weird whenever I talk about you. I swear his cheeks turn, like, bright red. And he's always asking what you're doing."

I snorted. "You're reading into things. He was literally just flirting with Amy at track practice."

Beck's eyebrows raised. "So you admit you watch him at practice."

I shoved him. "No, dummy. I admit to seeing him flirt with other girls at practice."

"The practice that you just happened to be watching."

"Oh my God, Hansen is a *friend*. Just like he's a friend to you."

"I can promise you that Hansen is not the same kind of friend to me that he is to you."

Maybe Beck was right. Maybe there was something different about the way Hansen looked at me. Sometimes, when I caught him watching me across the cafeteria, he didn't look away immediately—he just held my gaze, like he was trying to memorize something about my face. Or the way he always made sure I had a ride home, even if it meant he was late for practice, or the way he sat next to me at every stupid school assembly, his shoulder always touching mine, making little jokes under his breath just to make me laugh.

It was in the small things, too. How he always remembered I didn't like ketchup on my fries and ordered them plain. How he texted me when there was a song on the radio he knew I loved, or how he listened—really listened—when I talked, even when I was rambling about things no one else cared about. I thought about the time he waited with me outside the nurse's office when I got dizzy in gym, or the time he walked me home in the rain, even though he didn't have an umbrella and his new shoes got soaked.

The biggest thing was how he was always there for Beck. No matter how rough things got, no matter how many times Beck pushed him away or acted like a jerk, Hansen stayed. He was steady in a way that sometimes made me jealous. It felt like he was made of something stronger than the rest of us.

But then I remembered seeing him with other girls. Amy at track practice, laughing and leaning into him; Lila at that party last fall, her lip gloss smeared and Hansen's hands in her hair. He had never said a word to me about how he felt, not once. Not even a hint. If he really liked me, wouldn't he have said something by now? Or at least acted different, somehow?

The truth was, I was scared. I didn't know what I'd do if it was true—if Hansen liked me, if he wanted more than just friendship. I didn't know what I'd do with that kind of feeling. I didn't know how to carry it around. I had plans. Big ones that didn't leave room for relationships or distraction. If I let myself feel something for him, really feel it, I was afraid I'd lose my grip on everything else. And maybe, deep down, that was what scared me most.

So, I did what I always did. I laughed it off. I shoved the feelings down, and I kept moving forward. Because it was easier to pretend than to risk everything changing.

"Even if that were true, which it's not, I have too much going on to deal with a boy. I'm focused on my future," I said.

"You do know love can be a part of your future just as much as college."

"Yes, but it's easier this way. Less . . . complicated."

Beck looked at me for a long moment, then sighed. "Just don't forget that you deserve good things, Thea."

He nudged me softly. "Hey. Look at us. Talking about personal shit like sitcom siblings. I think we're going to be okay."

I smiled. "Yeah. We're gonna be okay."

We sat in the car for a while, watching the sun sink lower, painting the sky in streaks of orange and pink. I tried to memorize the feeling of the wind in my hair, Beck humming under his breath, the world wide open in front of us. I tried to hold onto it, knowing how quickly things could change.

On the way home, we left the windows down and sang until our voices cracked. For one perfect hour, it felt like things were perfect, like nothing bad could touch us.

I wish I could have bottled that drive and kept it somewhere safe. Because even now, years later, I can still feel the sun on my face and Beck's voice beside me, singing along. For just a little while, we were exactly where we were supposed to be.

Chapter Twelve

Now

The plate of cookies feels heavier with every step I take toward Station 218, my arms aching like I've carried it halfway across town. This is ridiculous. Hansen's mom literally owns a bakery. Like, *the* bakery in South Creek. Why would a bunch of firefighters want amateur cookies from me, especially when I can't even remember if I put in the right amount of sugar? My nerves had me double-checking the recipe three times, and still, I feel like I probably ruined them.

I hover awkwardly by the front doors, wishing I'd made Lucy taste one before I left. But then she would've asked why I was baking and where I was taking them, and that was a line of questioning I wasn't ready to field. Not when I barely know myself why I drove here. Boredom, grief, worry for Hansen—pick a reason.

"Thea!" someone shouts.

I turn, nearly dropping the plate. Riggins is leaning against one of the engines, grinning.

Ugh. Even though I know he works with Hansen, a part of me tried to forget. Ever since I talked to Juniper, my feelings toward him have been extra complicated.

"Are those cookies?" he asks, not bothering to hide his excitement. His gaze is fixed on the plate.

"They're supposed to be."

He doesn't wait for an invitation, just jogs up to me, peels back the plastic wrap, grabs a cookie, and pops it into his mouth.

"What the hell, Riggins?" I say while he nearly swallows the entire thing in one bite.

"You brought them for all of us, didn't you?" he asks with an annoying twinkle in his eye.

I roll my eyes.

"They're really good by the way," he says. Then he screams, "Hey, everyone! Thea's here, and she brought cookies!"

I cringe at his volume before glancing around. "Riggins, seriously. Keep it down." I'm not ready for all eyes on me, not yet—especially not Hansen's eyes. In fact, I'm second-guessing every single life choice that has gotten me to this point.

He just laughs, catching my wrist before I can yank the plate away. "Relax. Everyone's going to be really happy you're here."

"They don't even know me."

He smirks. "That's what you think."

I finally manage to swat his hand away. "You're annoying."

He shrugs. "I've been called worse. By you specifically."

"I will walk right out of here."

"No, you won't," he says, slinging an arm around my shoulders. I bristle, but he doesn't seem to notice. "You're too curious about what Hansen will think of you showing up."

I elbow him a little harder than necessary. "I don't need you reading into everything."

He just grins, undeterred. "Hey, I'm not judging. I'm just saying, you're not as mysterious as you think. Don't forget that I know you, Thea."

Before I can reply, an older man with salt-and-pepper hair steps out from an office. "Did I hear something about cookies?"

Riggins jumps at the interruption. "Cap, meet Thea Miller. She's Hansen's—"

I shoot him a warning look, cutting him off. "Hansen's nothing. I'm just Thea."

Captain Martinez shakes my hand warmly. "Nice to finally meet you, just Thea. Hansen's talked you up plenty."

My cheeks flush. Riggins leans in close, whispering, "Told you."

I shove him away. "Only good things, I hope."

Captain Martinez nods. "Only good." His gaze is kind, and I feel a little of my anxiety slip away. "Though he didn't mention you were coming by."

"Oh, he doesn't know. I, um, just wanted to drop these off. No need to bother him if he's busy. Or even if he's not busy."

"Hey, Hansen!" Riggins shouts over my protests, not even trying to hide his grin. "Get out here! Someone brought you cookies!"

I wince. "Subtle."

"Subtlety's overrated," he whispers with a wink.

Footsteps echo down the hall, and then Hansen appears, towel slung over his shoulder, hair damp from a shower. He's in his navy department T-shirt and a pair of gym shorts. He looks, for lack of a better word, hot. Even if there was a better word, I'm sure hot would still be an accurate one to use. This is the first time I'm seeing Hansen in his firefighting environment. I mean, I know what he looks like. What he's always looked like. But there's something about him here. About the way he just oozes confidence, even more so than when he's at the cabin, that makes him all the more attractive.

He stops short when he sees me, surprise flickering across his face.

"Thea?"

"Hey." My smile feels awkward, but I hold the plate up like a shield. "I come bearing gifts."

God, I feel like an idiot.

He glances at the cookies, then at me, and a slow smile builds. "You came all the way here to bring me cookies?"

"Don't make it sound like I trekked across the desert for a week. You're just down the street from Lucy's. And these aren't just for you. They're for everyone."

He studies me for a moment, an unreadable expression on his face. "Well, either way, I'm happy you're here." He gestures toward the kitchen. "Do you want to come meet the rest of the crew?"

"Sure."

Why not keep this awkward train going?

I follow him, and Riggins trails behind us like a puppy. We step into the kitchen, where a handful of firefighters are gathered around a scarred wooden table.

Hansen clears his throat, and they all look his way. "Guys, this is Thea Miller. Thea, this is Sam, Joseph, Nina, and Graham." He points to the four firefighters sitting at the table.

"Nice to meet you all," I say.

They all give me a pleasant smile. Then the youngest looking one, who Hansen introduced as Sam, stands up with a grin. "So, this is Thea. The girl Hansen has been spending so much time with."

"I'm the one he's renovating a cabin with, yes. I brought cookies. Consider it a thank you for not kicking Riggins out yet. I know Juniper appreciates her father having a job."

I set them on the table, and, predictably, Riggins grabs another. "Hey, as long as I get cookies, I can take a little abuse."

Sam leans in, smirking. "So, Thea, are you single?"

I almost choke on air.

"Sam. What the hell?" Hansen says.

"Yes. I am," I answer.

Sam just laughs. "Sorry. I just believe in shooting my shot."

Hansen's jaw tenses, and there's a flash of something sharp in his eyes. I nudge him, whispering, "Down, boy."

He backs off immediately, and I turn back to Sam. "I'm flattered, but firefighters aren't really my type."

The room laughs, and even Captain Martinez cracks a smile. "I like her."

Hansen clears his throat awkwardly. "Well, I think Thea's got places to be." He's already guiding me out of the kitchen as the rest of the crew calls out their goodbyes, and Riggins yells, "Come back any time!"

Once we're alone in the bay, Hansen stops. He looks almost shy as he rubs the back of his neck. It's honestly adorable. "Sorry about them. They mean well, but they're a lot."

"They're fine." I hesitate, glancing back through the glass. "Riggins may be a twelve-year-old menace trapped in an adult man's firefighter body, though."

Hansen's face softens. "He means well, too. Even when he's being an ass."

"Thanks for introducing me. They seem like a good group."

"They are. And hey, thanks for the cookies. Seriously."

"That's what renovation partners do, right?"

He chuckles. "Is that what we are?"

"Unless you have another name for it."

Hansen smirks, and the nerves in my stomach fizz into something dangerously close to giddiness.

"We'll brainstorm," Hansen says.

Before I can say another word, the loud, jarring blare of the alarm sounds. In a second, Hansen's whole demeanor shifts to focus. He gives my arm a quick, warm squeeze. "Gotta go. Thanks for the cookies. I'll see you in two days."

He flashes me a grin as he jogs away, leaving my heart hammering louder than the siren.

Chapter Thirteen

The rain starts just after midnight. It rattles along the windows and turns the streetlights outside Lucy's house into blurry halos. I lie in bed, sheets twisted around my legs, listening to the thunder roll over the hills. Every few minutes, lightning flashes and illuminates the whole room. Then it goes dark again.

I try my best to be rational and not check my phone. We got the storm warning on our phones at dinner. It didn't take Lucy all of five seconds to call me out. "Promise me you won't drive up to that cabin tonight, Thea. No matter how bad the storm gets."

I assured her I wouldn't. And I've tried to mean it. I've tried to sit still, to believe the forecast might be wrong, that the work we've done on the cabin will actually hold. I keep telling myself I have to be smart. Lucy is right. The roads will be dangerous, and what can I even do in the middle of the night? But every time thunder rattles the windows, I picture water seeping through the floorboards, undoing months of work. I lie there for hours, wide awake, until the anxiety finally wins out over common sense.

When Lucy's footsteps turn quiet and the yellow glow disappears from under her bedroom door, I count to fifty then slip out of bed, pull on some jeans, and put on rain boots. I grab my keys and quietly close the door behind me, heart hammering like I'm sneaking out to meet a boy past curfew.

The drive out of town is a blur. The rain is relentless, battering the windshield so hard I can barely see the yellow lines. Branches whip across the headlights, and puddles bloom out of nowhere, sending up sheets of water that slap against the undercarriage. I'm half convinced I'm going to get stuck, but I keep going.

By the time I pull up the gravel drive, the rain is coming in sideways, the wind howling through the trees, making the whole place look haunted. I sit for a second, engine idling, palms sweating against the steering wheel. Then I see it. The outdoor lights Hansen placed on the porch are on. And there's another car already here. It's Hansen's truck, with the headlights off, and wipers frozen mid-swipe. I wonder if I'm hallucinating.

But I'm not. It's him. Of course it's him.

I grab my hood, duck out into the rain, and sprint for the porch as water soaks through my clothes in seconds. The air is thick with the smell of wet earth and pine needles, the storm churning the old familiar scents into something new. Above me, I catch a flash of movement. Someone is on the roof.

And it can only be one someone.

"Hansen?" I yell, my voice nearly swallowed by the wind. Lightning cracks, illuminating his outline as he crouches near the chimney.

He glances down, rain streaming off his nose, and my heart drops.

"What the hell are you doing here?" he shouts.

I push back my hood, feeling the rain soak through my hair. "I think the better question is what the hell are you doing on the roof in a thunderstorm!"

He shakes his head and disappears from my view. It's not until a few moments later that I see a blur of movement as he climbs down a ladder placed on the side of the cabin. He's soaked to the bone with his hair plastered to his forehead, and his brown eyes are bright in the storm light.

I don't know whether to laugh or scream at him. "Why aren't you at work?" I ask instead.

He peels off his gloves. "I was. I came straight here after. Got the storm alert and was worried about the roof."

"And you thought it was best to then get on said roof while lightning is coming from every which direction?"

I'm so panicked my hands are shaking. Scratch that, my entire body is shaking.

"I'm fine, Thea. I promise. I know what I'm doing."

"Oh, that's really funny because I don't think you do."

His eyes narrow. "What about you? Why are you here?"

"I was also worried about the roof. Well, about everything, actually."

He glances upwards, then back to me. "It should be okay. I patched it as best I could. There's a tarp over the worst of it, but with this wind, I wouldn't bet on it holding all night."

Thunder rumbles, shaking the porch. I shiver, and Hansen grabs my arm. "We should get inside."

I nod, heading toward the door.

The inside of the cabin is somehow worse than I expected. The floorboards are slick under my feet, and there's a damp, old smell. Water pools near the front door, seeping under the threshold. The kitchen is a disaster with a steady drip-drip-drip from the ceiling.

"Shit," I mutter.

Hansen is already moving, grabbing a stack of sandbags from near the back door. "Help me get these around the doors. If we can slow it down, maybe we'll buy ourselves a little time."

We work in near silence, the only sound the rush of the storm outside and our own harsh breathing. The sandbags are heavy, awkward, and cold against my arms. We wedge them tight against the doors as water pools at our feet. Every time I think we're getting ahead, another leak pops up. By the kitchen window, under the stairs, in the corner where the floor sags. I grab every bucket I can find, lining them up under the worst drips.

Lightning continues to flash and illuminate the chaos. I glance at Hansen, who's wringing out a towel with a tight jaw. There's mud on his face now, and his hands are raw and bleeding. He looks as exhausted as I feel.

"You okay?" I ask.

He nods, but it's clearly a lie. "Just worried about the flooding."

"This place has survived a hundred storms."

He shoots me a look that's half exasperated and half defeated. "Yeah, and I'm guessing it's flooded every single time, Thea. We can't keep patching holes forever. I should have known to fix the roof first. I should have ripped up the entire thing and had it replaced, but every estimate was too much, and I kept thinking I could put it off a few more weeks until I found someone reasonably priced."

"You didn't know we'd get a storm like this."

"I've lived in South Creek my entire life. I should have known."

"Hansen, this isn't your fault."

He doesn't answer right away. He just sinks down onto a chair and stares at his hands. The muscles in his jaw are tight, like he's keeping in words he can't quite get out. The storm fills the silence as rain pounds the roof and wind shakes the windows.

I just watch him. The way his shoulders hunch forward, how his eyes are fixed on the warped boards, as if he can keep the water from rising just by willing it. He's not angry. Not at me, not really even at the storm. He just looks . . . sad.

He drags a hand through his hair, leaving a streak of dirt across his forehead, and I see it so clearly. The guilt, the self-blame. It's etched into every part of him. I'm not sure Hansen has ever been capable of not blaming every bad thing that happens in the world on himself.

I slide down to the floor, not caring that my jeans soak up the water pooling there. "You ever just want to walk away?" I ask quietly. "Because I wouldn't blame you if you did."

He lets out a breath that's half laugh, half sigh. "Sometimes. But then I think about Beck. About you." His voice catches, and he shakes his head, staring at the floor. "I don't know. I hope it's worth it. I want it to be worth it."

"Do you think it will be?" I ask, and he looks at me with his dark eyes.

"I hope so. I really, really hope so."

A tear slips down my cheek as another clap of thunder shakes the cabin. I swipe it away before he can see. "Should we stay? In case it gets worse?"

He watches the steady drip from the kitchen ceiling. "I was planning to. Someone should. Just to keep an eye on it."

"Then I'll stay too."

He shakes his head as he stands up. "You don't have to. I can handle it. You should go home and get some sleep."

I push myself up. "I'm not leaving you here alone. If this place goes under, I want to be here. Besides, you look like you're about to pass out from exhaustion."

"You really don't have to."

"I know. But I'm still going to."

He gives me a tired smile. "Stubborn as ever."

I ignore his maybe-a-compliment, maybe-an-insult comment and flop onto the old couch in the living room. The cushions are damp, but not soaked, and I pull my knees up, hugging them to my chest.

"I've got some blankets and jackets in my truck," Hansen says. "Hang on."

I watch him disappear outside and into the rain. When he returns, he's carrying a pile of things. He shakes the rain from his hair and hands me a sweatshirt first.

"Here. Figured you'd want this more than a wet coat."

I pull the brown sweatshirt over my head. The second it settles around my shoulders, I'm hit with the scent of Hansen. It's not cologne or detergent, just that unmistakable, impossible-to-name smell that belongs to him alone. The sort of scent we all have that lingers in a car or on a borrowed shirt. I wonder if he has any idea how good he smells naturally, or how much it gets to me.

When I look up, Hansen is just standing there, watching me with a smile.

"What?" I ask, probably a little too defensively.

He shakes his head. "Nothing. You just look really cute in that, is all."

Heat crawls up my neck, and I roll my eyes, trying to play it off. "Just give me a blanket. I'm freezing."

He laughs before draping the blanket around my shoulders. It smells like him too. For a moment, I seriously consider just freezing to death just so I don't have to be overwhelmed by how much I love his smell. How much I've missed it. How much I've missed him.

But I decide freezing to death just to avoid Hansen's scent is a tad dramatic, so I wrap the blanket around myself, tucking it close.

Hansen stands by the kitchen doorway, hovering like he doesn't quite know what to do with himself. The storm outside rattles the windows, but inside it feels quieter somehow.

"You know, you can sit on the couch with me," I say, patting the cushion next to me. "There's plenty of room."

"I'm fine here."

"Hansen." My voice is firmer. "Just come sit on the damn couch with me."

He hesitates, caught between wanting to argue and the exhaustion etched across his face. Finally, he gives in, crossing the room and lowering himself onto the far end of the couch, leaving a solid cushion of space between us. Even so, I can feel the heat off him, and suddenly I'm not so cold anymore.

A streak of lightning flashes, lighting up the room and his face. He's so handsome it almost hurts. I wonder if he has any idea what he does to me, just sitting there.

I clear my throat, desperate for a distraction. "Lucy's going to absolutely lose her mind when she finds out I came here tonight."

A grin tugs at his lips. "Oh, she totally will."

"I could always blame it on you," I tease, curling deeper into the blanket. "Think she'd set off a glitter bomb in my car?"

I groan, squeezing my eyes shut at the memory. "God, I totally forgot she did that. Poor Harry Hicks."

Hansen settles a bit more into the couch, finally looking relaxed. "Didn't he kiss you at prom and then ditch you for someone else the same night?"

I open my eyes and meet his. "No. I mean, yeah, okay, he did. But it was just a kiss. It's not like we were dating."

"Still."

"Still, nothing. I wasn't even upset." That's a big fat lie. And the truth is so much messier.

Though no one asked me to prom, Lucy and I agreed we'd go together. Okay, Lucy wanted to go, and she basically forced me to go with her. We bought the dresses, put on the makeup, everything. In the end, I actually felt . . . pretty. I was excited. When we got there and I saw all the couples dancing, it was impossible not to feel left out. I was only sixteen, but I already felt so far behind. I hadn't kissed a boy. Hadn't even had my first crush. Unless you counted the pathetic one on my brother's friend. Which I chose not to.

When Harry Hicks asked me to dance, I felt like I was on cloud nine. He saw me. He liked me. He chose me. But the wholesomeness of it all lasted all of four seconds. Harry didn't see me. He just wanted to sleep with me. Everyone saw him grab my ass, and I didn't have the strength to push him away. And I didn't have the strength to push him away when he kissed me either, because honestly . . . it still felt nice to be wanted. Even if it was only physical.

When he asked me if I wanted to "go somewhere more quiet," I knew what that meant. Surprising myself, I said no. I knew I wasn't ready for that step yet. He was nice enough about it, but the next Monday at school when he bragged to everyone that he slept with Sarah on prom night, I couldn't help but feel hurt.

Hansen scoffs. "Beck sure was upset. He wanted to murder Harry. So did I when he told me."

I snort. "Thank you for wanting to protect my honor, but I was fine. It was just a kiss. Not a big deal."

"It was your first kiss."

"You don't know that."

"I do, Thea."

I stare at him. "Fine. And?"

"*And* it should have been with someone who made you feel special. Not someone like Harry."

The words hang there, and I'm not sure what to do with them. "You really believe that stuff? That love should feel . . . special?"

He laughs. "Yeah. In fact, I kind of think that's the whole point."

I turn so I'm facing him and cross my legs. "Okay. So, tell me then, have you ever been in love?"

He's quiet for a second, his brown eyes illuminated by the soft glow of the lantern in the corner. "Yes. Once."

My mouth moves before my brain can catch up. "Was it with Kayla?"

He blinks, then actually laughs. "You mean the girl I dated in college? No, it definitely wasn't her." He narrows his eyes. "How do you even know about her?"

"I met her once. Lest you forget the Christmas break I came home, and Beck dragged us all to that bar that had a live Santa who really just turned out to be a drunk old guy with a white beard. But she was practically all over you that night. Actually, let's take out the word *practically*. She *was* all over you that night."

Hansen raises an eyebrow. "Sounds a little bit like you were jealous."

I snort out the most dramatic laugh. "I absolutely was not." *Liar.* "It's just . . . I'd never seen you with a girl before, so I wasn't expecting it." *Liar again.*

"I'm honestly surprised you even noticed."

"Of course I noticed. What, you think I go temporarily blind every time two people start dating?"

"No," he says with a laugh. "And we weren't dating."

My nose scrunches. "So, you were just sleeping together?"

"I didn't say that."

"You didn't have to. The way you were kissing her that night said it all."

He leans in closer, and there's a mischievous twinkle in his eye. "It sounds like it really bothered you."

"It didn't." The defensiveness in my voice is not doing me any favors. "I was just curious. That's all."

As fast as someone flipping a switch, the energy shifts between us. It's like we're walking into dangerous uncharted territory, and I'm not sure what waits on the other side.

"I wasn't in love with her," Hansen says.

"Okay."

"What about you? Have you ever been in love?"

I sigh. It feels like a loaded question. My first reaction is yes. But I also never let myself fully think about my feelings for Hansen. Not to the point of admitting I was in love with him. "No," I settle on. "There was a boyfriend once I could have maybe fallen in love with. But it didn't get that far."

His hands tighten a little on the blanket that's now draped over his lap. I pretend not to see it. Tell myself it means nothing. But it's there.

"And how did it end with Mr. Could Have Maybe Fallen In Love?"

"We're happily married with six kids and a dog named Buster," I say. He gives me a look. "We broke up, obviously. But it was amicable."

"What was his name?"

"Who?"

He rolls his eyes. "Your high school math teacher. Obviously your ex-boyfriend."

I purse my lips at his retaliatory sarcasm. "Cam. We dated three years ago. He was nice."

"So . . . he was a dick."

I frown. "No, he really was nice. Everyone liked him. Even Beck, and he was hard to please."

"And where is he now?"

"Married to his secretary. And she's pregnant, too. I checked." Hansen's eyebrows shoot up, so I add, "No need for the look. We were never that serious. I mean, I'm pretty sure he was in love with me, but like I said, I couldn't ever get there."

The second the words are out of my mouth, I hear how they sound. Hansen opens his mouth, but I quickly shoot him down. "I don't mean in that way."

"So, he could get you there?" Hansen asks with a raised eyebrow.

I shrug. "He did fine. But that's not the point. It just never felt right. Maybe I was too much in my head."

"Or maybe it was the lack of orgasms."

My cheeks heat, and I grab a pillow and throw it at him. He laughs as it hits him and falls to the ground. "What about you, Mr. Romantic? Who's the mystery woman after Kayla who stole the love of South Creek's hottest fireman?"

"That's a far reach."

"My mother's book club would beg to differ. All the women in there have massive crushes on you."

"Well, they'd be disappointed. I don't have the best track record for relationships."

"Oh, don't tell me you're married to your job. Such a cliché."

He hesitates, and I don't miss the way his jaw flexes. "It's not that."

"What is it then?"

I've spent years wondering why Hansen hasn't found the love of his life and settled down. I know he's dated here and there—at least that's what Lucy has told me—but it's never been anything serious.

"Maybe I'm also too much in my head," he admits.

I nod, completely understanding. "I hear that happens from lack of orgasms."

That makes him smile.

Once again, the energy shifts. My skin feels hotter, and years of unanswered questions swirl between us.

"Was it worth it though?" I ask him. "Loving whoever she was?"

He's quiet for a long time, staring at the far wall where lightning throws shadows. "Yeah," he says finally. "It was."

We stay like that for a while. Eventually, the rain lessens outside, and the thunder roars seem farther away. Then he moves to stand, looking even more tired than before. "You should try to get some rest, Thea. If you can."

"What about you?"

He offers me a small smile. "I'll be fine."

"You can't stay up all night."

"I'll sleep soon. I promise."

I roll my eyes, but then a yawn slips out before I can stop it.

He grins. "Go to sleep, Thea."

I want to protest more, but the warmth of the couch and the steady rhythm of the rain are pulling me under. My eyelids are heavy, and every bone in my body aches with tiredness.

"Fine," I mutter, curling up and pulling the blanket tighter. "But only because I might actually pass out."

He laughs quietly, and the sound follows me as I drift toward sleep, the storm fading into the distance, and Hansen watching over me in the dark.

Chapter Fourteen

When I open my eyes, the only sound is the slow drip of water into a metal pot somewhere in the kitchen. Sunlight streams through the windows, and I'm still tucked under a blanket on the couch.

It takes me a second to remember why I'm here. Then it all comes back. The storm, the buckets, the sandbags, the rush of adrenaline that lasted until I finally dropped, too tired to think.

Hansen.

I glance around, expecting to see him sprawled out on the floor or curled up on the other side of the couch, but he's nowhere in sight. His blanket is folded neatly on the back of the chair. I grab my phone and see that it's only 5:33 a.m.

My brain shuffles through every possible scenario. What if he left? What if something happened in the night?

I jump up from the couch and shove my boots back on before stepping outside and bracing myself for whatever chaos the storm left behind.

The air is clean, but the yard is a wreck. Pools of water glint in every dip and hollow, and the driveway looks more like a riverbank with mud streaked everywhere, and branches tangled in the grass. The sight of it all knots my stomach tight. This is going to take forever to fix.

I'm still taking it in when Hansen's truck pulls up. He hops out, holding a cardboard tray with two coffees in one hand and a brown paper bag in his other hand. His hair is covered by a backwards baseball cap, and he looks like he didn't sleep a minute, but his smile is still there.

"You're up early," I say as he walks up the steps.

He lifts the tray. "Couldn't sleep. Figured I'd see how bad the road was. And," he hands me a cup and the bag, "thought you could use some breakfast after the night we had. Hope you still like mocha and jalapeño bagels."

I just stare at him. It's been years since he's heard my coffee order, or my intense love for jalapeño bagels. I try to play it cool, but my voice wavers as I say, "Yes. Those are still my favorite."

I take a sip, and it's perfect. Just the right blend of espresso, milk, and sweet chocolate. "Thank you."

He smiles like it's nothing, then he leans against the porch railing, keeping his eyes focused on the mess in the yard. "Should we go back inside?"

"If we stay out here, we can pretend all the damage inside isn't real."

He laughs. "Good point."

We fall quiet, then listen to the quiet drip of water from the roof. There's a stillness when I'm with him, like the world stays quiet just for us. There's no pressure to talk, no rush to move—just the quiet and the strange, beautiful certainty that I'm exactly where I'm supposed to be.

Then he looks at me. "Are you okay? After last night?"

I look out over the damage. "I'm okay . . . ," I settle on, then turn to him. "You?"

He nods, but I can see the exhaustion in his eyes. "Yeah. I'm good."

I take another long drink of coffee. "Come on. Let's get this over with."

※※※※※ ※※※※※

The damage is worse than I thought, but not as bad as it could have been. The weeks after the storm are a blur of trips to the hardware store, spending money I don't have, and work. Hansen is there as much as his schedule allows, and I do what I can. We find someone willing to redo the roof within our budget, and I spend my time cleaning up the yard, sealing up holes, and drying out anything that was water damaged.

And somewhere in the middle of all the fixing and hauling and hammering, I realize I'm starting to enjoy it. Not the constant stress or the endless repairs, but the routine of it. I can get out of bed every morning with a purpose. Knowing that I'm making something broken a little less broken, even if it's only temporary. And I think Beck would really like that.

Then there's the Hansen of it all.

Every time we're together, time moves differently. We talk about nothing and everything. He even makes me laugh. And I notice, more and more, that when he's around, the ache in my chest loses its grip. Not gone, exactly, but lighter—like I can breathe just a little deeper.

But there's a part of me that's terrified of that. I worry that letting myself feel good, even just a little bit, means I'm betraying Beck. That I'm letting go of something I promised myself I'd never let go of. There's guilt in every moment that feels easy, as if Beck might slip away for good if I'm not careful. And underneath that, there's fear, too. Because if I let myself admit that I care about Hansen, if I open that door again, I'm just inviting that possibility of losing someone else. I don't know if I can survive that twice. Not with him.

❧❧❧❧ ❦❦❦❦

It's late in the evening on a Thursday when we finally finish our work. The sun is dipping behind the trees, finally giving us a break from the intense heat. I'm sweeping sawdust off the porch when Hansen comes up behind me. He's wearing a gray T-shirt and his usual backwards baseball cap, because of course he is, and there's a shadow along his jaw. I've learned that he doesn't shave on the days he doesn't work. And I hate how much I love the stubble.

"I think we should call it," he says.

I stop sweeping, honestly a little surprised. Hansen usually has to pry himself away from here. "You sure? I can keep going."

"I know you can, but I'm starving, and I know you're exhausted."

Now that I've stopped moving, I notice the ache in my arms and lower back. But I also know Lucy is out of town for work, and being here is better than sitting alone in my bed and letting my brain spiral.

Hansen walks over to me and grabs the broom out of my hand, then places it against the wall. "Let's go get something to eat."

I look down at my oversized T-shirt, biker shorts, and day-five hair that's currently fighting for its life in a slicked-back ponytail. "Have you seen what I look like?" I ask, scrunching my nose.

His eyes do this thing that's slow and deliberate. It's like he's tracing the outline of me in a way that makes my skin go hot. I have to force myself to look away. "I have," he says, and there's a softness there, something teasing but also real.

"And you still want to be seen in public with me?"

"We'll just go to the diner. Though, for the record, I'd take you anywhere looking like that."

I scoff. "You wouldn't."

He steps closer, putting his hands on my shoulders. "Try me sometime." Then he guides me toward the door. "Come on. Dinner's on me."

"Well, just lead with that next time."

My voice sounds confident, but inside my thoughts are not nearly so easy. I can feel myself getting tangled up in the small, stupid details. How his hands feel on me, the way he looks at me when he thinks I'm not paying attention. It's dangerous, this feeling. I should leave. I should run. I should do what I always do. That way no one gets hurt. But instead, I go with him.

Fran's diner is a small one that's been around longer than I have. It's got squeaky vinyl booths and a jukebox that's been broken since I was twelve. I haven't been in years, not since Beck used to drag me after track meets and then ditch me for his friends. Now it's almost empty, just a couple of regulars and a waitress who's probably seen every mistake anyone in this town has ever made.

"Geez. Blast from the past," I say as we walk inside.

"This okay?" Hansen asks.

"Sure. It can't possibly be as frightening as when I used to come in high school."

We slide into a booth by the window. The waitress comes right away, and Hansen orders a coffee and a cheeseburger. I get pancakes, because why not.

The waitress leaves, and Hansen leans forward, putting his hands on the table. There's a look in his eyes I can't quite place.

"What's with that look?" I ask, crossing my arms.

He smirks. Then: "Tell me what you want to do with the cabin."

I frown, caught off guard. "What?"

"The cabin. That place where we've been working our asses off. I want to know what you would do with it."

"We've already talked about what we're doing."

After Hansen and I started working together, I gave him Beck's notebook. The one that convinced me to come here in the first place. We decided to follow his plans for the cabin. Starting with the wood flooring and all the way down to the firepit.

Hansen nods, but he's not letting it go. "I know that. But what about you? Is there anything you would want to do with it?"

"I don't know," I admit. "It was always Beck's thing. I never really thought about what I wanted. Why are you even asking me this now? Isn't it a little late?"

Hansen takes a sip of his water and shakes his head. "No. We're just finally getting to the part of the renovation where we aren't in survival mode. We're actually creating something. We can do whatever we want now."

I stay quiet.

"Come on," he says. "You must have some ideas."

"Does it matter? We aren't even the ones that will live there."

Hansen sits up straighter and lets out a deep sigh. "Play a game with me?"

"No."

"Perfect. Pretend that it's not the cabin that you grew up with. Pretend that it's a cabin you just won on a game show, and now you get to have it free and clear."

"What kind of shitty game show gives me a cabin but makes me renovate it?"

"You aren't renovating it. Someone else is. You just have to tell them what to do."

I sigh. "Hansen."

"Thea." He leans forward. "Tell me."

I want to keep arguing. Or at least insisting that I don't care what we do with the cabin, but the little nagging part of me that *has* thought about what I would do with it peeks its head out. "I guess . . . I guess I would want it to feel like a place people actually want to be. It always felt so cold. My grandpa liked it dark, so maybe if it were brighter, lighter . . . not so much like a bunker, more like a home."

Hansen's eyes soften. "Lots of light. That's doable."

"Yeah. And more of an open kitchen. We could knock that one wall down, and it would open the entire room and give way more light into the living room."

"Knock the wall down. Consider it done."

He grabs a nearby napkin and pulls a pen from his jacket pocket. "New cabinets?"

"Of course."

"What color? Don't say white."

"What's wrong with white?"

"Too sterile."

"We could do gray."

He smirks. "Millennial gray?"

I groan. "Point taken. Blue, maybe."

"I like blue."

He nods, scribbling it on the napkin. "Noted. Blue cabinets, more light, open kitchen."

We fall quiet, and I dangerously let myself imagine it: the cabin bright and warm, music playing, Hansen in the kitchen.

Then, out of nowhere, Hansen looks up. "Have you ever thought about keeping it? The cabin, I mean. After all this work?"

The question hits me like a punch to the gut. My chest tightens, and I swallow, trying to keep my voice steady. "No. That wasn't the plan." I hear how flat I sound, how unconvincing.

He looks down at his water, tracing the rim with his thumb. I study him, searching for the truth in his face, but he's impossible to read sometimes. "But you've thought about it?"

"Yeah. I have." He meets my eyes. "But I won't."

I have no idea what to say to that.

"How much longer do you think the renovations will take?" I ask. The project's already eaten up two months, and my bank account is a literal horror movie.

He blinks, and something flickers in his face, but it's gone before I can catch it. "If I could work on it more, maybe we'd finish sooner. But with my shifts, probably by the end of the year. Is that okay?"

"That's fine."

"If you need to leave again—"

"I don't need to leave," I blurt out. "I told you I was in this, and I meant that."

He nods. "Okay."

"Great."

I look out the window at the clear sky. My hands are shaking, just a little. I want to stay. I want to run. I don't know how to want both at once.

Chapter Fifteen

THIRTEEN YEARS AGO

It didn't take long to get to the cabin from the city, but that day it felt endless. The air in the car was thick and stale, and I couldn't get comfortable. I pressed my forehead to the window until I left a greasy smudge, but I didn't care. I watched the trees flick past. Maple, pine, birch, all blurred into a green wall. I counted highway markers and tried to pretend I was somewhere else.

Mom drove, her knuckles white on the wheel, her eyes rarely blinking. She hadn't said much since we'd left. Every time I'd tried to talk, she just nodded or sighed or kept her eyes glued to the road. She was good at that—pretending. Sometimes I thought it was her only real skill.

The passenger seat was empty. I kept glancing at it anyway, half expecting Beck to be there with his headphones crooked over one ear, foot up on the dash, humming whatever song he'd been obsessed with that week. The car felt lopsided without him. Lighter, but not in a good way. Like something important had been cut out and left behind.

We hit a patch of bumpy road, and the silence finally broke.

"Are you hungry?" Mom asked, eyes fixed ahead. "We can stop and get something before getting there."

"No," I said, even though I was. I was always hungry when I was nervous, and my stomach had been gnawing at itself since we left.

She let the question die, like I knew she would. She wore her work blouse, with the sleeves rolled up. She smelled like coffee and the same perfume she'd been wearing my entire life.

I thought about asking her for the hundredth time why Beck couldn't come. Not the real reason, the one neither of us could say out loud ("He stole an entire bottle of whiskey from Dad's liquor cabinet and got drunk"), but some version that would make more sense to me. Something that didn't feel like punishment for both of us. But I already knew what she'd say: "It's just for a month, honey." Or, "He needs time with your father." Or, worst of all, "Just focus on yourself."

I picked at my cuticles until they bled.

The last turn was always the worst. The road narrowed, the trees got denser, and the sunlight turned watery and strange. I counted the potholes out of old habit. When the cabin finally came into view with its peeling paint and sagging roof, I felt that familiar twist of dread. It was ugly and small and always smelled of mildew.

I hated it.

Mom killed the engine and turned to face me. "Help me get the bags?" she said, like we were normal. Like we were the kind of family that needed help because there was so much to carry.

I got out, slammed the door harder than I needed to, and grabbed my backpack. The air was hot and damp, and the porch step creaked under my weight. I considered jumping up and down on it to see if it would break, but I didn't have the energy.

Grandpa's car was out front. He never left, as far as I could tell. He was like moss, clinging to the cabin, growing meaner and harder to scrape off every year.

The front door swung open before we reached it. Grandpa stood there with crossed arms, and his mouth was set in a line so thin it was nearly invisible. He looked the same as always: plaid shirt, jeans, suspenders, boots caked with mud. He didn't bother with a greeting.

"You're late," he said, not to me, but to Mom.

Mom gave him a brittle smile. "Sorry, Dad. The traffic was bad."

He grunted. "You say that every year." He glanced at me, eyes sharp as broken glass. "Where's the boy?"

I stared down at my shoes.

"I told you, Dad, Beck is staying home with his father this trip. He's going to have him work in the shop. But Thea is here, and she's really excited. Right Thea?"

My stomach twisted. I wanted to say no, but I knew better.

"Yeah," I said.

Mom just tightened her jaw, lips pressed together.

"Let's just get inside," she said.

The cabin reeked of cigarettes and booze. The windows were closed, trapping all the air inside. The living room was cluttered with old magazines and bottles, and that same wood stove stood cold and gray in the corner. Grandpa's brown leather chair sat dead center, facing the TV.

I dropped my bag by the stairs, already counting the hours until I could leave.

"Put your stuff in your room," Mom said. "Then come down and help me get started with dinner."

I didn't answer. I just grabbed my things and headed up, taking the stairs two at a time. The hallway was narrow and dark, and the room I shared with Beck was at the end. The door stuck as I tried to open it, and I had to shove it with my shoulder.

Inside, the room looked exactly the same as last summer: two twin beds with faded quilts, a warped dresser, and a window that looked out over the sloping backyard.

I set my bag down and shut the door, twisting the lock even though it didn't work. Then I sat on the bed, stared at the ugly floral wallpaper, and tried not to cry.

I could hear my mother and Grandpa's voices downstairs. Beck's bed across from me was empty and silent.

I dug my battered notebook from my bag and found a pen still stuck in the spiral. I flipped it open, stared at the first blank page, and started to write.

Dear Dipshit,

I knew he wouldn't read this. Or maybe he would and just laugh at me. But I had to do something, because if I sat there any longer, I was going to lose my mind.

I kept writing.

If you can't tell from my strong opening, I'm still pissed you didn't come with us. But probably even more pissed that you stole from Dad to get drunk. Like, come on. I know you have a fake ID. Why not just use it to buy alcohol like a normal kid? Or at the very least, not get caught. (Don't tell Dad I said that.) Now I get to spend the month listening to Mom cry about how much she misses you.

The pen scratched across the paper, and the words poured out in a rush.

I finished and signed the letter. Then I folded it, set it on the nightstand, and stared at it.

I had actually never sent a letter I'd written before. It was just a way to get my anger and frustration out. But there was something different about it this time. I wanted Beck to know what I felt. So, the next day, I walked to the post office and sent it.

Sleep was nearly impossible to come by after the letter was gone. Every time I closed my eyes, I saw Beck's face reading it. Would he be angry? Sad? Nothing? It was stupid to send it. But in the morning, I woke up and wrote him another one anyway. The words poured out faster this time. I told him everything. How I didn't sleep, how Mom forgot yet again how much I hated scrambled eggs, how mad I was, and how much I missed him, even when I didn't want to.

The days started to fall into a pattern. Wake up, write Beck a letter, stuff it in the battered blue mailbox at the end of the driveway. Pretend I wasn't checking for anything when I walked outside later, heart pounding in my throat. Nothing ever came.

I told myself it didn't matter, that these letters were for me. That I was just writing into the void, and that was fine. But every day when I pulled open the mailbox and found it empty, something inside me wilted a little more.

Three weeks. Twenty-one letters. I started running out of things to say. I started telling him about the weather, about the way the light came through the kitchen window, about how I tried to make his favorite grilled cheese but just ended up with a mess. Sometimes, I was angry. Sometimes, I just missed him.

Then, on a Tuesday, there it was—a letter. Thick paper, folded messily, with my name across the front. My heart stuttered. It was Beck, finally, finally writing back. But as I looked closer, I realized the handwriting wasn't his.

I quickly ripped the letter open. And it wasn't from Beck. It was from someone entirely different. The very last person I expected.

It was from Hansen.

Hey Thea,

Okay, I know I'm probably not the person you were expecting to hear from. To be honest, I'm not sure how you'll react to me writing you. I just couldn't watch another one of your letters go unanswered. So, here I am, taking a page out of your notebook. (Starting off strong with an absolutely hilarious writing pun.)

In case you were wondering, or worried, Beck's doing just fine. Your dad is working him pretty hard in his shop, but I think it's good for him. Anyway, how's your summer? I hope you don't miss us all too much (actually, that's a lie. I do hope you miss at least me.)

Write me back. If you want. Or not. It's fine.

Currently googling how to end a letter,

Hansen

I read it twice. Three times. I didn't realize I was smiling until my cheeks started to hurt. Suddenly everything else, the empty mailbox, the ache, the anger, faded out. There was just this letter, and the weird fluttery feeling in my stomach.

I took out a clean sheet of paper, smoothed it flat, and started to write.

Dear Hansen,

First and foremost, I refuse to acknowledge your writing pun. Except to say it was terrible. And the tiniest bit clever. (Don't let this go to your head.)

Second, I guess I should say thank you for writing me back. You've made what's been an incredibly lonely summer just a little more bearable.

Also, thank you for the update on Beck since he won't respond to me. It means a lot.

In worse news, my grandpa caught a fish and wants to teach me to gut it. So, basically living the dream. Try your best to contain your jealousy. Anyway, enough about me. How is your summer?

With Love,
Thea

Three days later, there was another letter.

Dear Thea,

Had a dream about you gutting a fish. Except that the fish wasn't a fish, it was me. And honestly, not the worst dream I've ever had. When you get home, you'll definitely have to show me how it's done.

My summer's okay. Yesterday was my dad's birthday. My mom tried *to pretend it was just another day, but she spent half the afternoon staring out the window, and the other half crying. I made him a cake. He always loved cakes. It tasted like shit.*

I keep thinking he's going to come home and yell at me for leaving my shoes by the door. Isn't that dumb?

Anyway, your dad is letting Beck out of the house now. We've been running every morning. I think he really misses you.

Write me back if you aren't too busy being elbow deep in fish guts.

Hansen

Dear Hansen,

First, that dream sounds more like a nightmare. I hope you haven't lost too much sleep over it.

Second, I'm really sorry about your dad's birthday. I can't imagine how weird and hard that must be for you and your mom. It doesn't sound dumb at all that you think about him still coming home. I think that's a really normal thing. And I bet he would have loved the cake, even if it did taste like shit.

Grandpa is now making me try pickled herring for breakfast. I told him I was allergic, which isn't true, unless you count emotional allergies.

With Love,

Thea

Chapter Sixteen

Now

The date on the calendar stares at me. August 1st. Tomorrow is Beck's birthday. What would be his thirtieth birthday. I can't even think about it. It feels too big. They say the firsts are always the hardest. And I know I'm not ready to face this one. Beck always enjoyed his birthday. He loved getting presents, eating cake, and all around just having everyone together to celebrate something. There were so many years where despite all the shit going on around us, his birthday would come, and it was like it was all forgotten. We'd get together, and it was just us. Enjoying this crazy existence on earth, having fun.

His last birthday was anything but that. We'd barely spoken the weeks leading up to it, and I stared at the date on the calendar much like I do now, not knowing what to do. That day, I almost called him no less than three million times. Hell, I almost flew back to South Creek, where I knew he was at my parents' house. But I didn't. Instead, I sent a text. A simple text.

Happy Birthday, Beck. I love you.

That's all.

And he never responded.

Maybe that's why today feels so heavy. Why I'm positive that tomorrow will be even worse. The urge to call my parents is gnawing at me. I haven't spoken to them since my mother told me she couldn't support me with the cabin. And I haven't wanted to. Not until today. Not until this moment.

Searching for some type of comfort, I grab my phone to call them, but instead am met with a string of missed calls and texts from Hansen. My heart stutters. I glance at the time. It's almost nine in the morning. I was supposed to meet him at six.

Shit.

Forgetting all about my parents, I shove the phone in my pocket and bolt for the door.

When I finally reach the cabin, it's quiet inside. "Hansen?" Nothing.

I drop my bag next to the door and wander through the rooms. The living room is empty, as is the kitchen. I head for the stairs, hoping he's not upset with me for being late. Hansen loves a schedule. And an early morning start time.

Halfway up, I hear a thump above me, and the soft scrape of wood on wood. I stop, then tiptoe the rest of the way, peering around the stairwell. At the end of the hall, the attic hatch is open, and all I can see is Hansen's feet on the top step of a ladder.

"Hansen?" I call out again. "Sorry I'm late."

He steps down the ladder so I can see his face. "Jesus, Thea—are you okay? I tried calling." He's gripping the ladder too hard, and there's worry etched all over his face. Guilt twists in my stomach.

"I know. I'm sorry. I just . . ." *was agonizing about tomorrow and how to handle all the emotions I'm feeling.* "Overslept."

He studies me, searching my face, and I see the fear there, the way he was probably running through every worst-case scenario. Finally, he lets out a shaky breath, wipes his hand across his face, and manages a smile. "You scared the shit out of me."

"I know. I'm sorry."

"I'm just glad you're okay."

I bite my lip, and my mind floods with questions.

Does he remember what tomorrow is? Is it hurting him as much as it is me?

"Can you hand me the flashlight in my toolbox down there? This one just crapped out on me," Hansen says, throwing a flashlight to the ground.

I grab it and hand it to him. "What are you doing up there?"

"Checking the insulation," he says before climbing back up and disappearing into the attic. It's quiet, then there's a shuffle and thud as something slides across the boards. "The insulation guy is supposed to come out in a few days. I just wanted to get a head start."

He appears again, but this time with a small cardboard box in his arms. "Just found this wedged behind a rafter." He climbs the rest of the way down and sets it on the ground.

It's just a plain box, crumpled at the corners, with a strip of faded masking tape across the top. "What is it?"

"No clue. It was all the way at the back. Maybe it was your grandfather's?"

"It's probably just alcohol then." I look at Hansen. "Should we open it?"

"Your call," he says, and I feel like he's thinking the same thing I am. What if it isn't my grandfather's? What if it was Beck's?

"I'll open it."

I kneel, and my hands shake as my fingers brush the rough cardboard. I peel back the old tape to reveal a box full of envelopes. Envelopes with Beck's name written in my handwriting across the top.

My heart drops to my stomach.

"What are those?" Hansen asks.

"They're letters," I whisper, grabbing one out. "My letters. The ones I wrote to Beck the summer I came here without him. The summer you and I wrote to each other." I stare at the water-stained pieces of paper. "He actually kept them. All of them. He told me he threw them out. Said they were embarrassing."

I flip through the stack of envelopes. They're all opened. Some even have bent corners, like they've been read a hundred times.

I pick up the first one dated May 29th.

Dear Dipshit,

If you can't tell from my strong opening, I'm still pissed you didn't come with us. But probably even more pissed that you stole from Dad to get drunk. Like, come on. I know you have a fake ID. Why not just use it to buy alcohol like a normal kid? Or at the very least, not get caught. (Don't tell Dad I said that.) Now I get to spend the month listening to Mom cry about how much she misses you.

And don't even get me started on Grandpa.

Is Dad making you do endless chores? Or work in the shop? Because if so, you deserve it. I hope you think about how your actions have consequences next time, Beck. And not just for you, but for everyone around you.

With no love,

Thea

Tears start to form in my eyes, but I grab another.

Dear Beck,

I haven't left my room all week. Mom's barely even noticed. She's been shopping with Grandpa and basically rearranging the entire cabin. It's hideous. Even more so than before.

Only three more weeks left.

Hope you're having fun with Dad. (Not.)

with barely any love,
Thea

I drop the letter and close the box. My chest aches. I always thought he'd thrown these away. That he'd never read the harsh words I wrote him.

But he kept them. Every single one.

"Why would he keep these?" I mutter, half to myself.

"Maybe they meant more to him than he let on," Hansen says.

"I don't get it. He never answered. Never even told me he'd read them."

Hansen's voice is barely above a whisper. "Maybe he just . . . needed to know someone cared."

I laugh, and it's harsh and ugly. "Yeah, well, fat lot of good me caring did. He left anyway."

"Thea—" he starts, but I stand, cutting him off.

"I don't even know why he killed himself," I blurt out. "He didn't leave a note. He didn't ever say he wanted to die. I mean, I know he's always struggled with life, but he never talked about . . ." My voice breaks. "One minute he was here, and the next he was gone. If I had known," I continue. "If I had only known."

Hansen doesn't respond, and my eyes land back on the box. "I can't keep these. They're just reminders that I failed."

I grab the box and start for the stairs. Hansen blocks me. "Thea, just stop for a second."

"No." I push past him and nearly trip as I stomp down the stairs.

I don't look back at Hansen, but he follows close.

"Wait," he says. "Just think about it. You might want them later."

"I won't," I spit, stepping outside into the already unbearably hot summer heat, my sights set on the giant dumpster in the driveway.

"I know why you were late," Hansen blurts out behind me. My entire body stops, and I clutch the box a little tighter.

I slowly turn to face him. "What?"

He sighs. "Today. I know why you were late. I know what tomorrow is. I know that it's—"

"Don't say it, Hansen."

"His birthday," he finishes anyway.

Pain grips me in a chokehold. I swallow a sob. "That has nothing to do with what's happening right now."

"I think it does. You're upset—" I let out a laugh, but Hansen keeps going, "—which is okay, Thea. But I don't want you to regret this. I don't want you to regret throwing them away."

I look into Hansen's warm brown eyes. They're pleading with me. And all I want to do is give in. Fall apart right here and sob until there's nothing left. But the guilt is too strong. It overcomes me like a poison spreading through my veins.

"You know what I remember?" I say. "When my Dad found out Beck took the whiskey, I was so angry. I didn't even ask why he did it. I just blamed him. I told him he was selfish. I wrote it in these letters, too. Over and over. 'You deserve it.' 'You should think about your actions.'" My voice cracks. "And he read them. He kept reading them. Maybe he even read them before he—" I can't say the words. I just press the box to my chest and squeeze my eyes shut.

The world goes quiet, except for the far-off bark of a dog. The sun is blinding, and I can picture Beck's hands holding these letters, the hours he must've spent rereading every line.

"He knew you loved him, Thea," Hansen says, and my eyes open. "He hurt you that summer, and you had every right to be upset."

I shake my head. "No." The box is heavy in my arms, but I turn and continue to walk toward the dumpster. I reach the edge and stop.

"I won't regret it."

Without another thought, I let the box go.

It lands with a dull, final thud.

I press my hand to my eyes as the tears start to fall harder. Silence settles over everything. I breathe and wait for the regret to come. But all I feel is empty.

Maybe that's all that's left.

Chapter Seventeen

I wake before the sun, but I don't open my eyes. Not yet. If I keep them closed, I can almost pretend none of this is real. That today isn't August 2nd. That the sharp, relentless pain isn't waiting for me, pressing down on my chest so hard I can barely breathe.

I curl tighter under the covers, ignoring the sweat dampening my shirt, or the way my legs are tangled in the sheets. My whole body feels too heavy, like I've been replaced from the inside out with cold, wet sand. The world outside my room doesn't feel real. It could be Mars, for all I care.

My phone buzzes on the nightstand. Once. Then again. I don't move. Even the thought of reaching for it makes my throat close up. I don't want to read messages, don't want to be anyone's sister, daughter, friend, anything.

Then there's a knock at the door. I don't answer. It gets louder, then softer, then I hear Lucy's muffled voice. "Thea? I'm coming in, okay?"

The door opens, but I don't even bother looking her way. The mattress dips as she sits beside me, and she gently puts her hand on my shoulder.

"Hey," she whispers. "I brought you some coffee." She sets it on the nightstand. "I know today must be hard, especially with everything that happened yesterday. Do you want to talk? Or I found that dumb movie where they get stranded on an island together. The one you used to make me watch when we were kids. We could ditch our responsibilities and introduce it to Juniper."

I bite my cheek, blinking back tears. "I'm sorry, Luce. I can't."

"Okay." She squeezes my shoulder, then leans forward and presses a kiss to my forehead. "You take all the time you need. I'll be right out there if you want to talk." She leaves the door cracked slightly behind her.

I fall back asleep after she leaves. I'm not sure how long I'm out, but when I wake up, the light behind the curtains has changed. My full coffee is still on the nightstand, next to my phone. The phone I know must be filled with missed messages. I try to sit up, and my head pounds, the room spinning a little. I stare out into nothing. I think I hear voices outside. Lucy and Juniper's, maybe.

Then Beck's face fills my mind. Too vivid, too alive. I see him in his car, those last moments. Did he suffer? Was he scared? If I could ask him now, would he regret it? The pain hits like a fist. I clutch the bed, trying to ground myself, but tears spill over before I can stop them.

Then, my bedroom door opens again. I glance up, and Hansen is there, standing in the doorway. He doesn't say anything.

"You shouldn't be here," I croak, and my voice is raw from all the crying.

"And yet here I am."

He sits next to me on the bed. I want to push him away, or maybe I want him to hold me tighter than anyone ever has. I let out a sob that should embarrass me, but right now, I don't care. Hansen's hand finds mine, and that's all it takes. I collapse into his chest, sobbing.

"Shh," he murmurs, cradling my head. "I've got you."

"I don't think I can do this," I manage, my voice cracking.

"I know. I know." His hand strokes my hair. "Just take it one second at a time."

It still hurts so badly that I can barely breathe. But I'm not alone. Not in this moment. So, I let myself cry until there's nothing left.

✻✻✻✻✻ ✻✻✻✻✻

The next time my eyes open, I'm a little disoriented. There's sunlight pouring through the bedroom window so bright I have to squint, so it's clearly morning. I remember Hansen's arms around me, the feel of his shirt against my cheek, and the way I cried until I was empty. And then, how he held me until I fell asleep in his arms. I roll over, half-expecting to find him there, but it's empty. There is, however, a fresh cup of coffee on the nightstand, and beside it, a bottle of headache medicine and a glass of water.

I sit up, moving slowly so as to not anger the headache already forming behind my eyes. My mind echoes with Hansen's voice: *Just take it one second at a time.*

One second at a time, I tell myself. Just this. Just sitting up. That's all I have to do.

I swallow the medicine. *One second at a time.*

I make it to the shower and let the water run hot over my body, washing away the ache, the tears, and the sweat of yesterday. I shampoo my hair. I wash my face. I stand there until my skin is red and my head feels clearer. *One second at a time.*

I dry off. I pull on clean clothes, brush my hair, and look at myself in the mirror. My eyes are swollen and red, but I look more alive than yesterday. It's not much, but it's something. *One second at a time.*

When I go back into my bedroom, my phone lights up as if it's been waiting for me to return. I brace myself for what I'm going to see. Several missed calls from my mom. A text from an old coworker in New York asking me how I'm holding up today. A text from Lucy asking if I need anything. And a message from my dad. From this morning. Guilt eats at me as I read it.

Dad

> Thea, I hope all is well. Your mother tried to call you yesterday a few times. She was worried when you didn't answer. But we called Lucy, who told us you were just sleeping off a headache. We miss you, honey. Hope you're doing all right and that we can see each other soon. Love, Dad.

My heart jolts, then sinks. I read it again, then flip the phone face down on the bed. I know yesterday had to be hard for them. Just like it was me. But I can't face them. Not yet.

When I leave my bedroom, the house is quiet. Lucy isn't in the kitchen, which is strange considering she's always awake first thing in the morning. It's Sunday, so she isn't at work. I peek into her office and find her slumped over her laptop, the screen glowing with a marketing presentation. I close the laptop gently, cover her with the throw blanket from the couch, and leave her to sleep.

Back in the kitchen, I can tell Lucy has been cooking, which is a common way she deals with stress. I start the dishes, scrubbing away the evidence of yesterday. I keep moving, one second at a time. I search my phone for a pancake recipe since they are Juniper's favorite. I measure flour, pour milk, crack eggs, whisk it all together. I try to lose myself in the rhythm, focusing on the movements, the sensations, the small sound of batter sizzling in the pan.

I'm sliding the last pancake onto the plate when the front door opens. It's not Juniper or Lucy—it's Hansen. He steps inside, looking like the calm after a dark storm. His eyes land on me, and something in his face softens. I have no idea if I should feel relieved or mortified after yesterday. Both, probably. My skin prickles, and I'm annoyingly aware that I chose to put on pajama shorts and an old T-shirt.

Hansen doesn't hesitate. He strolls into the kitchen, gaze flicking from me to the pancakes and back again. "Hey, you're awake."

I blink, trying to act casual and not think about the way his arms felt around me last night. "And you're here again."

"I told Lucy I'd come by after work." His eyes linger on me for a beat too long, and I have to look away before I say, or think, something dumb. "How are you feeling?"

"Uh, better," I mumble, suddenly fascinated by the pancakes. "And . . . a little bit like I'm hungover."

He leans back against the counter. "I want to take you somewhere today."

I shoot him a look. "Aren't you tired? You just worked all night. And isn't the insulation guy coming to the cabin? And—"

He pushes off the counter and, without warning, takes the spatula straight from my hand. His fingers brush mine, and it's a stupid, fleeting touch, but it shoots straight through me. "Just trust me, Thea." His voice has a rough edge now. "Go get your shoes on. I'm driving."

I stare at him. "Is this a kidnapping?"

He smiles. "Kind of. But you'll like it. Promise."

"I need to get changed."

"You look perfect."

I have no idea what to say to that. My heart is pounding. I hope he can't hear it.

Thankfully, a pair of footsteps behind us pulls our attention away. Lucy appears, yawning, the blanket still wrapped around her shoulders. She stops dead when she sees me at the stove and Hansen just a few inches away from me. Her whole face lights up. "You're up! And you cleaned. And you're making breakfast. And you're with Hansen. So many things to go over, so little idea where to start."

"You mind if I steal her away today, Lucy?" Hansen asks.

Lucy's green eyes widen. "Do I? Absolutely not. It will make me feel significantly less guilty that I have to unexpectedly work today." She waves me away from the stove. "Go on. I can clean this up. You two go . . . wherever it is you're going. I'll make sure Juniper knows you made the pancakes."

I hesitate. The safe and easy comfort of my bed calls to me. But Hansen is waiting, patient as ever, and there's a comfort with him too. A familiar one I've been trying to ignore but that I'm so tired of fighting.

"Trust me?" he asks, his voice soft, his dark eyes shining. He smiles, and I can't help but smile back.

"Okay."

Chapter Eighteen

The drive is quiet, but not the kind that feels heavy or forced. Hansen seems content to let the silence settle. He keeps his hands loose on the steering wheel and his focus on the road. I press my forehead lightly against the cool glass and let the blur of trees lull my nerves, though curiosity keeps clawing at me.

Finally, I can't help myself. "Okay, I've held it in long enough. Can I know where we're going now?"

A hint of a smile pulls at his mouth, one side lifting in that way it does when he's trying to tease but not quite commit. "You really don't mind spoiling the surprise?"

I turn to face him, arching an eyebrow. "Obviously, or I wouldn't be asking."

He glances my way, eyes steady and playful. "Just wait a few more minutes, Mrs. Impatient."

I roll my eyes, but I can't help noticing the road we're on. Something about the way the trees lean in, the dip in the pavement. It all feels familiar. My heart starts beating quicker. Old oaks line the road, their branches low enough to almost brush the roof of the truck, and wildflowers crowd the ditches. I know this route. I know what's coming, but I can't bring myself to say it out loud. The anticipation knots itself in my stomach.

When we pull into the small lot, I look up, blinking in disbelief at the faded wooden sign. South Creek Butterfly Conservatory.

I lose my words for a second. The glass building sits in the sun, completely unchanged. The memories hit so hard, I have to grip the seat to keep steady. Beck and I used to come here every year, sometimes twice if I could convince him. He'd complain, roll his eyes, but he never actually said no. I swallow, trying to force down the grief.

Hansen switches off the engine, then looks over with a gentle, tentative expression. "Thought you might want somewhere that felt familiar." His voice is quieter than usual, and it tightens something in my chest.

My nod is small, but the gratitude behind it isn't. "How'd you even know?"

He shrugs, looking away and then back again. "You told me once. I hoped you'd still like it."

The urge to cry catches me off guard. Instead, I open the car door and step into the warmth, letting the air rush around me. We walk inside together, Hansen pays, and we enter.

The conservatory is warm and thick with the scent of earth and flowers. Sunlight streams through the glass ceiling, painting everything gold. Butterflies float by in bursts of color. We start down one of the winding paths, taking slow steps. It's all just as I remember: wild, lush flowers in every shade, benches tucked beneath arching branches. I pause beside a bush crowded with purple blooms. A monarch perches on a petal, its wings trembling.

"I can't believe I'm here," I whisper. "Beck used to complain every time I dragged him here. He'd act like it was torture, but he always ended up loving it. Especially when one landed on me. I think he just got a kick out of me geeking out."

Hansen's watching a blue morpho as it circles overhead. "He liked seeing you happy."

We walk for a while in silence. There's no one else here, so the only sounds are the hum of the greenhouse and the soft brush of our shoes on the path. I let my fingers trail the railing. The moss is cool and rough beneath my palm. It feels good to move, to be somewhere that's mostly good memories.

At a little pond dotted with lilies, Hansen sits on a bench, his elbows braced on his knees. I lower myself beside him, hands tangled in my lap.

I'm so twisted up in memories and gratitude that I don't really know what to say. I settle on something easy. "So," I start. "How's your mom? I keep meaning to ask."

A smile tugs at his lips, the corners of his eyes crinkling. "She's good. Practically lives at her bakery now."

"Lucy raves about her place. If her baking's anything like I remember, I bet the whole town's addicted."

"She's happier than I've seen her in years. Bakes every day, feeds anyone that's willing. She even got a bee tattoo, if you can believe it."

"Yes, I absolutely can."

"She asks about you all the time." He's watching me now, not the butterflies.

I study the lilies, trying to hide my smile. "What do you tell her?"

"That you're a millionaire with a ten-story house and your own butler."

"Damn. You went straight to millionaire?"

"Didn't want to oversell it. Billionaires are bad news."

"Oh, definitely."

"She believes it, though."

"Of course she does. Makes total sense that a millionaire like me would be living in her best friend's guest room and fixing up an old cabin with her son."

His laughter rings out, open and real, and my heart flutters.

"What about your parents?" he asks. "How are they?"

A sigh slips out before I can stop it. "You probably know better than I do. I've seen my mom once since I got back. She didn't love the idea of me staying. Definitely didn't love that I'm renovating the cabin. I think . . . maybe it was easier for them when I was far away. I was safe, but not their problem up close."

He's quiet for a moment. "I'm sure they've missed you."

"Maybe." I nudge a pebble with my shoe, watching it disappear into the grass. "She called a few times yesterday. My dad texted this morning.

I want to answer, and I just . . . can't. Maybe I'm being unfair. They lost their son. That's not something you recover from. But it feels like they only started caring about me because Beck's gone." The words stick in my throat. "Sometimes it feels like the wrong kid got left behind."

"You matter just as much as Beck, Thea."

I look at him, surprised by how close we've gotten—physically and emotionally. It's scary, how easy it is to let the walls drop in here, with him. Outside, the world feels too big, too loud, but right now, it all shrinks down to something small enough to hold. The thought of caring for him this way again terrifies me, but I don't think I can push it away anymore.

I force a smile, reaching for lighter ground. "Enough about me. Tell me what it's like being a firefighter."

"It's pretty much what you think."

I raise an eyebrow. "Hot men fighting fires all day?"

Hansen's head snaps up, startled. "Wait. Did you just call me hot?"

My eyes roll. "You know what you look like, Hansen."

He laughs, but it's more out of disbelief than confidence. "Yeah, but you've never said it out loud before."

"Yes, I have."

I've certainly thought it enough times.

He shakes his head. "No. You haven't."

"Oh my God, do you need a compliment that badly?" I nudge his shoulder, but he just smirks at me, not letting it go. "Fine. I think you're very hot, Hansen. There. Happy?"

His smirk softens into something real, almost shy. "Thank you. And just in case you've never heard me say it out loud before either, I think you're also very hot, Thea."

I wasn't expecting that. I mean, he's called me beautiful before, but it's never felt like this. It's never felt so real. My cheeks go hot, and I try to play it cool, but I can feel a ridiculous grin tugging at my mouth. "Well, thank you for the official confirmation."

I need to get the conversation back on track, and far away from talking about how attractive we find each other, before I explode.

"So, back to my question. What's it actually like being a firefighter?"

He shakes his head, amused. "It's hard work. There are long days and unpredictable nights. Sometimes you get this rush, like nothing else. But you're also seeing people on the worst day of their lives. It sticks with you. I like being useful. I like actually helping. But . . . it takes a toll."

The night I saw him running flashes in my mind. "Do you talk to anyone? When it gets bad?"

He looks at me, almost surprised. "You mean, like, a therapist?"

I nod. He exhales, rubbing the back of his neck. "A couple of the guys do. Graham, one of the firefighters you met, his mom's a therapist, actually. He's always repeating stuff she says."

"Have you ever thought about going yourself?"

He pauses briefly. "I've thought about it. You?"

I laugh. "Honestly? No. The idea of telling a stranger all of my dark thoughts and secrets sounds like torture. Not sure I'm cut out for it."

"You tell me your secrets."

"You're not a stranger. And I definitely don't tell you everything."

He drifts a little closer. "Fine. Tell me one."

"What?"

"Tell me one of your dark thoughts or secrets. Right now."

"Hansen," I protest, but I can't keep the smile off my face.

He matches my tone, playful. "Thea."

"I can't just . . . pull one out of thin air."

He raises an eyebrow, unconvinced. I turn to face him fully, willing to play along if only to distract from the heavy stuff.

"All right, if you're so sure. What about you? What's Hansen Reed's deep, dark secret?"

He thinks for a second, then glances at me sideways. "I went to New York once and stood outside your office."

My mouth drops open. "What? When were you even in New York? And how did you know where I worked?"

"Lucy told me. She told everyone, actually. And my cousin was getting married. She lives in New Jersey, but her fiancée's family is from the city. My mom and I went for the weekend, and before I even realized, we were outside your office."

I stare at him, trying to picture him standing outside the offices of Peterson & Weston. "Why didn't you come in?" I ask.

"You and I weren't talking. I just imagined what would happen if you walked out and saw me."

"What would you have said if I had?"

"I have no idea. I played out a dozen scenarios in my head, all of which ended horribly."

I let out a shaky laugh. "Wow."

Would anything have changed if I'd seen him that day? I'm honestly not sure.

"I hated that job," I confess. "The one you stalked me at."

He scoffs.

"My boss was a creep. He never took me seriously. Spent more time staring at my ass than listening to anything I said."

Hansen's jaw tightens. "I'm sorry, Thea. Now I wish I had run into him that day instead of you. And by run into, I mean punch."

I laugh.

"I thought you were happy out there," he says.

I shake my head. "I wanted to be. And don't get me wrong, some parts were okay, but most of the time it felt like a really long, really lonely vacation. It never felt like home."

"Was there anything you did love about it?"

I let the memories sift through, searching for something that matters. "There was this diner near my apartment. They made fresh bagels every morning, but they'd sell out so fast. I used to get up at four just to grab one before work. Those mornings, before the city was really awake, when everything was quiet—that's when I felt most at peace. Reminded me of how quiet South Creek could be."

"Sounds peaceful."

I gently shove his shoulder. "What about you? Ever think about leaving here?"

He shakes his head with no hesitation at all. "No. Not because I couldn't be happy somewhere else, but . . . this is home. I'm pretty sure I could spend my whole life searching and never find this feeling anywhere else."

His words hit deeper than I think possible. "Yeah. I get it."

He shifts, snapping his fingers like he's just had an idea. "Hey, remember that thing we used to do?"

"You'll have to be a little more specific."

"When we'd pick a word for how we felt. No explanations, unless we wanted to. Just . . . the word."

I give a skeptical look. "I'm pretty sure we did that, like, twice."

He's unbothered. "Let's do it now."

I wrinkle my nose, but he's not letting up. "You're serious?"

"Very."

I sigh. "Fine. But you go first."

He's quiet for a moment, searching for the right word. "Unperturbed."

I blink. "That's your word?"

"Yes. Look it up if you don't know what it means," he says in a playfully mocking tone. "Your turn."

I let my mind wander. There are a hundred words I could pick, but only one feels true. "Tired."

Hansen doesn't push. He just smiles, leaving it at that.

At the car, Hansen opens my door, then stops. "Still on for the cabin in the morning?"

I let out an exaggerated breath . "I guess it's back to reality, huh?"

"We could run away. Go to New York and just eat bagels all day."

A smile tugs at my lips as I shake my head. "No. I've already tried that. It never goes quite the way you hope."

Chapter Nineteen

THIRTEEN YEARS AGO

The first week of school, I found a letter taped to my locker. The paper was folded in a neat square, the edges already soft from being carried around in someone's pocket. I recognized Hansen's handwriting before I even opened it.

Dear Thea,

Happy first week of school! Do you hate it as much as I do?? Mr. Patterson told the entire precalculus class that he won't be handing out As this year. So basically, I should give up my dreams of ever going to college. Even though I respect you heavily for it, I'm not sure how you can enjoy math.

Barely hanging on,

Hansen

I couldn't help but smile. I imagined him scowling at his desk, pencil tapping, math book open but ignored. During free period, I wrote him back, pressing hard enough for the pen to leave an imprint on the next page.

Dear Hansen,
Sorry about Mr. Patterson. If it helps, he hates everyone. Except me. Maybe I can put in a good word for you. Just whatever you do, don't mention Beck's name. They've never been fans of each other. Hope your day gets better.
With Love,
Thea

The letters kept coming, sometimes tucked into the spine of my chemistry book, sometimes taped crookedly to my locker. They weren't every day, but often enough that I started looking for them, hoping for a few sentences scrawled in blue ink.

Dear Thea,
I saw you at track practice today. You were sitting in the stands, writing. Were you writing me a letter? I hope so. Honestly, junior year has been harder than I thought, and these have become the best part of my day. It's nice to have something to look forward to. Beck and I are going to Amber's this weekend for a party. You should come. She's really chill and her parties are always pretty fun. Let me know.
Hansen

Dear Hansen,
As much as I would love to see all of my classmates get wasted and make really stupid choices at a party, this weekend is my math competition. It's about two hours away but will really help me secure a scholarship.

With Love,
Thea

That night, I sat cross-legged at my desk, with a stack of practice questions for the math competition in front of me. The house was quiet. Beck was at a doctor's appointment, Dad was at the shop, and Mom was reading in her room. I'd just started working through a particularly nasty geometry proof when the door to my bedroom burst open.

I threw my head back, startled, and saw Hansen standing in the doorway. His hair was still damp from running, and he wore his track shirt and a pair of gray shorts that, I'll admit, did unfair things for his legs. I tried to focus on his face, which was just as distracting. "Can I help you?" I asked, trying to sound annoyed. "Beck isn't here."

He grinned, and my heart stuttered in my chest. "I'm here to see you," he said, like it was obvious. "Why didn't you tell me that math thing was this weekend?"

"I did. In my letter."

He walked in and flopped onto my bed like he owned the place. "I know that, Thea. I mean, why didn't you tell me sooner, and in person?"

I shrugged, fiddling with the corner of my worksheet. "Because it's not that big of a deal."

He laughed like I'd just told the best joke. "Not a big deal, my ass. I've heard you talk about this competition before. It's huge."

I looked away, embarrassed. He reached out, grabbed the back of my chair, and pulled me closer until our knees bumped. "What are you doing?"

He leaned in, his eyes bright. "Tell me it's a big deal."

"Hansen."

"Thea."

I tried to pull away, but he kept me there, so close I could smell the salt from his run, the faint hint of laundry detergent on his shirt. "Tell me," he insisted, his voice softer now, "that it's a big deal to you."

"My mom's going to kill you if she finds you in here."

"A noble way to die." His voice lowered. "Tell me, Thea."

The air felt charged, like the moment before a thunderstorm. I tried to fight it, I really did, but something about the way he looked at me broke through my defenses. "It's a big deal to me."

Hansen's whole face lit up. "Then I'm coming."

"No, you're not. It's two hours away."

"That's not that far. Are your parents coming?"

I hesitated, looking down at my lap. That was answer enough.

He nodded, like he'd expected that.

"It's fine, really. I get that no one wants to spend a Saturday with a bunch of math nerds," I said.

"Speak for yourself. That sounds like my ideal day."

I rolled my eyes, but I felt lighter. He pushed my chair back and stood, stretching his arms over his head. "Give me the details. Promise?"

"What about Amber's party?"

He shrugged. "There will always be more parties. Besides, I usually just go so I can make sure Beck behaves himself."

That I could understand.

"See you soon!" he said. Then he bounced out of the room, leaving the door wide open. I tried to go back to my practice problems, but my mind kept wandering. I couldn't stop replaying the conversation, the way he'd looked at me. I barely got any work done that night.

Saturday morning, I woke before my alarm, my nerves making my hands shake as I packed my backpack. As I padded down the stairs, I heard voices by the front door. Hansen and Beck were waiting at the bottom of the staircase, both with bags slung over their shoulders. Beck's hair was sticking up in every direction, and Hansen was bouncing on the balls of his feet.

"Hey," I said, surprised.

They both looked up at me. Beck beamed. "Hey! You ready for this road trip?"

"You're coming too?"

"Of course I'm coming." He threw an arm around Hansen's shoulder. "I can't wait to watch you kick some serious ass. Also, I call the backseat so I can sleep the whole way there!"

Before I could say anything else, the front door flew open.

"Sorry we're late. Junie had the blowout of the century." Lucy, carrying a bundled-up Juniper in her arms, came walking through the door, and Riggins followed.

"What—Lucy? What are you doing here?"

Lucy adjusted Juniper on her hip. "Nice to see you too, Thea," she said, but her eyebrows were up, amused. "Riggins needs to use the bathroom, and I wanted to see your face when you realized we're coming with you."

I blinked, still trying to catch up. "Coming with me where?"

"To your math thing!" Riggins said, smiling. Fatherhood, even at the young age of sixteen, had most definitely agreed with him. "Hansen told us about it. Said you needed a fan club."

My face went hot. I glared at Hansen, who wasn't hiding his smile at all.

Lucy looked at me, and I could tell she was a little hurt. "You didn't even mention it, Thea."

"I'm sorry. I just didn't want you to feel like you had to come. With Juniper and everything."

Lucy rolled her eyes, but she was smiling. "Please. We want to be there. Always. Just because I have a baby doesn't mean I'm made of glass. Right, Junie?" She bounced Juniper gently, and the baby giggled, her cheeks round and pink.

Riggins nodded, coming to stand behind Lucy and putting a hand on her shoulder. "She's right. And Juniper's already smarter than half the math team, so she'll fit right in."

I laughed, the tension draining out of me. Lucy stepped forward and handed Juniper over, just like she always did when I needed it most. I tucked Juniper against my chest, and she reached up, grabbing a fistful of my hair in her chubby hand.

"Hey, baby girl," I cooed, bouncing her gently. "You ready to see Aunt Thea crush some nerds?"

Juniper blew a spit bubble and grinned up at me, and the nerves melted away. Lucy brushed a strand of hair behind my ear. "You got this, Thea. We're all here, okay?"

I nodded, suddenly feeling steadier.

"All right, enough talking and more going!" Beck yelled before darting out the front door.

After Riggins relieved himself, we piled into the car, grateful that it was big enough to fit us all.

And later that day, South Creek High School took home first place. When my name was called, I looked up into the stands and saw them all on their feet, cheering louder than anyone else. And I didn't even care about the people who hadn't shown up. I had what mattered.

Chapter Twenty

Now

Over the next few days, the good news dries up, replaced by a steady drip of bad luck.

Monday, it starts with mold. The guy from the company doesn't even try to sound reassuring. "You've got mold in the wall," he says, flashing his light at a dark patch behind the drywall.

"No, we don't," Hansen says. "I checked. There was no mold."

The guy just shrugs. "Well, you must not have looked hard enough, because it's there."

Wednesday, the county office calls. Apparently, we're not getting the permit for the deck Beck wanted. "It's too close to the trees," the woman says, as if she's reading off a script. "They won't approve it."

I nearly drop the phone. "What kind of bullshit excuse is that?"

Thursday, the plumbing backs up. When the plumber comes out, he says it'll be almost a thousand dollars to fix. It feels endless, hopeless, like the universe is playing a joke at our expense.

And yet, I get out of bed every day. Even when the pull of the covers is nearly enough to keep me down, even on the mornings Hansen is putting out fires at his other job. I get up. I get dressed. I do what work I can. If it's a cabin day, I'm there by six, hands already aching before we start. The work is never easy, but by the time the day ends, I feel lighter, as if the bad news can't quite stick once I've sweated it out.

Maybe it's the hammering. Or the demolition. Maybe it's Hansen, and how everything feels just a little less sad when he's around.

One especially early morning, I look up from patching a hole in the floor. "I need to get a job," I tell Hansen. "One that actually pays. Not just doing odd jobs here and there that pay a few hundred dollars."

He pauses, wiping his hands on his jeans. "We'll figure it out, Thea. I'll pick up more shifts at the station. I can pull from my savings."

I shake my head. "No. You don't have to do that, Hansen. I won't let this place drain us both dry."

He smiles. "It will all be over soon." He says it like a promise. I try to believe him. Soon we'll sell the place, take the money, and that'll be that. I can go back to college. I can leave if I want.

The first swing of the sledgehammer that day feels refreshing. We're finally taking the wall down to open up the kitchen, and Hansen wants me to make the first blow. I brace my feet, grip the handle, and slam it into the drywall. A shudder runs up my arms, dust billows out, and a chunk of wall falls away. My heart thuds, loud in my chest.

I glance over my shoulder at Hansen. He's kneeling by the window, prying off old trim. He looks up at the sound, eyebrow raised. "You're gonna have to hit it harder than that if you want it down before winter."

I purse my lips at him, then swing again. The wall groans, the crack spreads, and a strange thrill shoots through me.

"Atta girl," Hansen says with a smile plastered on his face.

I swing again, feeling the hammer's vibration all the way up to my teeth. "It's coming down."

"Sure is," Hansen says. "Need a break?"

I lower the sledgehammer and wipe my forehead with the hem of my shirt. "Not yet. This feels good."

He laughs deeply. "Then keep going."

Before I can hit the wall again, a car door slams shut outside. I freeze, sledgehammer poised in mid-air. Hansen peeks out the window. "Expecting someone?"

I shake my head, anxiety blooming in my chest. Maybe it's the plumber here to actually tell us he found a tunnel to an underground rat colony. Or the mold guy telling us that the entire cabin is actually just one big mold monster. Nothing would surprise me anymore.

But the front door squeals open, and Lucy barrels in, arms loaded with bags. "Everyone decent? I come bearing caffeine and extra hands!"

I nearly drop the sledgehammer. "Lucy! What are you doing here?"

She dumps her stuff on the couch, brushes off her hands. "You told me you were demoing a wall today. That's basically an invitation."

Hansen crosses his arms, and he looks genuinely happy to see her. "Lucy."

She shoots him a grin. "Hansen. Glad I could come to your rescue. No offense, but this place is not looking good."

"Lucy," I scold, but she waves me off.

"It's fine. We'll have it looking amazing by the end of the day." She reaches into her bag and pulls out goggles, gloves, and a hard hat. "Now, where do you want me?"

"Did you just pull a hard hat out of your bag?" Hansen asks with a look of surprise.

"Sweet Hansen," Lucy places the hat on her head. "You should know by now that I'm not showing up anywhere unprepared."

Before I can chime in, more footsteps crunch up the steps. The door swings open again, and in walks Riggins, wearing a faded fire department T-shirt and lugging a toolbox the size of a toddler. Two more guys trail behind—a tall one with deep black hair and a stone-cold face (Graham, if I remember right), and a redhead with freckles and a happy grin (Sam, I think).

"Hey, Thea," Sam says, waving with his work glove. "We heard you were tearing down walls."

"And battling a mold infestation," Graham adds, setting down a battered Shop-Vac.

I blink at them. "What is happening?"

Lucy beams. "I may have told Riggins to get more people. And they were more than willing since you brought them cookies, which I, your best friend, knew nothing about." She says *cookies* like it's a bad word.

"Sorry," I say, then quieter, "Are you really okay with this? If it's too much for him to be here, I totally understand."

She smiles. "It's fine. I'm the one who called him. Many hands make light work, or whatever the saying is, right?"

I just stand there, sledgehammer in hand, surrounded by people who—what? Thought I needed help? Decided to give up their Saturday just to show up? For a second, I don't know what to do with myself. I want to laugh, and cry, and hide all at once.

Riggins puts down his toolbox and claps his hands. "Point us toward the destruction."

"It's the wall in the kitchen," I say, and the three guys and Lucy start heading that way.

When they're out of sight, Hansen catches my eye. "You okay?"

I nod, swallowing hard. "Yeah. I just . . . didn't expect this."

He grins as that stubborn piece of hair falls across his forehead. "That's the best part."

※※※※ ※※※※

The next few hours blur together in a rush of noise and dust and laughter. The firefighters start to make quick work of the walls while Lucy and I set up a makeshift workbench outside, pulling nails from salvaged boards and tossing the warped ones onto a growing pile. We take turns with the sledgehammer, each of us getting a chance to bash at the stubborn wall dividing the kitchen and living room. It's slow going—the studs are old, the plaster thick, the whole place rattling with every blow. But with every swing, the wall starts to come down.

At one point, arms aching, I step back to watch. Hansen stands in the center of the chaos, hair falling into his eyes, shirt streaked with grime. He lifts the hammer, shoulders flexing, and brings it to the wall in a clean, practiced arc. The wall shudders, splits, and an entire panel crashes to the floor.

The guys cheer. Riggins whistles.

"Who needs CrossFit?" Lucy pants.

"I think I just inhaled mouse poop," Graham says, mock-gagging.

"Adds protein," Riggins replies, slapping him on the back.

I laugh so hard I have to lean against the newly exposed beam. For the first time in months, something loosens inside me—a knot untying. I'm not alone, not invisible. These people see me and showed up anyway. The thought of ever leaving them feels impossible.

Once the demo is done, we all pitch in to clean. We sweep, vacuum, and wipe down every inch. We drag out garbage, old wood, dead rats—everything that doesn't belong.

Hansen moves between us all. More than once, I catch myself watching him. The way he looks, the way he moves. Every time he catches me staring, he winks, and I don't bother to hide my smile.

❧❧❧❧❧ ❦❦❦❦❦

It's seven when we finally call it. The cabin looks different. It's more open and alive. The wall is gone, and the studs are stacked in a neat pile by the steps. It's clean and ready for us to start building instead of just tearing away.

Lucy drops down beside me on the porch, stretching her legs. "Not bad for a couple of people who have never done this before."

I nudge her. "You didn't have to come, you know."

"Sure I did. You'd do it for me."

A pang of guilt shoots through me. There was a time I would've done anything for Lucy. Then I lost sight of that. But I know I never will again. "Yeah," I say quietly. "I would."

Riggins plops down on the other side of Lucy with a flushed face and looks at her with a softness I haven't seen in a long time. He nudges her, she elbows him back, and the moment passes.

After taking some things back to his truck, Hansen returns and leans against the porch railing. When our eyes meet, he tips his head, motioning me inside.

"I'll be right back," I say to Lucy. She nods, and I follow him inside.

Everything inside the cabin is different now. It's lighter, just like I wanted. The kitchen and living room are one big open space, and it feels like a place people would want to be.

Hansen stands in the center of the empty room. "We're doing it, Thea."

I look around at the bare beams. "We're definitely doing something."

He turns to me, earnest. "How are you feeling? With all of this?"

"Good. I think. Excited for it to be done."

He smiles. "Me too."

"What's your word today?" I ask, knowing that's easier than asking him directly how he's feeling.

He squares his shoulders, trying for serious. "Exultant."

I snort. "Show-off."

"It means happy."

I shake my head, letting out a long breath. "I think mine is grateful."

He looks at me, and steps closer. "That's a good one."

We're close, but not touching. The silence is comfortable, but charged in a way that makes my skin prickle. I want to reach out, run my fingers along the stubble on his jaw, tell him that I want this. That I'm done fighting my feelings. That I want him to make me feel better. Even if just for a second.

But I'm scared. Because this—us, this place, all of it—it actually matters to me now. And I keep thinking, what if it goes wrong? What if I let myself be happy and I just lose it too?

His eyes dip to my lips, then rise back up to my eyes. My breath catches, and I'm about to take a step forward when my phone dings in my pocket.

"Sorry," I say, pulling back a bit. I get the phone out of my pocket, and my heart stutters when I see the name attached to the message: Mom.

I stare at the screen for what feels like an eternity before finally reading the message.

Mom

Thea, we'd like to talk to you about going through
Beck's things. When can you talk?

My chest tightens. The room blurs around the edges. I can't breathe.

Hansen notices. He grabs my arms. "Hey. You okay?"

I shake my head. "It's my mom. She—she wants to talk about Beck's
stuff." I look up at him. "I knew we'd have to do it eventually. I just . . . I don't
think I can."

"You don't have to. Not before you're ready," he says. "One second at a
time, remember.

I nod. "One second at a time."

Chapter Twenty-One

Both Hansen and Lucy are working the next day, so I hole up in my bed and chip away at a couple of side gigs. The money isn't much, but it's enough for now. I cycle through listings for PhD programs, scroll through job postings in South Creek, then go back to PhD programs again, trying to imagine a future that makes sense. Around four in the afternoon, my phone buzzes.

Hansen

> Hi, Thea. It's Hansen.

I snort and nearly drop the phone. We've texted before, but it's always been about the cabin.

Me

> Hi, Hansen. It's Thea.

There's a pause, then:

Hansen

> Wow. What a plot twist.

Me

> Just keeping the suspense alive.

Three dots pop up, disappear, reappear.

Hansen

> What's your word of the day?

My thumbs linger above the screen.

Hansen

> First thing that comes into your head. Don't over-think it.

Me

> Sleepy.

Hansen

> Easy.

Me

> Is that your word, or are you mocking me?

Hansen

> Logy is my word.

Me

> You just took my word and made it sound more dramatic.

Hansen

> I'm nothing if not a plagiarist.

I grin. Another message pops up.

Hansen

What happened today?

Me

Oh, you know. Just job hunting. Future plotting. Existential spiraling. The classics.

Hansen

You're going to figure it out. You're going to be amazing.

Me

Thanks. What about you? How's work?

Hansen

It's fine. Same old.

I'm about to push him for more when another message comes in.

Hansen

What's one thing you've always wanted to do?

I pause.

Me

Does it matter?

Hansen

More than you think.

Me

> Fine. I want to get my PhD and work in theoretical mathematics. It's the study of abstract mathematical structures that form the basic framework for the rest of mathematical sciences. Basically, I'd be doing research. Maybe even teaching.

He doesn't answer right away, and suddenly I'm painfully aware of how nerdy that sounds. I've spent most of my life feeling awkward about loving and being good at math—a subject people either glaze over or actively hate. Beck often made fun of me for it, and my parents didn't even pretend to be interested. But Hansen never made me feel weird. Still, when his reply doesn't come after several minutes, I wince.

Me

> Are you actively trying not to laugh at me?

His reply comes a few seconds later.

Hansen

> No, sorry. One of the guys needed me. I would never laugh at you, Thea. Theoretical math sounds amazing.

> Tell me more.

So, I do. I give him as much information as I can without overloading him. He asks questions and actually listens. By the time I finally put my phone down, the world outside is silent and dark. For the first time in a long time, I fall asleep easily.

The next day, he texts again. This time, his word is *stout*. Mine is *moody*. This becomes our routine. A new word every day, sometimes a whole conversation built around it. Doesn't matter if he's at work. Doesn't matter if we just spent the whole afternoon at the cabin together. Sometimes the conversations are short, but they're always there.

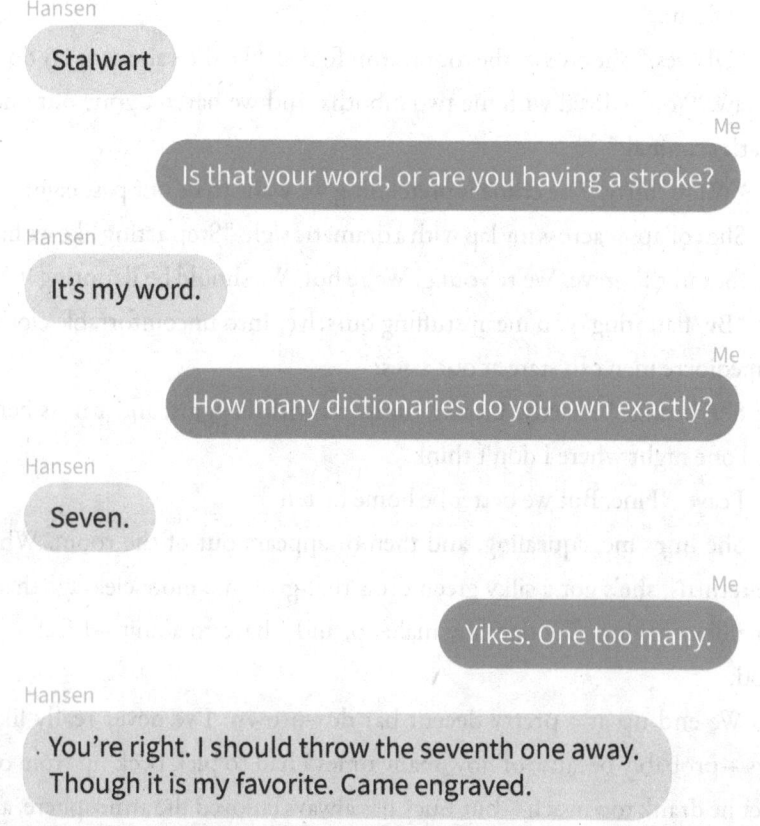

Hansen

Stalwart

Me

Is that your word, or are you having a stroke?

Hansen

It's my word.

Me

How many dictionaries do you own exactly?

Hansen

Seven.

Me

Yikes. One too many.

Hansen

You're right. I should throw the seventh one away.
Though it is my favorite. Came engraved.

I laugh loud enough that Lucy glances over her shoulder from the full-length mirror she's using in my room.

"What's so funny?" she asks.

"Nothing," I say, tossing my phone onto the bed like it might burn me. But she keeps watching me in the glass.

"Fine, keep your secrets." She turns back, adjusting her top. "Is it bad I want my boobs so high they touch my chin tonight?" She squishes them together and grins.

"Nope. Your boobs, your business."

She smiles at me. "I knew you'd get it."

"What's the occasion for the boobs being so high?"

She catches my eye in the mirror, and there's mischief there. "I'm going out. And you're coming with me."

"Uh, no."

"Uh, yes." She crosses the room, arms folded, like she's about to lay down the law. "You've lived with me two months, and we haven't gone out once. That's criminal."

"We're thirty. The crime is pretending we want to be out past eight."

She collapses across my lap with a dramatic sigh. "Stop acting like we have one foot in the grave. We're young. We're hot. We should be flaunting it."

"By 'flaunting' you mean stuffing ourselves into uncomfortable clothes so mediocre men can stare at our asses?"

She beams. "Exactly. Please? Juniper's with Riggins, and I miss her. I need one night where I don't think."

I cave. "Fine. But we better be home by ten."

She hugs me, squealing, and then disappears out of the room. When she returns, she's got a silky green dress that gives me more cleavage than I remember having. She does my makeup, and I have to admit—I feel really good.

We end up at a pretty decent bar downtown. I've never really liked bars—probably because of how many times I had to pick Beck up from one after he drank too much—but Lucy has always enjoyed the atmosphere, and I know she could use the night out.

We snag a table by the window, and Lucy orders herself a cocktail with a fancy name and me a virgin piña colada.

Halfway through her drink, Lucy blurts out, "So, Archie texted me."

I arch an eyebrow. "Archie as in—"

"Archie Soto. High school Archie. The one who had the super loud laugh and always wore those green shorts."

"Oh, that Archie." I whistle. "That's a blast from the past."

She grins but twists her straw nervously. "Yeah. I ran into him at the store the other day. I guess he's moved back into town after his divorce. But he, uh, he asked me out."

"And?"

"And he's hot. So, I said yes. I deserve to have fun."

"You do, Luce. You deserve a whole parade of hot men if you want."

She laughs, but it's brittle. "Yeah, but now I'm kind of freaking out. I haven't been on a real date since . . . well, Riggins."

I lean in. "It's normal to be scared. You can change your mind at any time."

She shrugs, staring into her drink. "I know. And it's been two years since the divorce. Riggins and I—God, we were together a decade. What if I forgot how to do this? What if I'm just . . . broken?"

"You're not broken. You're just . . . bruised. You can heal from bruises."

She lets out a shaky laugh. "Listen to you. Dr. Thea Miller."

"I won't be that kind of doctor." I watch her twist her straw, and I can't help myself. "Lucy, can I ask you something?"

Her eyes move up. "Sure."

"Do you . . . even want to date again? I mean, really. Not just Archie, but . . . anybody?" I'm careful because I've wanted to respect her boundaries about the divorce. It was heartbreaking to say the least, and I know she doesn't like talking about it. Which is strange considering how much Lucy enjoys talking. But Riggins? She keeps her feelings about him locked up tight.

She lets out a slow breath. "Of course I want to date, Thea. I mean . . . I loved Riggins. I'll always love him, probably. But we grew apart. It wasn't some big betrayal, we just . . . turned into different people. Getting married at sixteen will do that. But I want to try again. I want to move on. And I think Juniper wants me to move on, too. She's always bringing up me going on dates or trying to set me up with her friends' single dads."

I nod. Juniper hasn't brought up the conversation we had about her hating her dad. And Lucy hasn't mentioned anything about it either, leading me to believe that Juniper still hasn't said anything to her. Even though I think Lucy should know, it doesn't feel like my story to tell.

"Okay," I say. "Then I say do it. Go out with Archie."

She smiles, and her eyes start to shine. "Jesus, did you ever think it'd be like this? Us, single, one of us divorced, thirty, and trying to remember how to flirt?"

"No. But I'm not trying to flirt. You are."

She snorts. "You should be trying. With Hansen."

I shake my head. "We're just friends."

"And the early bird gets the worm."

"What?"

"Oh, sorry, I thought we were just saying random clichés now."

I roll my eyes, but I'm smiling. "Point taken."

Lucy leans forward, suddenly serious. "Come on, Thea. Give me something."

I take a slow, deliberate sip, trying to buy time, but my heart's pounding. "Okay, fine."

Lucy lights up like I've handed her a winning lottery ticket. "I knew it. I fucking knew it! You like him. I mean, I've always known that you like him, but now you finally admit it! You want Hansen and his sexy firefighter body and that dorky baseball cap he always wears."

"Lucy, stop."

"I will not. I have been waiting for this day since you met him."

"No, you haven't."

She holds up her hand as if taking an oath. "If I'm wrong, may God smite me where I sit." She glances theatrically at the ceiling, waits, then shrugs. "See? Still here. Unsmote."

I laugh. "You're impossible."

"And you're in denial. What finally made you realize it?"

I hesitate. Do I really want to say this out loud? My chest is tight. "Realize what?"

"That you're in love with him and he's in love with you."

"Lucy, no one said anything about love. We're talking about a crush, maybe. That's it."

"A crush you've both been nursing for fifteen years."

"He hasn't had a crush on me for fifteen years."

Lucy rolls her eyes so hard I'm surprised they don't get stuck. "Thea, I love you more than anyone except my kid and maybe Elijah Wood, but you are . . . spectacularly dense sometimes."

My mouth drops open. "I am not dense."

"You are. But it's okay. We all knew you had to get here on your own. If I'd pushed, you would've just shut down. So I waited. Patiently. For you to realize you have the hots for Hansen."

I open my mouth, ready to argue, but nothing comes out. She's right. I've spent so long shoving my feelings into some dark corner, pretending they weren't there, pretending he could never like me back, that now, letting myself even think about Hansen feels dangerous. Like I'm stepping out into sunlight after years underground. It's blinding. And yet, not surprising at all.

"It's terrifying," I admit, "It's always been terrifying."

Lucy's face softens. "Yeah. I know, honey."

"We're both so . . . broken. What if I let myself feel this, and it just destroys me? What if lose him again?"

Lucy reaches across the table and squeezes my hand. "You know, a very smart and annoyingly attractive doctor once told me we aren't broken, just bruised. And bruises heal."

I let out a shaky laugh. "She sounds like an idiot."

Lucy shakes her head. "Nope. She's the smartest person I know. And that's saying a lot, because my best friend went to Berkeley."

"What if he doesn't feel the same way?" I ask, finally voicing the vulnerable thought out loud. "Maybe I've just misread things or—"

"Thea," Lucy interrupts me. "You've spent your whole life thinking that no one wants the real you. It makes sense that you wouldn't see that Hansen does. But he does. He always has.

"You don't have to figure it all out tonight," she continues. "You and Hansen . . . you've both had your share of pain, but that doesn't mean you don't get to be happy. Just . . . take it one day at a time. Let yourself want what you want. There are a million scary things in this world, but falling for someone who makes you happy? That's one of the good ones. That's worth it."

My throat tightens, but I nod. Lucy's right. She so often is.

"What would I do without you?"

Lucy shrugs, putting her drink up to her lips. "Probably live a peaceful, drama-free existence. But then you'd be so bored."

We talk for hours. About work, love, Juniper, the weird neighbor down the street that we're pretty sure is breeding hamsters. The city glows outside the window and people come and go from the bar, and I just let myself be in the moment. I let myself feel it all.

Eventually, Juniper video calls Lucy with a question, and I excuse myself to the bathroom. It's down a narrow hall, past the dartboards. Just as I'm about to reach the door, someone calls out my name.

"Thea? Thea Miller?"

I turn. There's a tall man with sandy hair. He's older than me, late forties, maybe. But his face is familiar in a way that makes my chest tighten.

"Sorry, I didn't mean to startle you," he says. "It's Josh. Josh Hamilton. I was in rehab with Beck."

"Oh, hi," I manage. My voice sounds far away

He smiles, awkward, and uncertain. "Wow. This is such a small world. How are you? How's Beck? Is he here?"

My throat goes dry. "No. He's . . . not here."

"Oh." He laughs. "Guess that makes sense. An alcoholic in a bar isn't the best idea. I'm only here because my sister just got a job as a bartender. So, how is Beck?"

I shake my head, fists balled tight at my sides. "Actually he—he died. A few months ago."

Josh's expression crumbles. "Shit. Thea, I'm so sorry. I had no idea."

"It's okay."

"Can I ask what happened?" His question knocks the air out of me. It's not the first time someone has asked, and it won't be the last, but tonight it hurts in a new way.

"He . . . took his own life."

Josh's eyes go wide. "Fuck. I'm so sorry. I shouldn't have pressed—"

"It's fine. I, uh, have to go." I push past him, forgetting all about the bathroom. I make my way back to Lucy. She takes one look at me and grabs my hand.

"Are you okay?"

I blink a few times, trying to get my bearings. "Yeah, I just . . . ran into someone who knew Beck. They didn't know he had died though."

Lucy's face falls. "I'm sorry, honey. Should we go home and stuff our faces with ice cream?"

I nod.

At home, we change into pajamas and collapse onto the couch with pints of our favorite ice cream flavors. Lucy puts on some reality show with too-tan, too-loud contestants. We talk. We eat. After a while, the show gets so ridiculous we start to laugh, and it feels good.

Later, when the lights are low and the cinnamon roll candle has nearly burnt out, Lucy leans her head on my shoulder. "Thanks for coming out with me."

"Thanks for making me go," I say. Even though I ran into Josh, I'm grateful for the time with Lucy.

Outside, the night is still. Inside, it's just us. Two women, a little bruised, but a little better than they were yesterday.

Chapter Twenty-Two

I'm crouched in a corner of the cabin's kitchen holding a flashlight and watching Hansen waist-deep in the cabinet under the sink. He's been trying to fix the plumbing for hours. Or maybe it just feels that way.

"Try it now," Hansen calls.

I reach up and twist the faucet on. Nothing. Not even a single drip.

"Nope," I say, leaning in so he can hear me. "Still dry."

With a grunt, Hansen scoots out from under the sink with hair plastered to his forehead and his shirt damp with sweat. He swipes the back of his hand across his forehead, leaving a smudge of grime behind. His expression is somewhere between exhaustion and frustration.

"Still?" he echoes, settling down his wrench.

"Yep."

"Okay. Maybe the shutoff valve is stuck. Or broken." He squeezes his eyes shut and presses his fingers to the bridge of his nose. "Or I've done something in my life to anger a plumbing god and now I'm paying the price."

"Oh, yeah. It's for sure that one."

He opens his eyes to shoot me a look, but there's a flicker of a smile at the corner of his mouth. Even though he may be irritated, and covered in who knows what, his smile still gives me butterflies.

"Can you check the water in the bathroom?" he asks.

I nod and push myself up from the floor. In the bathroom, I twist the knob on the sink. Still nothing.

I'm about to call back to Hansen when my phone starts buzzing in my back pocket. I pull it out, squinting at the screen as a string of texts from Lucy light it up one after another:

Lucy

Help.

Abort. Abort.

This was a bad idea.

Please save me.

I think I made a mistake.

"Shit," I mutter.

"Everything okay?" Hansen's voice makes me jump. I look up to see him leaning in the doorway with folded arms and a brow furrowed just enough to show he's concerned.

"No." I hold up the phone. "Lucy's on a date, and I don't think it's going well. She wants me to come get her."

Hansen doesn't hesitate. He reaches into his back pocket and pulls out his keys.

"Come on," he says, already turning for the door. "I'll drive."

The Steak House is a nice restaurant about fifteen minutes outside of South Creek. Lucy spent nearly an hour this morning picking out what she wanted to wear. I could tell she was nervous, but she still seemed confident. Excited, even.

I step inside and do a quick scan. Every table is packed with men in jackets and women wearing beautiful dresses. My baggy T-shirt and sweatpants draw more than a few raised eyebrows. Some people even openly stare; others just smirk into their wine glasses.

"Any word from her?" Hansen asks behind me.

I shake my head. "She stopped texting ten minutes ago. I've been trying."

"Can I help you?" a hostess intercepts, approaching us with a clipboard and a tight smile.

Her eyes flick from my sneakers to Hansen's battered hoodie, then back up to our faces.

"Yeah, hi." I force a smile. "We're looking for our friend. She's got long black hair and is wearing a purple dress. She was here for a date?"

Hansen jumps in. "We're just here to give her a ride home. That's all."

The hostess hesitates, glancing between the two of us. Then, thankfully, her expression softens a little. "You can go get her," she says, stepping aside. "Just . . . please don't disrupt the other guests."

I nod. "Thank you."

We move deeper into the restaurant. Hansen stays close, his hand resting gently at the small of my back. The room is dimly lit and filled with couples eating and laughing. Under different circumstances, it might be a nice place to have a date.

Lucy isn't at any of the tables, but then I spot Archie, her date. He's wearing a gray suit, with perfectly combed hair except where he's run his fingers through it. He's jittery, bouncing his knee, looking everywhere.

When he spots me, he bolts up so fast his water glass nearly tips over. Relief floods his face. But he still looks like he might throw up.

"Thea," he breathes as we approach. "Thank God."

"Where's Lucy?" I ask, not bothering with small talk.

He gestures toward the back hallway. "She's in the bathroom. Everything was going really well, and then she just ran off. I tried to check on her, but she told me to go away. I don't know what happened."

"I'll talk to her," I say, then turn to Hansen. "Can you stay with him?"
He nods.

"I didn't mean to upset her," Archie blurts. "I'm really sorry."

Hansen rests a hand on his shoulder. "It's okay. Thea's got her."

I don't waste any more time getting to the bathrooms. They are tucked down a short, dim hallway. The bathroom is empty except for the last stall with a closed door. Behind it is a faint sniffling just loud enough for me to hear.

"Lucy. It's me."

She goes quiet. Then the lock clicks.

I ease open the stall door. Lucy is perched on the closed toilet seat, her makeup is smudged, and eyes are red. She doesn't look at me.

I crouch in front of her and place my hands on her knees. "Lucy, what happened?"

"It's not what you think," she says. "Archie was perfect. He said all the right things. Maybe it was the drinks, or maybe it was just—God—I don't know. I felt something tonight. I felt alive. For the first time in years. And when he reached across the table and kissed me . . ." Her breath catches. "It was everything I wanted. But then I just . . . broke. Suddenly I was cheating on Riggins. Which is so stupid because we're divorced, and he's probably off screwing every girl he can, but I panicked. Archie stopped, but I just . . . ran."

I squeeze her knee. "You didn't do anything wrong, Lucy."

She lets out a bitter laugh while wiping her eyes with the back of her hand. "I feel so stupid."

"You're not stupid. You're just not ready. There's nothing wrong with that."

She finally looks at me, and my heart breaks. Lucy's always been the strong one. Much stronger than I've ever been. But I think I forgot that strong doesn't mean invincible. Sometimes it just means hiding the cracks a little better than the rest of us.

And maybe I used that as an excuse. I mean, when Riggins walked out . . . I didn't even come back to South Creek to be with her. I stayed away. Told myself she was fine, because that's what she said. I wanted to believe it. Looking at her now, I see everything I missed. I see the weight she's been carrying, alone, for longer than I realized.

I hate myself for not seeing it. For not coming home when she needed me.

Lucy swallows a sob. "I thought I was over him. I thought I'd moved on." Tears fall down her cheeks. "But I just miss him so much."

I reach up and brush her hair back from her face. "I know, honey. I know."

She presses her face into her hands and begins to sob.

And I let her.

Eventually, when her breathing evens out, I grab her hand. "Come on. Let's get you home."

She clings to my arm as I help her to her feet. "Archie's still out there with Hansen. Want me to send them away?"

She shakes her head. "No. It's okay."

She stumbles, and I catch her, slipping my arm under her shoulders, steadying her as we walk back out into the dining room together.

Archie and Hansen are still at the table, Archie's knee bouncing a mile a minute. When he sees us, his face crumbles with worry.

"Hey. Are you okay?"

"I think I've had too much to drink," she says.

"I'm going to take her home," I say. "Thanks for watching out for her."

"I'm sorry, Archie," Lucy says. "I just . . . I'm really sorry."

Archie tries for a smile, but it doesn't quite land. "It's okay, Lucy. Really."

Hansen steps forward. "Why don't you head home? We'll make sure she gets home safe."

Archie hesitates, glancing at Lucy, but ultimately nods. "Yeah. All right. Take care, Luce. Call me if you need anything." He gives her one last lingering look before disappearing into the crowd.

Hansen puts a steadying hand on my back. "Let's go."

Outside, the air is thick with humidity and the lingering scent of cigarettes. Lucy doesn't say anything as we guide her to the truck. She lets me ease her into the back seat, her head already tipping against the window. She's asleep before I finish buckling the seatbelt.

I close the door gently, then slide into the passenger seat. The truck engine rumbles low as Hansen pulls away from the restaurant.

"She gonna be all right?" Hansen asks, glancing at her through the rearview mirror.

I blow out a shaky breath. "Yeah. She just needs to sleep it off."

I close my eyes, rubbing my temples, trying to press back the headache building behind my eyes. The night feels endless.

"What about you?" Hansen asks gently. "Are you okay?"

"I'm fine." I stare out the window at the blur of passing lights. "I just . . . I hate seeing her like this. I hate what loving someone can do to a person. How much it costs." My voice drops. "Sometimes I'm not sure it's even worth it."

"You don't mean that."

I let out a sharp, humorless laugh. "I really think I do."

He's quiet long enough that I think he won't answer before he says, "I think you think being alone is safer. That if you don't let yourself care about anyone, they can't hurt you."

I turn toward him, filled with anger I can't quite justify. "Yeah, well, being alone is better than feeling like this. I'm tired of pretending I want to be happy when I—" My voice caves in on itself. The words jam up in my throat.

He waits. The only sound is the engine's hum and Lucy's soft, uneven breathing in the back seat.

"What do you want, Thea?" he asks, so quietly I almost miss it.

I shake my head, fixing my gaze back to the window. "Nothing. I don't want anything."

From the corner of my eye, I catch him looking at me. "You know it's okay to want to be happy."

Guilt burns in my chest. I can't meet his eyes. "If I let myself be happy, even for a second, it feels like betraying him. Like I should be miserable, because he's not here to be anything at all."

"I like to think we can have both," Hansen says. "The pain and the happiness."

"It sure doesn't feel that way."

I'm silent for a beat, then my voice breaks again.

"Why would I even deserve to be happy, anyway? I wasn't there when Lucy's life fell apart. I left Beck when he clearly was still struggling. And every time someone needed me, I was . . . somewhere else, doing nothing. So how am I supposed to let myself want anything good? How can I want love when all I've ever done is fail the people I love?"

Hansen exhales slowly through his nose. "Thea. You didn't fail them. You loved them. That doesn't mean you always did the perfect thing. No one does. God knows I certainly haven't. People grieve, they run, they freeze up. That doesn't make you a bad sister or a bad friend. It makes you human."

His hands tighten on the wheel. "And this story you keep telling yourself—that you don't get to want things, that you have to carry the guilt forever—that's not the truth. That's punishment. You don't have to keep punishing yourself just because you survived something someone else didn't."

I blink hard, my throat tightening.

"You think love is dangerous," he adds. "I get it. It is. But maybe it's not about avoiding the hurt. Maybe it's about choosing someone who'll help you carry it. Someone who stays."

The car goes quiet again, but the silence feels different now. Not empty. Just . . . still.

I don't answer. I can't. But something inside me shifts. Like a door that's been jammed shut for years creaking open just a little.

"All we can do is try to be a little better than we were the day before," Hansen says. "And you're doing that. And that matters."

I want to ask if he's doing that, if he takes his own advice about guilt and punishment, but then Lucy's driveway comes into view, and there's a familiar car parked there.

"Is that Riggins?" I ask.

"Yep," Hansen says, already unbuckling. He's out of the car before the engine's even off. I follow, the night air cooler than I expect, waking me up a little.

Riggins stands on the porch, eyes darting to us. He looks sick, and all thoughts of my conversation in the car with Hansen go out of the window.

"Is Lucy in there?" he asks.

"She's asleep," I say. "Is everything okay with Juniper?"

"Yeah. She's with my mom. That's not why I'm here. Someone called me from the bar and said Lucy left drunk, with some guy."

"She didn't leave with some guy. She left with us."

His jaw tightens. "She wasn't answering her phone. I panicked. Then Tim called from the bar—"

"She's safe," I cut in. "She just needs to sleep. You can talk to her in the morning."

Riggins shoulders deflate, all the fight leaking out of him. "Sorry. It's been a long day."

"It's all right," Hansen says, coming up beside me. "Go home. We'll get her inside."

Riggins lingers, glancing between us, clearly torn on whether to stay or go. But finally, he nods and heads for his car, slamming the door harder than he means to. His taillights fade down the street.

Hansen and I exchange a look. The kind that says, *Let's not unpack that right now.*

I help Lucy out of the car, and she stumbles into me, mumbling, "Sorry I ruined your night."

"You didn't," I whisper, guiding her up the stairs and into bed. "Get some rest. We'll talk in the morning."

She nods, already falling back asleep. I close her door softly behind me.

Hansen is out front on the porch swing when I come back down. I quietly take the spot next to him, hugging my knees to my chest.

"She's asleep," I say.

He turns. "You're a good friend, Thea."

Even though I try to fight it, because the moment feels dangerously intimate, I look at him. The pain and anxiety I've felt all night eases just a touch when our eyes meet, and my heart skips a beat.

"I'm really trying to be now."

He shifts closer, the swing creaking. The air feels charged with all the heavy things I wish I could say. "I meant what I said in the car, Thea. You're allowed to want happiness."

He's so close now I can see the tiny freckles over his nose, the way his mouth softens when he looks at me. My gaze drops to his lips, and my heart nearly bursts out of my chest. I want to close the gap. Maybe it would make the ache in my chest go away. Even for a second.

"You are too." And I believe it. For him, at least.

He leans in, just barely. "Being with you makes me happy. And fuck, I may not deserve it, Thea. Actually, I know I don't, but when I'm with you, things feel a little less empty."

My heart pounds against my rib cage. His gaze flicks to my mouth, then back to my eyes. Then his hand finds my face. His touch is so gentle it almost undoes me. He cups my cheek, eyes never leaving mine, and his thumb brushes slowly along my skin. Goosebumps ripple across my arms.

His breath brushes against my lips. My heart is loud in my ears.

And then—I stop.

I pull back, just slightly, just enough to break the spell.

His hand falls away slowly, like he doesn't want to let go.

"I'm sorry," I whisper. "I'm just—"

"You don't have to explain."

I try anyway. "It's not you. I'm just a mess. Everything's a mess. I'm just trying to figure it all out."

"It's okay, Thea." And he says it like he gets it. Like he understands exactly what it costs me to want something, and how hard it is to reach for it when you're still carrying everything you've lost.

We sit like that for a while, with just the night sounds around us. Eventually, he clears his throat, and a smile tugs at his lips. "Stop me if this is too forward, but my mom's having a barbecue this weekend. She wanted me to invite you. Just a warning, there will be a million people. But also, a million pounds of food.

I perk up. "*The* Winnie Reed wants me at her famous barbecue?"

He smiles. "Yeah. I've had to stop her from showing up at the cabin every weekend, but she's been dying to see you. But only if you want to go. I know meeting the whole Reed clan is . . . a lot."

I shake my head. "Are you kidding? Meeting a million Reeds is literally my dream." He rolls his eyes, and I shove his shoulder with mine. "I'd love to go, Hansen. I've missed your mom."

His smile is the most honest thing I've seen all night. It makes me want to take everything back, just so I can kiss him.

"Good." He stands, offering me his hand. "Come on. Let's get you inside before the mosquitoes carry us off."

I take his hand and let myself enjoy the feel of it in mine. I don't know what comes next with Hansen, or with Lucy, or with me. But maybe for tonight, just believing Hansen is enough.

Chapter Twenty-Three

THIRTEEN YEARS AGO

The "Why do you want to attend our university?" essay glared back at me for the third time that night. My chair squealed every time I shifted, a familiar soundtrack to years of late-night cramming and way too much caffeine. I was chewing on the end of my pencil, squinting at the screen, when my bedroom door crashed open. Not a knock, never a knock. I was pretty sure Beck didn't believe in knocking.

He barreled into my room like he always did, with nothing but raw energy. This time, though, he wasn't alone. Hansen followed behind him with that smile I'd gotten so used to. The one that made my stomach weak. He nodded at me and gave me a lopsided wave that, for a second, made me forget how to breathe.

Beck's eyes landed on the stack of college stuff spread across the desk. I lunged, but he was faster. He always was. He snatched the top paper and held it above his head.

"What's this? 'Congratulations on your academic achievements . . .'" Beck read in a ridiculous posh accent, then started rifling through the pile. "MIT? NYU? Berkeley? Jesus, Thea, you taking over the world or something?"

I made another grab for the pages, but he just backed up, laughing. Hansen leaned in the doorway, watching.

"Give them back, Beck," I said, trying to keep my voice even.

"Seriously, Thea, you applying everywhere?" Hansen asked, raising an eyebrow. There wasn't any judgment in his voice, just honest curiosity.

I finally yanked the stack free and shoved everything into a folder. "Just . . . keeping my options open."

Hansen whistled, low and impressed. "Honestly, you should. Nobody in this town's half as smart as you."

Beck flopped onto my bed, sprawling out like he owned it. "No, it's awesome. You're gonna crush it out there." He looked back at Hansen. "Maybe she'll forget all us losers back here, huh?"

He tried to play off his comment, but in his eyes, there was something raw. Something I would've missed if I didn't know him so well. I glanced at Hansen, who watched Beck, then looked at me, like he saw the whole conversation happening underneath the words.

"You really think I should go?" My voice came out soft. I stared at the carpet, then, stupidly, at Hansen.

He didn't hesitate. "Yeah. You'd be crazy not to. You'd kill it at any of those places."

Beck went quiet for a second. I could feel him watching me, like he wanted to say something else, but all he did was smile. It was big and blinding. "Duh, you should go. Get out while you can, Thea. Someone's gotta graduate college. Lord knows it won't be me."

"You sure? You're not just saying that? These places are like, hours away."

He shrugged. "Positive. If those colleges want you, that means something." Then, like he couldn't handle sincerity for more than a second, he grabbed a pillow and hurled it at me. "Now enough nerd stuff. You're coming to the party tonight."

I groaned, slumping back in the chair. "No. I have to finish these essays."

He scoffed and rolled his eyes dramatically hard. "Yeah, sure, because you never rewrite them anyway. Come on, I already told everyone you were coming."

"Why would you do that?"

He just smirked. "Because you like my friends."

I rolled my eyes. "By 'friends' you mean the idiots who get drunk every party and end up throwing up in my car?"

"Yes, exactly. Hansen's coming too. You can just hang out with him. He never gets drunk."

I risked a glance at him. "You're really going?"

He shrugged. "Guess so."

Beck grinned like he'd just solved world peace. "See? You can ride with him. He volunteered."

Hansen nudged Beck with his foot. "I did not volunteer. You just said your car was full of junk and you wouldn't have room for Thea and me."

"Same thing."

Hansen shook his head, but he smiled at me. "I'll take you, if you want."

I looked between them, feeling the walls close in.

"Come on, Thea. You never do anything fun. And if you actually leave South Creek and go to one of these fancy colleges, then you're really never going to have fun."

Hansen's voice was quieter, but it drowned out my brother's. "You should come, Thea. If nothing else, we can find the pool table and you can teach me how it's really just all about math to win."

"It really is just all about math," I muttered. "Fine. But if you two ditch me, I'm leaving and telling Mom everything."

Beck whooped, jumped up, and grabbed me in a bear hug. "You're the best, Thea. Seriously."

"Yeah, yeah. Get out so I can change," I grumbled, but I was smiling, and they both knew it.

Hansen lingered for a second as Beck bounded out, already celebrating. "See you in ten?"

I nodded, and he slipped out after Beck, leaving the room quieter. I gathered up the college brochures and tucked them out of sight. Just for tonight. Because tonight, I was going to a party. I started digging through my closet, hunting for something that didn't scream, "I'd rather be at home writing college essays." I landed on a blue tank top Lucy swore made my eyes look brighter and the jeans she claimed made my ass look "like someone who does squats regularly." Which I absolutely did not. I checked the mirror. For a second, I almost believed I did.

I was halfway through fixing my eyeliner (why was winged eyeliner so hard?) when something slid under the door. There was no knock. Just a folded piece of loose-leaf paper. I stared at it for a second, then bent to pick it up.

Dear Thea,
Hey.
Hansen

I snorted, clapped a hand over my mouth to muffle it, then grabbed a pen from my desk and scribbled back.

Dear Hansen,
Hey.
Thea

I folded it up again, slid it under the door, then waited, suddenly nervous. Outside, there was a quiet shuffle. Then the paper snuck back under.

Dear Thea,
If you want, I can make up an excuse to get us out of this party. Sore throat? Stomach issues? My mom called, and she's in desperate need of our help? I can put on the show of a lifetime. Whatever you want, just name it.
Hansen

I rolled my eyes, but I was smiling. The kind of smile I was so grateful Hansen couldn't see.

Dear Hansen,
As much as I would enjoy you putting on a show, I'd
rather be there to make sure Beck doesn't get too
drunk.
Thea

There was a longer wait for the next letter this time. It was just long enough for my stomach to do a slow flip. When the note finally came back, it just read:

Can I come in?

That made my heart skip. I glanced in the mirror, checking my hair, the way the tank top sat on my shoulders. I looked . . . good. Confident enough. I opened the door.

Hansen was right there, leaning just a little like he'd been about to knock and lost his nerve. He looked at me, and for a split second, I forgot about Beck, the party, the whole rest of the world.

His eyes took me in slowly, starting with my face and then moving down my body. He stopped for just a second at my chest but quickly brought his eyes back up to mine. If I didn't know any better, I'd say he was blushing.

"You look really pretty, Thea."

Great. Now *I* was blushing. "Thanks."

We stood there, just the two of us, and the half-opened door and the note still crushed in my palm. It wasn't awkward, exactly. It was just quiet. A good kind of quiet.

He broke it first. "You know, you don't have to go just because of Beck. He's a big boy. He can take care of himself."

I shrugged. "I know. It's just . . . easier this way."

He looked sad about that. Not disappointed, just . . . sad, like he understood but wished things were different. "I really hope you get into one of those colleges, Thea. You deserve a big life."

That made my heart squeeze in a way I didn't know was possible. Because maybe it wasn't just Beck who wanted me to go. Maybe it was Hansen, too.

Before I could say anything, Beck crashed back into the hallway. "Hey, you guys ready?" He stopped when he saw us, then his eyebrow raised. "You guys good? There's some strange vibes."

"We're good," I said way too fast.

Beck smiled. "Perfect. Let's go!"

And just like that, we were off.

Chapter Twenty-Four

NOW

Hansen pulls into Lucy's driveway fifteen minutes early. He sits in his car, engine off, staring straight ahead.

"Is he just talking to himself out there?" Lucy asks, peering through the curtains like a nosy neighbor.

"Lucy, stop spying on him," I say.

She clicks her tongue, dramatic as ever, and drops the curtain. "You're no fun."

Last night feels like a half-remembered dream. After Hansen left, I checked on Lucy. She was awake, crying again, so I crawled in beside her. We talked and cried. It ended up being the kind of late-night unraveling that leaves your eyes puffy but your heart feeling a little lighter. I told her how sorry I was for not being there for her when she got divorced. She told me it was fine, but I pushed. Eventually, she caved and told me the truth of how much she's been struggling. She told me just how angry and hurt she's been by me in the past. It was hard to hear, and hard for her to say, but exactly what we both needed.

We finally fell asleep close to five in the morning and didn't wake up until two in the afternoon.

I decided not to tell her the part about Riggins showing up, but I did tell her about almost kissing Hansen on the porch. She freaked out (to be expected) and insisted I take an everything shower and wear her favorite dress—the blue one with little white flowers and a low-cut back. It's almost too nice for a family barbecue, but it's so cute I don't really care.

After I curl my hair and put on a bit of makeup, the doorbell rings. My stomach drops.

It's just a barbecue, Thea. Stop freaking out.

"He's here!" Lucy screams as she comes barreling into my room.

I hold up my hand to try and stop her visible enthusiasm. "Calm down, tiger. I'll answer it."

She sighs but follows closely behind me as I walk to the front door.

When I open it, Hansen stands there, framed by the glare of the sun. He's in worn jeans and a faded blue T-shirt, nothing fancy, but somehow, he looks better than anyone has a right to at four in the afternoon. His hair is a little tousled, and that single piece is falling down in front, and he has a bit of stubble.

He looks up at me, and my heart flips.

"Hi," I manage.

He takes a long, slow look. Like he's memorizing the way my hair falls or how the dress skims my collarbone. "You look beautiful."

I smile. "Thank you. It's Lucy's."

"Well, you should never give it back."

Lucy yells from behind me, "Agreed!"

Hansen points inside. "Are they coming with us?"

"No. Juniper's at play practice, and Lucy's got work."

"Thanks for thinking of me, though!" Lucy says, grabbing my shoulders and peeking around me.

I pat her hand. "Don't wait up," I whisper, just to give her something to hang onto.

We step outside into the thick air of the late summer afternoon. The sun is warm on my bare shoulders, and every nerve in my body is alive and restless. I can feel Hansen's presence beside me, the way his arm brushes against mine as we walk to his car. I feel like I'm made of glass and just might break if I'm not careful.

The ride to his house is quick and easy. Hansen stops at a local stand selling flowers so I can grab some for his mom. His childhood home is only a few streets down from mine, tucked at the end of a quiet road—the kind where lawns are a little too green and kids still play outside. The window's down, and even before we pull into the driveway, the smoky smell of barbecue drifts in, thick enough to taste. It makes my mouth water almost enough to distract me from the knot in my stomach.

As we park, the sound from the backyard drifts to my ears. There's laughter, kids shouting, even a dog barking. It's the sound of a real, happy family. Even though I hate it, there's a pang in my chest. A longing I've carried since I was a kid peering through other people's windows. When Hansen used to invite Beck and me to his house growing up, I could never bring myself to go. I felt too jealous. This is the kind of house I always wanted to belong in, the kind of noise I used to envy.

Before I can even reach for my seatbelt, Hansen's out of the car, moving around to my side. He opens my door with a flourish, leaning in so close I can see the gold flecks in his eyes.

"We could still turn around, you know," he murmurs, his voice pitched low for just the two of us. "She hasn't seen us yet. We can make a run for it."

"Relax, Hansen," I say, pushing past him and stepping out of the car. "I want to be here."

He drags a hand over his face. "Okay, then let's have a word. Or a signal. Just in case you want to bail."

I narrow my eyes. "I think it might be you who needs the distress signal." I cross my arms. "Are you nervous?"

"Yes," he says quickly. "I haven't brought anyone home in a long time."

"Oh, is that what you're doing? Bringing me home?"

He smirks, but there's a softness in his eyes. "Let's go, smarty pants."

"Good, because I can't waste this dress on nothing."

His fingers brush my lower back, just above the dip of the dress, and it sends a jolt of electricity up my spine. He leans in, voice barely above a whisper. "Wasting that dress would truly be a crime."

I do my best to compose myself as we walk up to the porch, which is crowded with wind chimes, potted plants, and shoes kicked off by the door. A golden retriever barrels out the front door and nearly knocks me over. Hansen kneels to greet her. "Thea, meet Daisy. My mom got her a few months ago."

Daisy ditches Hansen without a second thought and heads to me, licking my hand, tail thumping. "It's very nice to meet you, Daisy."

Then Winnie Reed steps outside, her gray hair pulled back into a bun and her cheeks flushed from the heat. "Hansen Reed! If you rile that dog up again—" She stops, eyes landing on me. "Oh, my goodness. Thea." She pulls me into a tight hug.

"Hi, Mrs. Reed."

"Please. We've known each other long enough. Call me Winnie."

I hand her the flowers. "These are for you."

She beams. "Aren't you sweet? Come on, let's get you fed before the boys eat everything in sight."

Hansen gives me a look like, *last chance to bail,* but I smile and follow Winnie inside.

The house is basically what I used to imagine it might be like. Colorful, loud, and full of life. Kids race down the hallway, chasing each other. There's an '80s playlist blaring in the kitchen, and even more shoes piled up by the door. Winnie wastes no time introducing me to a parade of cousins and neighbors, most of whom seem to already know who I am. They crowd around, talking over each other, and I do my best to breathe.

Hansen stays close, our shoulders touching. At one point, he grabs my hand and squeezes. I almost pull away, but I don't. He mouths, "You okay?"

I nod, though I'm not sure it's true. I'm not built for crowds, not even happy ones. But seeing how much this matters to him makes me want to try.

"So, you're the one renovating the cabin with Hansen," a woman says, a toddler perched on her hip.

"That's me." I do my best to summon a smile.

"He's shown us pictures," an older man chimes in, his arms folded across a stained apron. "You two should be proud of how much you've accomplished."

People agree, and the knot in my chest loosens a little. But there's a dull ache, too. This is so far from my own family, who can barely manage a group text, let alone a backyard barbecue.

We're ushered outside, into the backyard where the grill sizzles and smoke curls into the sky. Kids dart between tables with laughter. Winnie corrals everyone toward the food. "Everyone eat before the kids find the brownies and forget about dinner!" She hands me a plate stacked high with potato salad, grilled corn, and a burger the size of my face.

"Still okay?" Hansen asks as we find a table in the shade.

"Yeah. Your family is . . . really nice," I admit. "Your mom seems to be doing really well."

He smiles. "Yeah. I think she is." It's a sentiment that should make me happy, and for thirty-year-old Thea, it does. But for fifteen-year-old Thea, who watched how heartbroken Hansen was about his father, it makes my heart ache for him. That he had to see his mother so far lost in her own grief that he felt like his feelings didn't matter as much, like he was to blame.

But I know now isn't the time to bring that up. So, I smile and take a bite of my burger. The smoky and juicy flavor explodes in my mouth. "Fuck, that's good," I blurt, then immediately scan for kids, wincing.

Hansen just smirks. "Glad you like it."

We eat a bit before a woman plops down across from us, and my fork freezes halfway to my mouth. She's gorgeous, with long blonde hair that falls in perfect waves, skin like porcelain, and eyes so dark they almost match Hansen's. She glances at me, then at Hansen, and her mouth twists into a knowing smile.

"So, Thea, how'd you meet Hansen?" she asks, and her voice matches her appearance exactly. Silky, yet somehow sultry at the same time.

"April," Hansen warns. And all it takes is that one word for me to realize they know each other.

"What?" the woman, whose name is apparently April, says. "I'm just asking her a question."

"It's okay." I meet his eyes for a second, then put my attention back to her. "We actually grew up together. He was best friends with my little brother." Hansen's hand finds my knee under the table. It's a gentle touch, but electric.

April's mouth drops open, and there's a hint of recognition in her eyes. "Thea. That's right. I knew I remembered the name. You're that Thea."

I glance between her and Hansen, confused. "What Thea?"

Hansen shakes his head. "Nothing."

April smiles, leaning forward. "Just the Thea Hansen talked about all the time."

I stare at him, but he won't meet my gaze. I look back at April, searching her face for a joke. There isn't one.

"Makes total sense you two would be dating now," she says.

I laugh, not realizing how loud and surprised it was going to come out. "No, no. We aren't dating. We're just friends. Always have been." The word *friends* feels wrong coming out of my mouth, especially after last night. After how much I wanted to kiss him. After how strongly my body is reacting to his hand on my knee right now. But it's the only word I have.

April looks disappointed but shrugs. "Oh, I'm sorry. I just assumed."

"It's okay," I say, but my voice sounds thin. I don't have the strength to look at Hansen right now.

Gratefully, she doesn't push, just watches me for a second longer before the conversation drifts. More people join the table, and soon I can disappear into the chatter. I find myself watching Hansen when he isn't looking, cataloguing the way his eyes crinkle when he laughs, the way he always checks to see if I'm still there.

After a while, and way too much lemonade, I excuse myself to the bathroom while Hansen heads to the kitchen to help his mother with the dishes. The house is quieter now as it's getting late, and most of the guests have left.

The bathroom is small, decorated like a beach house with seashells on the counter and palm trees on the shower curtain. I stare at my reflection, trying to calm the riot in my head. My cheeks are a little sunburned, and my curled hair is now falling into a flat mess at my shoulders.

When I step out, April is in the hallway, her head down looking at her phone. I hope she won't notice me, but she glances up before I can sneak past.

"Oh, Thea. Hi again."

"Hi."

She smiles, but it doesn't seem genuine. "Gosh, I'm actually glad I ran into you again. You slipped away before I could talk to you some more."

I gesture toward the bathroom. "Nature called."

"That it did." She laughs, but it's brief. "So, you and Hansen really aren't dating?"

"Nope."

"Just sleeping together then? I'd one hundred percent get that."

"No. We aren't sleeping together." Even saying it out loud makes my face go hot.

You are truly pathetic, Thea.

She twirls her phone. "You know, he probably told you this, but Hansen and I dated a while back."

I freeze. I'm not surprised. She's beautiful. And seems exactly like Hansen's type. "No. I actually didn't know that."

She nods, lips pursed. "Oh, well. We did. What was it, like five years ago now?" She leans in, and her perfume fills my lungs. It smells amazing, because of course it does. "Between you and me, I kind of fell in love with him. He's easy to do that with."

I stand there, not sure what to do with any of this. She doesn't sound hurt, or like she's telling me all of this to be petty. More like she just genuinely wants to talk about it.

"Unfortunately, I don't think he ever quite felt the same way. At least not about me." She smiles. "Oh well. Guess he'll always be the one that got away."

She touches my arm, gentle. "Just be careful, okay? He's the best man I've ever known, but he can have a real hard time opening up." Then she slips away, leaving me alone in the hall with my heart thudding.

What the hell just happened?

I'm not naïve. I know Hansen has been with other women. As he should be. He could be with one now for all I know. It's not like we're dating. We're just two people who happen to be forced together by a terrible thing. And yet, the image of April and Hansen together makes my stomach hurt.

Instead of heading to the kitchen to find Hansen, I wander down the hallway, looking for a place I can have a moment by myself without the risk of running into another girl Hansen has dated. I walk until I find myself outside a bedroom with the door ajar. I know it's Hansen's old room the second I see it. There are trophies lining the shelves, and faded posters of bands I know he was into taped to the wall. I step inside, needing the quiet.

In the middle of the room there's a bed made up for what I assume are guests now, but the walls are still lined with Polaroids, ticket stubs, pieces of his life I only ever saw from the outside. I run my fingers over a corkboard, tracing the edges of old photos. There is one of him with his dad, smiling at a lake. Another of him and his mom at the opening day of her bakery. There's even one of Hansen and Beck at a high school football game, faces painted, their laughter frozen in time. The ache in my chest sharpens. I miss Beck, wishing he'd had this kind of childhood, wishing I wasn't always on the outside looking in.

Then my eyes catch on a photo tucked in the bottom corner. It's from the state math competition my junior year. I'm standing next to Hansen in the auditorium, his arm is around my shoulder, and I'm smiling from ear to ear. I remember this photo so vividly. I remember the whole day. How happy I was. Not just because we won, but because of how loved I felt.

"Finding anything interesting?"

I jump at the voice and turn to see Hansen standing in the doorway.

"Well, you caught me before I could go through your drawers."

He laughs, stepping inside the room, then shutting the door behind him.

"Your mom really kept everything," I gesture at the trophies and photos.

"Yeah. She's the sentimental type."

"I think it's really sweet." I touch the photo of him and his father. "You look so much like him."

He smiles, but there's a sadness to it. "Yeah, I think so too."

I then point to the photo of Hansen and Beck. "I've never seen this one before."

"South Creek High against West Ridge. We lost, by a lot." He laughs. "But Beck made out with Brenda Anderson under the bleachers, so the night was a win for him."

I laugh, my finger still pressed to Beck's smile.

"I never did go to a football game," I admit.

"You didn't miss much."

My eyes drift back to the corkboard, landing again on the photo of us. I hesitate, then carefully pull it free from the push pin.

"And you kept this photo?" I ask, holding it up between us.

Hansen glances at it, then steps toward me. "Yeah. I love that photo."

Heat crawls up my neck. "It was a good day."

He nods, his eyes on me and not the photo. "One of my favorites."

I set the photo on the desk. "Mind if I confess something a little creepy?"

He raises an eyebrow. "I'd prefer it, actually."

"I always wondered what your room looked like. And honestly? This is exactly what I pictured."

He walks to the bed and sits. "You should've seen it in its prime."

I wrinkle my nose. "No thank you. I know what teenage boys' rooms smell like."

"I'll have you know I showered every day. Sometimes twice."

"Alert the media."

I trace the comforter, then sit beside him. I swallow, fighting the urge to bring up April. I don't want to poison the moment, but if I don't say it now, I know it will just gnaw at me.

"So, I, uh, ran into April in the hall."

Hansen lets out a breath. "And?"

"*And* she told me you guys dated."

He nods, lips pressed tight. "I'm sorry, I should have told you. I didn't know she'd be here. Apparently, she's going through a bad breakup, and my mom invited her."

"It's okay. You don't owe me anything about your past. Besides, she was nice."

He raises a skeptical eyebrow.

"She was," I insist. "She told me you were the one that got away."

He nods, eyes on the floor. "She was a great girl. She deserves someone who can love her fully."

"And you couldn't?"

He looks up, those dark eyes locking with mine. "No."

My heart pounds. Whatever this is, I can stop it right now. But I don't want to. "Why not?"

"You have to know, Thea."

"I want you to say it out loud."

His eyes soften as they meet mine. "It was because of you."

The words I've waited so long to hear, settle between us. Part of me always knew—of course I did—but hearing him say it, hearing the actual words, is something else entirely. My mind races through every memory, every almost-moment that I used to chalk up to my imagination.

I open my mouth, but nothing comes out.

Hansen breaks the silence with a soft chuckle. It snaps me out of my trance.

"Why are you laughing?" I ask.

He shakes his head, rubbing a hand over his jaw. "It's nothing. It's just . . . Thea, I was crazy about you. Like, an embarrassing amount. So much so that I'd rehearse having conversations with you in my head and then mess them up anyway. I'd change my shirt three times before coming over to your house, just in case you saw me. I thought it was so painfully obvious."

For a while, I can only stare at him. All those years I lived half in love with the idea of him, convinced I was the only one. It's dizzying to realize I wasn't alone.

I want to say something witty, but all I can do is shake my head. "Well, it wasn't." Then curiosity gets the better of me when I ask, "When did it start?"

"Since that first day on the track."

I let out a sharp laugh. "You're joking."

He raises his hands. "I'm not. I swear."

"But April said you dated five years ago. I wasn't even talking to you then."

He sighs. "You're a hard person to get over."

I move a bit on the bed, putting just an inch more of distance between us. "Why didn't you ever say anything? Back then, I mean?"

"I really thought it was obvious."

"No. I don't believe you. It has to be more than that."

"Thea—"

"Tell me, Hansen."

He exhales. "I was afraid that if I told you, you would have . . ." He trails off, but I know exactly where the rest of his sentence is going.

"Stayed," I finish for him.

The way he's looking at me is all the confirmation I need.

"I'm sorry this is coming up now," he says. "There were so many times when I wanted to tell you."

"Do you know why I left South Creek? Why I *really* left?"

He shakes his head. "Tell me."

"You once asked me what word would describe what I was feeling. I said invisible. That's all I ever felt. Not wanted. Not seen. Not listened to. It didn't matter what I did or how good I was at something. I still wasn't enough. All I wanted, Hansen, was for someone to choose me. For someone to want me. There were times when I thought that person was you. But then you told me to go. Just like everyone else did."

"I told you to go because I saw the way you were treated. I saw how your family treated you. I wanted you to have a chance at a life you deserved."

"And I just wanted one reason to stay," I admit.

"I wish I could go back. Tell you how I felt. That I didn't want you to go."

He takes my hand, raising it up between us, tracing each finger with his own. Goosebumps prickle across my arm.

"What about now?" I ask, heart hammering. "What are you feeling now?"

He laces our fingers together. "I think you know."

I shake my head. "Apparently, I'm not very good at reading signs, so you're going to have to spell it out for me."

He smiles softly. "I care about you, Thea. So much it scares me."

My throat tightens. "I care about you too. So much it scares me."

We're close enough that I can feel his breath. I reach up to brush the rogue hair off his forehead. "What do we do with this?"

"Whatever we want."

I rest my forehead against his, eyes squeezed shut, trying to breathe through the storm inside. Everything is tangled. My wanting him, missing my brother, longing for something safe. The ache never really leaves, not even now. I wish I knew how to fully let it go. I wish I knew how to let myself want more.

"Tell me your word," I say, needing something to hold on to.

He smiles. "Relief."

His breath is warm against my lips. His thumb draws slow circles against my palm. My gaze drops to his mouth, and for a heartbeat, I just let myself want.

Then his hand slides to my waist. His touch is tentative at first, but that doesn't last long. He pulls me closer until our thighs are pressed together. Heat radiates between us, and I'm positive he can hear how loud my heart is beating.

I trail my fingers along his collarbone, then up the side of his neck, memorizing every inch. His hand moves lower, gliding over the small of my back, tracing the curve of my spine through the thin fabric. His fingers skim my hip, lingering at the place where my dress ends and bare skin begins. My breath catches. I want him to keep going. I want to freeze and give in, all at once.

"This is your childhood bedroom, Hansen."

He fakes surprise. "Is it? I hadn't noticed."

I roll my eyes. "Your mom is outside. Plus, like, a million other people."

"They're busy," he says in a low voice I've never heard from him before. It sends desire straight to my core.

But I force myself to pull back, just a little, even though every part of me aches not to. "Come on, big guy." I slide my hand into his and pull him to his feet. "Let's go help your mom clean up."

We make it out of Hansen's room before things can get any more dangerous. My cheeks are still burning as we head down the hallway, the sounds of the lingering barbecue drifting in through the open windows. I'm halfway to the kitchen when Hansen grabs my hand again, tugging me gently back toward him.

"Before we go back," he says. "I want to show you something."

I give him a look.

He gently squeezes my hand. "Just trust me."

I let him lead me out the back door and past the few people still talking in the backyard. We slip around the far side of the house, past a wooden gate I barely notice until Hansen unlatches it. He pushes it open and gestures for me to go first.

On the other side of the gate is a huge open field filled with wild grass and clover. I stop, a little stunned.

"Wow. This is incredible."

"Isn't it?" Hansen remarks. "All these years and it's never been touched."

I fold my arms across my chest. "And what exactly are we doing on the untouched land behind your childhood home?"

He doesn't answer right away. Instead, he lets the gate swing shut behind us and jogs a few steps ahead, turning back to face me. "Race me."

I blink. "What?"

"You heard me."

I stare at him, still not moving. "You can't be serious."

"Why not?" He's bouncing up and down now.

"For one, I'm in a nice dress."

His eyebrows raise. "You scared, Miller?"

I roll my eyes, but my heart is already pounding in my chest. "No." I grab the hair tie I always keep on my wrist and quickly put my hair into a ponytail. Then I slip my sandals off and toss them to the side. "Let's go, Reed."

He gives a little bow before saying, "First one to the flowers wins." Then he takes off running without a single warning. I chase after him, the grass wet beneath my feet, my dress flying in the wind.

Hansen is still faster. He always was. But I'm not bad, and I'm stubborn enough not to let him get too far ahead.

He glances back, slowing just enough to let me catch him, his laugher echoing across the open space. "You're gonna have to do better than that!" he calls, just as I reach out and almost grab the back of his shirt.

"Cheater!" I yell, pushing myself harder. My lungs are burning, my feet are slipping in the grass, but I'm smiling so big it hurts.

He lets me catch up again, then right before the grass meets the flowers, he stumbles to a stop, letting me surge past him. I skid to a halt, nearly falling over.

I turn, my chest heaving. "That doesn't count. You let me win."

Hansen just shrugs. "I got a cramp. Couldn't go any further."

"You liar." I shove him playfully, but we're both laughing.

And it's then, in the quiet of the early evening, that it really hits me. Not in a soft, slow, way but all at once. I'm in love with him.

I think maybe I always have been, ever since that first day fifteen years ago. I love how he makes me feel like I'm someone worth showing up for. I love how he always believes in my future, how he's always thought I could be whatever I wanted, even when I doubt myself. I love his patience, his ridiculous sense of humor, the way he can fix anything, the way he knows things about the world and about me. I love how much he loves everyone around him. I love how he sits with me in my grief, how we can exist in the silence together.

I love his body, his warmth, and that one stubborn piece of hair that always falls into his eyes.

I can tell myself that I don't deserve it, that happiness like this is reserved for people who haven't messed up so badly, who haven't run when things got hard or failed the people they love. But right now, I don't want to let him go. Because when I'm with him, the world feels easier. He makes me feel seen in a way nobody ever has. With him, I don't have to fight so hard to exist.

I can see, suddenly, what it would mean to have a life worth wanting. Not a perfect life, but one where I get to be happy, even if it's only for a while. I want it. I want him. And I don't want to let go.

"Thank you," I say to Hansen, feeling the lightest I've felt in years.

He raises an eyebrow. "For letting you win?"

I shake my head. "No. For giving me a really happy day."

Chapter Twenty-Five

I t's late, and I'm soaking in the bathtub when a text from Hansen pops
up, making my pulse jump.

Hansen

One word.

It's been three days since the barbecue. Three days since we sat in the
dark of his childhood bedroom, confessing things I never thought possible.
Since then, he's been working. Meanwhile, I've been flinging myself at every
possible distraction. Cleaning, reading, working, walking the neighborhood
with Juniper until my legs ache.

It hasn't worked.

Me

You first.

Hansen

Lugubrious.

The word makes me snort.

Me

Gloomy.

My phone rings a second after I've hit send.

"Hey. Hard day?" Hansen asks when I answer. It's been three days since I've heard his voice, and it's amazing how much I've missed it.

"I've had better. I miss you," I confess, even though it's terrifyingly vulnerable. But I'm sick of holding it in.

"Really?" Hansen asks, and there's a hopefulness to his voice that I desperately want to be real.

"Yes."

"I've really missed you too, Thea."

"Well, glad we've cleared that up."

He chuckles.

"How was work?" I ask.

He breathes heavily. "Long. There was a multiple-car pileup. It was really bad. Several of the cars started on fire. Two dead at the scene."

"Shit, Hansen. I'm so sorry."

"What's that thing they always say?"

"When life hands you lemons, chuck them right back?"

Hansen's low laugh fills my ears. God, I love that sound. "I was thinking something more like 'Life's a bitch.'"

"And then you die," I finish for him.

"Or you keep on living," he adds.

"Or you keep on living," I repeat.

There's a clatter in the background. It sounds like a garage door opening. "What are you doing right now?" I ask, suddenly desperate to see him, to touch him.

"Getting in my car."

"Why?"

"To come get you."

I sit up so fast that water spills over the edge of the tub, puddling on the tile. "I'm in the bathtub."

"Well, you have ten minutes to get out."

I scramble for my towel. "Why are you coming here?"

He's smiling through the phone. I can hear it. "I heard Lucy's place has great bathtubs."

"Oh my God, Hansen."

He laughs. "Just get dressed and meet me outside."

He hangs up before I can ask more questions. I wrap myself in a towel and peek out the door. The house is dark besides the light glowing through the crack of Lucy's office door. But as I get closer, I realize she's fallen asleep at her desk again. I move quietly past her office and into my bedroom. Once safely behind my door, I stare at the closet, paralyzed. What do you wear for a mystery night with the guy who's been living in your head for fifteen years?

I go for comfort on the outside, but my hands tremble as I pull out the only matching underwear set I own. It's pink lace that I bought on a whim in New York when I wanted to feel like someone else. The bra is delicate, and the underwear has a tiny bow that always makes me smile. I slip them on, then pull a gray T-shirt over my head and wriggle into black biker shorts. My hair is still wet, so I braid it quickly.

By the time I make it outside, Hansen's car is idling in the driveway, headlights painting the lawn in light. He's out of the car before I reach the porch.

"Why does it feel like I'm sixteen sneaking out to a party?" I ask, shivering in the night air. "Not that I ever did that."

He laughs, stepping closer. "Good. I always wanted to sneak out with you."

I raise an eyebrow. "You didn't."

"You have no idea the things I wanted to do with you, Thea."

The words hit me low in the stomach.

He opens the passenger door with a playful bow. "Your chariot awaits, ma'am."

I slide in. The car is cool, and the radio is playing something soft and slow. Hansen gets in, glancing over.

"Where are we going?" I ask, buckling up.

He smirks, one hand on the wheel. "Guess."

"The cabin?"

He shakes his head. "I think we spend enough time there as it is."

I frown, but he just says, "You'll see." He pulls away, and we drive out of town. It's late enough that the streets are empty, and the world feels quiet.

When he finally pulls up to a house, I realize we're at Mr. Henderson's, a South Creek resident who's been around longer than anyone. His house sits right on the lake, and he lets just about anyone and everyone come and enjoy it.

"What are we doing here?" I ask.

Hansen's already out, smiling. "Mr. Henderson's on vacation. My mom's watering his plants."

"So . . . we're watering plants?"

He comes around to my side to open my door. "No. We're getting in the lake," he says, as if it's obvious. "Then watering plants."

"What do you mean we're getting in the lake? It's nearly midnight!"

He just raises his eyebrows as he starts toward the house.

"This is how horror movies start," I mutter, following him. "'Let's go for a midnight swim at the place where all our childhood trauma lives.'"

He laughs, tossing me a look over his shoulder. "Name one horror movie where the killer targets nostalgic thirty-year-olds just trying to swim."

I try to think of one but come up blank. So, I follow him through the backyard. He unlocks the old gate with a little brass key, a piece of the past that Mr. Henderson refuses to let go of, and suddenly it's just us and the lake. The water is black and silver, moonlight flickering on the surface. The dock still leans to one side, warped with age.

Hansen stops just short of the water and peels off his shirt before tossing it to the side. My mouth goes dry. It's the first time I've seen him shirtless since coming back, and fuck me, he's perfect. He's all lean muscle and broad shoulders. He has a few more scars than I remember him having, but they suit him. I imagine running my fingers over every inch of him. I try to play it cool, but he's smirking.

"What are you doing?" I ask and my voice is anything but steady.

"We're getting in. That's kind of what swimming means."

"No, we are not."

He shrugs. "Okay, I'm getting in. You can watch and be jealous."

"I didn't even bring a swimsuit."

He gives me a long, slow look, eyes lingering in all the places that make me blush. "Wear your clothes. Or take them off."

My breath catches, heat blooming in my cheeks. He's looking at me like he just challenged me.

Fine. Two can play this game.

I hold his gaze, then pull my T-shirt off, throwing it onto the dock. He sucks in a breath when he sees the pink bra, and his face alone makes me glad I wore it. I keep our eyes locked as I slip out of my shorts. His chest rises and falls.

"Jesus, Thea," he whispers.

I smile, pleased with myself. "Jump with me?"

He grins, and we join hands before walking to the edge of the dock.

"On three," I say.

"One, two—"

On three, I drop his hand and shove him. He yelps, arms windmilling, and hits the water with a splash big enough to rock the dock. I'm laughing so hard I almost fall in after him.

He surfaces. "Dirty move, Thea!"

"Is it cold?"

"No."

"You're lying."

"One way to find out."

I groan but leap in. The water is shockingly cold, stealing my breath. When I surface, Hansen is close, his eyes bright in the dark.

"You liar!" I gasp. "It's freezing!"

He splashes me before swimming out farther. I don't chase after him. I just let myself float, enjoying the moment. It's like time has stopped. The rest of the world has fallen away, and I can just be. There are no expectations, no past, no future.

After a minute, Hansen swims up next to me. His eyes find mine through the darkness, and the mood shifts from playful to something much more intense. I splash him, and he splashes back.

Before I can overthink it, I paddle closer, so we're just inches apart. "Can you stand?"

He nods, so I loop my legs around his waist and put my arms around his neck. He inhales sharply when our skin touches. Then his hands find my lower back.

"You okay?" I whisper, not wanting him to slip.

"More than okay."

I smile, running my fingers through his wet hair while he trails his fingers up and down my back. When he grazes the clasp of my bra, it sends a shiver through me.

"Are you cold?" he asks.

I shake my head.

He takes that as a sign to keep going.

His touch drifts from my back to the curve of my bare arm. He traces a line to my shoulder, then slips down, following the length of my arm back up again, and I lean into him, barely breathing.

He hesitates for half a second, searching my face, and when I don't pull away, his hand slides down, skimming my side. His fingers find my hip, settling there for a heartbeat that feels impossibly long. I want to ask for more, but all I can do is press closer, my heart thumping hard enough I'm sure he can feel it.

He shifts, his palm gliding up, moving over my ribs, every inch sending sparks through me. By the time his hand reaches my stomach, my breath is coming quicker, my body desperate for him. And then—so gently I almost miss it—he lets his hand rest between my breasts.

I want him. I want him to keep going, and to never stop. I want every part of him, here in the dark, with the water holding us up and nothing else in the way.

My hands tighten around his neck, pulling him closer, and I can't help the soft noise that escapes me. He hears it, and his eyes grow darker, hungry in a way that matches everything I'm feeling.

His thumb brushes the skin just above my bra, and I can barely stand it. I need him. I need more.

"Hansen," I whisper, as I put my hands on his cheeks so our eyes are locked. "Take me back to your place."

"Are you sure?" he asks, his voice breathy.

"Yes. I don't want to waste any more time."

My lips are just about to brush his when something grazes my leg. Something slimy and very much alive. I freeze, panic flaring.

"Oh my God, something is touching my leg!" I shriek, shoving away from Hansen and scrambling for the dock.

"Thea!" he calls, but I'm halfway there, heart pounding. I haul myself up, not caring that my knees scrape on the wood. I'm on all fours, chest heaving, trying to banish the image of some ancient lake monster taking a bite out of me.

Hansen pulls himself out beside me, laughing. I glare at him. "It's not funny. There are scary things in this lake."

"You're right," he says, trying to look serious. "It's not funny. I'm sorry."

He gently rubs my back until my breathing returns to normal. When I finally feel somewhat normal again, I sit, tucking my legs under me. The dock light flickers on, casting everything in a golden glow. And I guess it's been too dark to notice until now, but when Hansen rakes a hand through his hair, I see it. His knuckles are raw and red, covered in angry marks. They look fresh, like he got in a fight and lost.

I grab his hand, turning it over. "Hansen. What the hell happened?"

He tries to pull away, but I don't let go. "It's nothing."

"It doesn't look like nothing. Your hand looks horrible."

His expression tightens. "It's just from work."

I narrow my eyes, studying the cuts, the bruises. This doesn't look like a work injury. It looks like he punched something—or someone. "Hansen." I grab his hand before he can pull away, but he still tries, and the rejection lands hard. My whole body goes tense with worry. "You can talk to me." I'm practically begging.

"I'm fine, Thea." He doesn't sound like the Hansen I know. The one who just held me in the water. The one I almost kissed.

I drop his hand, and he closes his eyes. "I'm sorry. I didn't mean to yell. I just . . . I'm fine. Really."

"Are you sure? Because that doesn't look fine."

He moves so his hand is hidden in his lap. "I know."

"You don't have to be okay all the time, Hansen."

He looks at me, and I can tell there's a lot he isn't saying. I almost mention the night I saw him running, but I let it go. Maybe he's being honest about work. Maybe he's not. Maybe it's something worse. Whatever it is, I want to hear it from him.

He chews at his bottom lip, staring out at the lake. "I love that you're worried about me, but I'm okay. I promise."

I let out a breath, feeling the frustration build. Part of me wants to push, to force him to talk to me. But I don't. I can't make him share if he isn't ready. I get that now. You can't help someone who doesn't want it.

"We should get back," Hansen says quietly.

He helps me up, and I let myself lean against him, wishing he'd let me carry some of the weight he's holding. Wishing he'd trust me the way I want to trust him.

Chapter Twenty-Six

ELEVEN YEARS AGO

I was half asleep when Beck's first text came in, followed by two more, the phone buzzing hard enough to rattle the cup of pens on my desk.

Beck

Let me in, Thea!

Just kidding! There's a nice girl here who's opening the door. (You really should get better security here.)

On my way up!!

Open your door!

Surprise! I brought Hansen.

He'd attached a picture of Hansen and him standing outside my dorm, both grinning.

I froze. Hansen. I hadn't seen him since I left for college in August, and the interaction had been anything but comforting. Beck had decided to throw me a surprise going-away party, and Hansen ignored me the entire time. I honestly thought I'd done something wrong because he wouldn't talk to me. He just stayed in the corner, pouting. When the party finally started to wrap up, he stood by the door and said, "Good luck, Thea." That was it.

Three years of knowing each other, and all I got was a *good luck, Thea*.

But now he was here.

Suddenly wide awake, I shoved the book off my lap and glanced at myself in the mirror. My hair was a mess. I quickly scraped it into a bun, hoping I looked casual enough to hide the fact I'd been holed up studying all day.

I'd barely gotten the door unlocked before Beck barreled in, hitting me with a hug that threatened to snap my ribs. He smelled faintly of an unfamiliar cologne, his laugh bouncing off my dorm walls.

"Thea!" he shouted, like it'd been years instead of weeks since we'd seen each other.

"Hi, Beck," I mumbled, trying to wriggle free.

Once he let go, Beck gestured grandly behind him. "And look who I found!"

Hansen stepped in with a little more caution. Then he gave me a small wave.

"Hey, Thea," he said, and I hated how much I'd missed his voice.

He looked different—older, somehow, even though it had only been a few months. His brown hair was longer than I remembered, falling into his eyes more than it used to. He looked . . . handsome. Stupidly handsome.

I tried to play it cool. Tried to keep my breathing normal and my voice easygoing. "Hey. I didn't know you were coming."

"Beck didn't give me a choice," Hansen said, flashing a smile that made me want to look away. I wouldn't, though. "Nice PJs."

I looked down, completely forgetting I was wearing bright pink Barbie PJs.

Perfect.

I cleared my throat, trying to change the subject. "Where are Mom and Dad?"

"They're at the hotel," Beck said. "They wanted to sleep after the drive." He threw his arm around my shoulders. "So, you've got us all to yourself tonight."

I slipped out of his grip again. "You guys didn't want to rest?"

Beck was already bouncing on his toes. "Are you kidding? I want you to give Hansen the full college tour since he's never been here. Never seen Thea in her element."

I sighed. "You sure?"

Hansen shrugged. "I'm up for it."

After I changed into something a little more appropriate, we headed outside. The campus was still damp and muddy from yesterday's rain, but that didn't bother Beck. He insisted I show them everything, firing off questions about my classes, my almost-never-there roommate, and whether I'd gone to any parties or games.

"This isn't really a party campus," I told him.

"Please. Every college is a party campus, Thea. You just have to know where to look."

Hansen kept quiet as we walked. He didn't seem uncomfortable—just content to let Beck fill any silence. When Beck finally admitted he needed a bathroom, he sprinted off, leaving Hansen and me alone for the first time.

"So," I said causally, and if I was being honest, I little awkwardly. "How's work?"

Hansen shrugged. "Hot."

Instead of college, Hansen had decided to go straight into the work force and gotten a job with a local construction crew.

"Is that . . . good?"

He smiled a little. "Yeah, it's good. It keeps me busy, but the paycheck is nice, so I don't mind."

"Good. I'm glad." I rocked on my heels, feeling way too nervous for someone who'd known him for years. This was Hansen, not a stranger. I'd interacted with him a billion times. Why did this time seem so different?

He cleared his throat. "Hey. I wanted to apologize for how I acted at your going-away party."

"Oh, we don't have to—"

Hansen interrupted me. "I want to talk about it, Thea."

That shut me up.

"It's not an excuse, but I'd had a rough week. And I don't do well with people leaving or saying goodbye. But I shouldn't have ignored you. I should've spent that last day with you instead of acting like a totally emotionless jerk."

"To be fair, you didn't look emotionless. The emotions just looked . . . pretty awful."

He smiled. "Yeah. It was shitty, and I'm sorry. I wanted to say it in person. That's kind of why I came."

"Well, it's okay."

"It's not, and you deserve a friend who doesn't act like that."

There was something in the way he said *friend*, but I decided not to read into it too much. "Well, thank you for the apology then."

His smile grew. "You're welcome."

"You've sort of made up for it though by sticking around for Beck. It can't be easy since he's still in high school and you're this cool working man now."

He laughed, shaking his head. "Beck and I are friends. It's not a hardship."

"Is he—" Just as I was about to ask Hansen how Beck was doing without me, Beck came skipping out of the bathroom.

"Done!" he yelled. "Now, let's get some lunch. I'm starving."

Just like that, the moment was over. We grabbed food and finished what had to be the least impressive campus tour in history. I found myself itching to get back to my room, back to the quiet comfort of my homework, but Beck was already grinning at me with that look, the one that told me we weren't anywhere near done yet.

"No," I said before he could even ask me anything.

"Come on."

"No. No parties."

"You know I can't come all the way here and not go to a college party. That's like blasphemy," he whined, hanging on my arm. "We have to go."

"How do you even know there's a party?"

He smirked. "I told you, Thea, you just have to know where to look."

"Well, I don't do parties."

"You do tonight."

"I really, really don't."

"Please! I've literally never asked you for anything in my whole life."

I barked out a laugh. "That's all you ever do. Besides, you're barely eighteen. I can't take you to a college party."

He sighed dramatically. "Why not? Tons of freshmen are eighteen. I'll blend right in."

"What about Mom and Dad?"

"*Pff*, I'll just tell them we're hanging out here watching a movie. They won't notice, Thea."

Without thinking, I glanced at Hansen, hoping he'd provide me with an escape.

"I'll go too," he said. "We don't have to stay long."

I couldn't tell if that was supposed to make me feel better or worse, but I knew Beck. He'd keep pressing me until I caved.

"Fine," I groaned. "But no one is drinking."

Beck whooped, clapping Hansen on the back. "Deal!"

The party was everything I'd grown to hate about college in one place: crowds, sticky floors, and music so loud it gave me a headache. Beck disappeared into a group of people immediately, acting like he'd known them his entire life. I hovered near the door, wishing I had not agreed to this.

Surprisingly, Hansen stayed beside me, close enough I could feel the warmth radiating off him. "You okay?" he asked loud enough so I could hear him over the music.

"I'm fine," I said.

"Let's grab something to drink," he suggested, steering me into the kitchen. There weren't as many people in there, but someone had spilled beer everywhere, causing my shoes to stick to the tile. Hansen handed me a can of ginger ale, unopened, and grabbed one for himself.

I sipped it, mostly for something to do with my hands. Out in the main room, Beck had already become the center of the party. He was telling wild stories, which I'm sure weren't true, and had people laughing and shouting. I envied how easy it was for him.

"He never gets tired, does he?" I said to Hansen.

"Never. He exhausts me too."

It made me laugh a little. Only a little.

As we drank our drinks, more people filtered into the kitchen, and I swore someone turned the music to max volume. Panic started to rise in my chest. There were too many voices, too many bodies touching me. My head buzzed, and my hands turned clammy.

Hansen noticed almost immediately. "Hey, let's get out of here."

I let him guide me down the hall until he found an empty bathroom and ushered me inside. The door clicked shut, and the noise dropped away, muffled, like we were underwater.

I gripped the edge of the sink, staring at myself in the mirror. "Sorry."

"Don't apologize." Hansen sat on the edge of the tub, patting the tile beside him. "Come here. Just sit with me."

And so I did. We sat in silence for a long while, the only sound the faraway beat of the music.

"Better?" Hansen finally asked.

I nodded. "Thanks. I know this is ridiculous."

"It's not. I'd rather be here, anyway."

I raised an eyebrow. "In some random person's bathroom at a college party? A college you don't even go to?"

"You honestly just described my ideal day."

I smiled, feeling the panic slip away.

"So, how's college?" he asked. "Besides the incredible parties."

I thought about it, searching for an answer that wasn't just 'fine.'

"I like my classes," I said. "I like having my own space."

He shoved my shoulder. "But?"

"No but."

"Sounds like there's a but."

"There's no but."

"I thought we were friends, Thea. Friends tell each other the buts."

Friends. There was that word again. I hated it when it came from him, even if I knew it was true. Even if I understood that's what we were, what we'd always been. It felt smaller than what I felt with Hansen. Like the word was a coat two sizes too tight, and I was supposed to pretend it fit.

I tried to swallow the feeling, but it never stayed down for long. "It's just . . ." I started, then trailed off. I could already feel my cheeks getting hot.

Hansen nudged me again. "Come on. I came all this way. Give me the but."

I laughed under my breath. "I guess it's just a lot lonelier than I thought it would be," I admitted. "I mean, I like being on my own. I really do. But I miss Lucy. And Juniper. And Riggins, even though he's such a dad now. And Beck. And—" I stopped, glancing over at him. "You."

He smiled, and it was so soft. So real. It twisted something in my chest. "We all miss you, Thea. Even Beck, though he'd rather die than say it out loud."

"Have you made any friends here?"

The question made me snort. "No. Not really."

He smiled. "Not even one?"

I shook my head.

"What about your roommate? Brittany, isn't it?"

"Brenda." I laughed. "She's nice. Just hardly ever there."

"What about guys? There has to be an endless amount of hot, smart guys here."

I shrugged. "There are good-looking guys here. Just . . . not my type."

He smirked a little, leaning in. "And what's that?"

You.

"It doesn't matter," I said instead.

"It so does actually. Come on, if Thea Miller could have her perfect man, who would he be?"

"Why are we talking about this now?"

"Because I want to know."

I rolled my eyes, but I could feel the flush creeping up my neck. "I don't know. I've always liked just being alone. Existing in the silence of the world. It's easier, you know?"

Hansen wasn't letting me off that easy. "That's not an answer to my question."

There was something about Hansen that always made me want to tell the truth. "I guess I would just want someone who can exist in the silence with me," I said, so quietly I wasn't sure he'd hear.

But he did. When I looked up, he was already looking at me, and I felt something passing between us. It was heavy, electric, and impossible to name. We just sat like that, eyes locked, and the rest of the world dropped away.

Eventually, I blinked, letting out a shaky breath. "What about you? What does Hansen Reed want?"

Hansen opened his mouth, then stopped, like he had to find the right words. For a moment, I thought he might say something that would change everything. But then he just smiled. "I just want someone who makes all the hard things in life a little easier."

That made me smile, even if it hurt a little. "That's a good answer."

The music thumped through the walls, and I decided now was as good a time as any to say the thing I'd been holding back.

"Hansen," I said. "Beck told me about the fight."

He blinked, shocked. "Beck should keep his mouth shut."

"Hansen—" I started, and he stood. "Didn't you just say we were friends? Friends tell each other when they get in fights."

He shook his head. "It was nothing. Just a stupid misunderstanding."

"He told me what day it happened. Your dad's birthday."

His jaw clenched, but before he could respond there was a sudden crash outside, the party's volume spiking. Hansen and I looked at each other.

I wasted no time moving out of the bathroom, and Hansen followed closely behind. Back in the kitchen, Beck was in the middle of it all, laughing and waving an empty red cup. Someone was yelling at him, but he just grinned at me, cheeks flushed.

"Hey, Thea! Hey, everyone! This is my sister, Thea!"

I grabbed his arm, furious. "Beck, stop." I lowered my voice. "You said you wouldn't drink."

He shrugged. "It's fine. I'm fine."

Hansen appeared at his other side, trying to grab Beck. "Let's get you out of here, man."

Beck shoved him back. "Hey, lay off."

"Beck, stop. You're drunk."

"I'm not drunk, Hansen!" he yelled. "I'm fine! Why don't you get out of my face?"

Hansen tried to grab him again, but this time Beck shoved him harder, and Hansen staggered back.

I stepped forward. "Hey," I said to Hansen. "You okay?"

"Yeah, I'm fine."

"Beck. Stop."

Beck looked around the room, then back at me. "Hey, everyone. This is my sister, Thea! She's really smart, and everybody knows it! I mean, she got into this fucking place!"

"Beck, you need to stop," Hansen said.

"And you need to get the fuck out of my face!" Beck screamed.

I felt tears start to form. Everyone was staring. Beck just smiled, like this was all a big joke. "What my sister won't tell you is that she really just wants to fuck my best friend."

"Beck!" Hansen shouted. "That's enough."

Beck and I locked eyes. I was crying. He looked at me like he didn't care what he was doing.

"I'm leaving," Beck said. Then he was shoving past people and out of the house so quickly I barely saw it.

Hansen was right by my side. "I'll go after him."

"No," I said. "Let him go. He can sober up in the fucking street for all I care."

I left the house, lungs full of sand instead of air. I stepped away until I was out of sight, out of reach, out of everything. Hansen caught up with me quickly.

"Thea," he said gently.

My voice was tight and broken. "I'm fine. I just . . . I thought he was doing okay. My parents told me he was doing okay. That his new medicine was working. That he wasn't drinking."

"He isn't. I mean, he wasn't."

"Maybe I need to come home."

Hansen shook his head. "Don't you fucking think that, Thea. Don't come home. Do you hear me? You're right where you belong. Beck will be okay. I'll make sure he's okay, all right? Just stay here. Please."

I looked into his eyes, and he wasn't just reassuring me, he was pleading.

If I could have done anything just then, it would have been to tell him what he meant to me, how even when everything else cracked open and swallowed me whole, just the fact of him existing was enough to keep me standing. But I couldn't.

The only thing I could say was, "Okay."

Chapter Twenty-Seven

Now

A voidance works. Until it doesn't. Until you're standing in the paint aisle of a hardware store, pretending that the most important thing in your life is the difference between Celery Mist and Avocado Dream, pretending just as hard as he is that last week never happened.

"Do you like this one?" I ask, waving a paint swatch at Hansen a little too hard. I'm not actually seeing the color. I'm seeing his hands from the other night, the angry marks that shouldn't have been there.

He barely glances up. "You mean the puke green color?"

I want to snap the card in half. Not because of the color, although it is rightfully hideous, but because he's acting like this is just another Tuesday.

"It's not that bad," I say, even though it is. I squint at the swatch, trying to make it into something it's not. "Maybe it's just . . . under these lights."

He finally looks at me, mouth twitching like he might laugh. "You hate it."

I cross my arms, defensive. "Well, maybe I don't hate it enough."

He picks up another swatch, but I can feel him watching me, measuring every word, every breath. "We've been here an hour, Thea."

"You could leave, you know. You don't have to do this with me."

He lets out a sigh. "I want to be here. With you."

That should be enough. It should. But it's not. Because he can say he wants to be here all he wants, but it still feels like I'm alone on this stupid paint aisle island, and he's standing on the mainland, waving cheerfully from a safe distance.

I stare at the paint options, but all the colors are starting to bleed together. "I don't even know what I want anymore," I admit.

He doesn't say anything, just stands there, and somehow that's worse.

So, I grab the ugliest swatch and shove it toward him. "Fine. Let's get this one. We'll paint it the color of a stomachache. It fits."

Briefly, I think he might argue, but ultimately, he agrees. "Whatever you want."

He starts toward the counter, waving the card overhead. I trail after him, fighting the urge to scream. The clerk looks between us, his eyebrows raised like he's watching a couple on the edge of a meltdown.

"Are you sure about this color?" the clerk asks.

No. I'm not sure about anything. "We're never sure," I say.

"Maybe just one gallon," Hansen says.

Which is how I end up outside, loading a gallon of vomit-colored paint into my car and wondering how my life got here.

"Why does paint have to be so expensive?" I mumble, but what I really want to ask is why everything feels so hard. Why do we have to act like nothing's wrong when everything is wrong?

Hansen folds his arms, watching me. "If you don't like it, we can choose another color. Nothing has to be set in stone."

I know that, and I know I'm being unreasonable, and yet, I can't seem to stop. I can't stop thinking about his hands. About how easy it was for him to lie.

We drive back in silence, the gallon of paint rolling around in the trunk every time Hansen takes a turn. I keep my eyes on the window, watching the same South Creek streets blur by, wishing I could crawl out of my own skin.

When we get back to Lucy's, I drop my bag at the door and don't bother looking at him as he follows behind me.

"You're mad at me," he says once the front door is shut.

I stop in the middle of the kitchen, grabbing the counter for support.

"Thea," he says when I don't speak. "I'm sorry about the paint. Will you please talk to me?"

"I don't know if I should."

"If that's how you feel, then you definitely should."

I laugh at the irony of it all. Then I turn around. "You want to talk? Fine. Let's talk. I'm mad. In fact, consider that my word for the day. I'm mad because fifteen years ago I met you, and it was like nothing else mattered but you."

"Thea—"

"No. You asked. Let me finish."

He falls quiet.

"Then everything happened, and I didn't see you for seven years. Seven years of wondering where you were, what you were doing. It was torture sometimes. Then I come back, and you're still you. I still have those feelings, even when I try to shove them down. And then you tell me you've always felt the same, and for the first time I wanted to try. Really try. But then I feel like you treat me like some stranger you have to keep secrets from."

He shakes his head. "Thea. I'm not trying to keep secrets from you."

"But you are." My eyes sting, but I don't look away. "If we're going to do this—whatever this is—I need to know you're actually here. Not just standing next to me physically, but here with me. I can't keep pretending I don't notice when you shut down."

He runs a hand through his hair. "I don't want to shut you out."

I step forward. "You remember what you said to me that night in the car? About punishing myself?" My voice shakes. "Well, I know you do the same thing. I saw you, Hansen. One of the first nights after I got back. I saw you running. Like you were trying to outrun something terrible."

He flinches, but I keep going.

"And now your hands . . . I'm not stupid. I know those marks aren't from work. You're hurting yourself. Just like you used to do when things got bad with your dad."

"It's not about that, Thea."

"But it is." I step closer, putting my hand on his chest. "Because you can't keep trying to be everything for me while you're nothing for yourself. I want you. All of you. Not just the part that takes care of me. I want to know what's actually going on inside, even if it's ugly. Even if it hurts."

He places his hand over mine. "Ever since the day I left you . . . I feel like I left something behind. Like some part of me never made it back. I try to be better, but . . ." His voice cracks. "I don't know how."

"Believe what you told me, Hansen. Believe it about yourself."

Our fingers intertwine, and he brushes some hair from my face. "I want to let you in, Thea. I do. But I don't want to drag you down with me."

"You already made that choice for me once; I'm not going to let you do it again."

The hesitation is clear in his expression, but eventually, he nods. "I'm sorry."

"Stay," I whisper. "Just stay with me. We don't have to talk. You don't have to be anything. Just . . . stay."

"I want to. I really do, but I have a shift soon."

I close my eyes, swallowing down the ache. "Will you call me? After?"

"The second I'm off. I promise."

He lifts my hand to his lips, pressing a kiss to my knuckles.

And then he's gone, the door clicking shut behind him. The house is quiet, but every part of me is still reaching for him, still hoping that wanting someone to stay is enough to make them do it.

Chapter Twenty-Eight

SEVEN YEARS AGO

I was still learning the sounds of my apartment. The scrape of trees against the window at night, the neighbor's air conditioner humming through thin drywall, the endless drone of distant traffic. It was all new. And hard sometimes. But it was real. It was mine. Only mine.

I was packing up the lunch I'd actually prepped the night before, trying my best not to rely on frozen burritos every day, when someone knocked at the door. It wasn't the landlord's sharp pounding, or the friendly double-tap from the girl across the hall. This one was fast and chaotic. I set the lunchbox down and opened the door.

It was Beck. Standing in my doorway, looking like he'd just crawled out of a war zone.

I barely recognized him. His hair had grown out, and it looked matted, as if he'd been sleeping wherever he landed. He also had a beard now and looked like he'd lost twenty pounds he couldn't stand to lose. I didn't know how long I stood there before I found words. I was shocked. The last I'd talked to him, which was only a week ago, he'd sounded good. Happy. He told me he was planning his next backpacking trip. He even asked me if I wanted to come along. This was a far cry from that version of Beck.

"Beck?"

He grinned, that same lopsided smile he'd had since we were kids, but it didn't touch his eyes. "Hey, Thea. Surprise."

I stared. "What are you doing here? I thought you were on your way to Greece."

He shrugged, the motion slow, like even that cost him something. His backpack sagged off one shoulder. "I was. But I wanted to see my favorite sister first."

I raised an eyebrow. "I'm your only sister."

He let out a laugh. "All the more reason."

I stepped aside to let him in. He shuffled past, studying everything—the Ikea couch, the tiny kitchen, the plant I'd most certainly killed in the window—as if it were a museum. He flopped onto the couch, throwing his backpack at his feet.

"I can't believe you're here," I said, shutting the door behind him.

He leaned his head back, and his eyes fluttered closed. "Yeah, me neither."

I took a step toward him. "Are you okay?"

He opened one eye. "Yeah. Just tired. Long trip."

"You sure?"

He nodded gently. I knew him too well . . . and I knew he was lying. Something was wrong, something big, but I didn't know how hard to push. "I just need a little breather, you know? Mom and Dad are a lot. And my therapist said it might be good if I came and saw you."

"Okay," I said, happy to hear he was still in therapy. "Well, I have to go to work in a bit, but you can stay here as long as you want. There's, uh, food in the fridge, Wi-Fi password's on the counter. Couch is all yours. Call me if you need anything at all."

He gave a tired thumbs-up. "Thanks, Thea."

I hovered, desperate to fix things, to make him okay through sheer force of will. But I couldn't. Not now. I grabbed my purse and keys and glanced back one last time before leaving. He was already curled up on the couch, eyes closed, looking almost peaceful for the first time in years.

Work dragged. Every time my phone buzzed, I half-expected it to be Beck. I missed a meeting, and my manager gave me a look that said, *Get it together*, but I just mumbled an apology and kept moving. I thought about calling Beck, checking in. But he wasn't a kid. He could take care of himself. He'd call me if he needed me.

The subway was delayed, so I got home well past eight. I'd tried calling Beck a few times to let him know I'd be late, but he hadn't answered. I'd figured he was still asleep. My apartment was dark, the only light a sliver of moon through the blinds and the night-light I had plugged in the bathroom. I dropped my keys in the little bowl by the door, kicked off my shoes, and headed for the kitchen.

But Beck wasn't still asleep on the couch. He was on the floor.

For one gut-wrenching second, I thought he was dead. He was sprawled on his back, mouth open, one arm twisted beneath him. Two empty pint bottles and a crumpled paper bag lay beside him. The air stank of alcohol. I dropped to my knees, shaking his shoulder.

"Beck. Beck, wake up." My voice came out shaken.

He didn't move.

Panic clawed at my chest. I shook him harder. "Beck! Come on, wake up!"

Still nothing. His skin was pale and clammy. I pressed my fingers against his neck. There was a pulse, weak but present.

With trembling hands, I fumbled for my phone and dialed 911.

"Nine-one-one, what's your emergency?"

"My brother—he's not waking up. He . . . he's drunk, I think. He's got a pulse, but he's not responding. Please, I don't know what to do."

The dispatcher was calm, guiding me through it. Don't move him. Keep talking. Wait for the paramedics. I did everything she said, but a part of me kept screaming, *This can't be happening. Not here, not now, not to us.*

The rest of the night blurred. Paramedics showed up in blue uniforms, moving Beck to a gurney. They asked questions I could barely answer. How much did he drink? Any medical conditions? What meds? I just kept shaking my head. "I don't know."

At the hospital, they let me stay in the waiting room. It was a cold, sterile place where time unraveled. I paced. I sat. I tried calling my parents, then hung up before the call connected. What was I supposed to say? "Hey, Beck almost drank himself to death while I was at work?" I couldn't. Not until I knew he was okay.

There was only one person I could think of calling. The only one who ever knew Beck the way I did.

I called Hansen.

He picked up on the second ring. "Thea? Is everything okay?"

There was no holding it together. "Hey, I—" My words failed, and a sob escaped me.

"What's wrong?"

"It's Beck. He showed up at my place, and he—I came home from work, and he was passed out. He drank too much. I called nine-one-one, and they took him to the hospital. I'm here now, but I don't know what to do."

He paused. "I'm coming."

"No. You can't. It's too far. I just needed someone to talk to. I didn't know who else—"

"I'm coming," he repeated, and hung up.

I wanted to scream, or cry, or both. Instead, I just sat, knees pulled to my chest, trying to disappear into the ugly blue vinyl chair while I waited for news. And somewhere in me, a small, cruel thought whispered, *Maybe it would've been easier if I hadn't gotten home in time.*

I hated that thought. And I hated myself for having it at all.

I didn't know how, but Hansen showed up the next morning. I was nearly asleep in the waiting room when the automatic doors opened and he stepped through. He looked as bad as I felt, with dark circles under his eyes and stubble he didn't usually have across his face. He spotted me right away and crossed the room.

"Thea."

I stood, feeling the first bit of relief since Beck had knocked on my door. Hansen pulled me into a hug, and I let myself fall apart. The tears poured out of me, and I sobbed uncontrollably into his shoulder.

"It's okay," he said as he smoothed my hair. "I've got you."

I wasn't sure how long I cried, but eventually, I stepped back.

"What happened?" he asked, still holding onto me.

I told him. How Beck just showed up, how he looked like hell, how I found him on the floor, the paramedics. Everything.

When I finished, he said, "He needs help, Thea."

I bristled. "He's just having a hard time. He'll be okay. He always is."

Hansen shook his head. "No. This isn't just a bad night. He could've died. And it isn't the first time. Not by a long shot."

I narrowed my eyes. "I know that."

"Do you?" His voice softened, but there was an edge. "You can't keep pretending this is normal. He needs help. Real help."

I looked away, blinking hard. "I'm not calling my parents. They'll just freak out. They always make it worse for him."

He sighed, running a hand through his hair. "You think ignoring it will make it go away?"

I glared. "He just needs time. He'll get it together. I'll help him get it together. I'll have him move in with me. I can make sure he takes his medicine and that he's not drinking."

"It won't work, Thea."

Those words stung. "It will. He's my brother, Hansen. I have to help him." More tears streamed down my face.

"You can't help him if you won't admit he's not okay."

"He's still in therapy," I argued. "He wouldn't do that if he didn't know he needed help."

Hansen shook his head. "He fired his therapist months ago, Thea. And I don't know the last time he refilled his meds."

My body recoiled. "You're wrong."

"I'm not."

I closed my eyes, hoping this would all just disappear. "It doesn't matter right now. All that matters is that he's okay."

Hansen didn't have the chance to speak again before a nurse came out to tell us we could see Beck now. Relief washed over me fast, and I forgot Hansen as I rushed to Beck's room.

He was lying on the hospital bed, smiling weakly when I entered the room.

"Hey," he said.

"Hey yourself," I said, trying to sound normal and not like I was a total mess. I perched on the edge of his bed, and more tears welled in my eyes at the sight of him. I reached out and placed my hand on his. He took it and squeezed.

"What the hell happened, Beck?"

He sighed. "I just needed to take the edge off. I didn't think it'd get that bad."

My throat burned.

Beck tightened his grip on my hand. "Hey, it's okay. I'm okay. It won't happen again."

I wanted to argue, but his eyes flicked past mine to the figure in the back of the room. "What are you doing here?" Beck's voice was harsh.

"He came because I asked him to."

Beck dropped my hand. "You shouldn't have done that, Thea."

"Well, you shouldn't have done this." He flinched at my words, and I instantly softened. "Let's just put this behind us, okay? We'll get you back to my place, you can rest, and then we'll talk."

Beck didn't say anything after that. Not when I brought his discharge papers. Not when Hansen helped him to the car, or on the drive back. He just stared out the window with an empty expression.

At my apartment, I helped Beck to the couch, and he passed out the moment his head hit the pillow.

I'd honestly thought Hansen had gone, but when I went to turn my porch light off, I noticed he was still standing outside waiting for me. I contemplated not going out there. I wasn't sure I had it in me to be lectured again, not after the long day. But I also craved his comfort.

So, I stepped out into the chilly night air, pulling my jacket tighter, and joined him by the fence.

"He okay?" Hansen asked.

I nodded. "Sleeping."

Hansen gripped the fence, then let out a long, slow breath. "He could've died, Thea."

"You've said that already."

He met my eyes. "I mean it. If you hadn't found him—"

"But I did find him."

He turned toward me, desperation in his eyes. "You don't understand. This isn't the first time this has happened, and it won't be the last. I've done everything I can think of. I've sat with him through withdrawals. I've cleaned up after him. I've lied to your parents to keep him out of trouble. I've lied to you. I've spent so many nights staring at my phone, waiting for a call that he's gone. I've begged him to get help. I've tried to drag him to doctors, to meetings, to therapy."

I was stunned by Hansen's words. "I didn't ask you to do that," I whispered.

"I know you didn't, but I wanted to do it, because I do love Beck. And I wanted you to have a life beyond South Creek."

"That isn't your choice to make."

He squeezed the fence. "I know. I know." His eyes met the darkness ahead. "Maybe it's because I could never help my mother that's made me want to help him so badly. And maybe that's the wrong reason. I don't know." He turned back to me. "But he's pushing me away over and over again, and sometimes I let him, because it's easier than fighting. He's been awful to me, Thea. I wish I could pretend it doesn't matter, but it does. I know he doesn't mean it, not really, but it still . . . it still gets in. I can't un-hear it.

"Last week," he continued, "he blamed me for my father's death for the first time."

Those words broke me. I almost reached out but decided against it at the last second. "I'm so sorry. He shouldn't have said that."

"I care about him, Thea. He's your brother, but he's my friend. I never wanted to give up. I never thought I would. But I'm tired. I'm so tired I can't sleep. I have dreams where I'm searching for him and I never find him, and I wake up feeling like I've failed him all over again. I don't even know who I am outside of worrying about him."

"Well, you don't have to worry about him now. I'm coming home. I'm leaving school, and I'm coming back."

"He won't let you."

"I won't give him a choice."

Hansen turned his body to face me. "What about you, Thea? What about how hard this is for you? I've watched you for years give up everything for Beck, and all he does is drag you into the darkness with him."

I tried to sound angry, but my voice came out weak. "I haven't given up everything. I went to college. I moved here."

"You did those things, yeah, but you're not really living. Not with this. Not with him swallowing you whole. You call him all the time. You worry about him. You're living like a ghost."

"So what, you want me to just walk away? Leave him to figure it out alone?"

"No," he said softly. "I want you to admit that this, what's wrong with Beck, goes beyond anything you can fix. That you can't save him by setting yourself on fire."

I shook my head, finally noticing the tears that had started to stream down my cheeks. "I can't. I can't do that, Hansen. I can't abandon him. He's all I have."

I covered my face with my hands, shoulders shaking. And then Hansen stepped closer. Carefully and gently, he reached out and took my wrists, lowering my hands. I let him, because I didn't have the strength to fight it.

He wrapped his arms around me, and I pressed my face into his chest, sobbing. He held me until the shaking slowed, until there was nothing left but the sound of my breathing and his heartbeat in my ear.

He pulled back just enough to press his forehead to mine. His hands cupped my cheeks, thumbs brushing away tears I couldn't stop.

"I can't stay and watch him destroy himself," he whispered. "And I can't watch him destroy you."

Everything else fell away, just for a second. There was only Hansen, looking at me with so much love and grief it almost undid me.

"So that's it? You're just leaving?" The words were jagged, torn from somewhere deep.

Tears gather in his eyes. "I'm so sorry, Thea. I'm so sorry. I wish I could do more."

I wanted to scream at him, to tell him he was a coward, that he was abandoning us when we needed him most. Part of me did hate him for it. But under that, deep down, was something worse—a cold, aching understanding. He had stayed. Longer than anyone ever had. Maybe longer than he should have. And I knew, if I was honest, that I didn't want to be in his place. I didn't want to have to choose between loving Beck and saving myself.

And just like that, I felt the world shift, some last bit of hope slipping from my hands. He stepped closer and pressed a soft kiss to my forehead, a gesture that nearly shattered me. Then he turned and walked away. I didn't try to stop him. I just stood there, broken, while he drove away into the dark.

When I was sure he was gone, I stumbled inside and collapsed on the floor, shaking with grief and rage and something like relief, all tangled together.

Beck slept on the couch, oblivious, and I wondered if this was what it meant to love someone. To feel so much pain, you wished you'd never loved them at all.

Chapter Twenty-Nine

Now

My laptop glows with the same job board I've been circling all week. Every posting is starting to blur together, and I'm pretty sure I have a cursed resumé at this point. I click open the PhD program requirements for the university just outside of South Creek. It must be just to torture myself, or maybe because some tiny voice inside me is desperate to hold on to something. The conversation I had with Hansen earlier replays in my mind like a bad movie. I'm not sure what I was thinking. That he'd open up to me and we'd talk and be together like we're a totally normal pair of people?

No. We're not two normal people. We're two broken people. And even though every moment with Hansen makes me feel a little less broken, maybe I've been too naïve. Too blinded to see that it won't work. That it can't work.

I'm halfway through adding "strong communication skills" to my resume for the sixth time when Lucy bursts through my door. She doesn't say good morning, just heads straight for my TV and flips it to the news. The anchor's voice is urgent.

"We're receiving live images now from the east side, where a five-alarm fire has broken out—"

I freeze. "What is this?"

Lucy's mouth forms a grim line. "A fire."

"No, I mean, is it . . . ?"

"It's them," she finishes for me.

My stomach drops.

The anchor starts talking about evacuations and the risk of collapse.

"Where's Juniper?" I ask Lucy.

"At her grandparents' house. They won't know unless I tell them. They don't watch the news."

The anchor's voice interrupts us. "We'll now cut to live footage from the scene."

The screen fills with smoke, thick and gray, blooming up from the skeletons of old brick buildings. Flames snap through broken windows, leaping story to story. Fire trucks cluster along the curb, and every few seconds, the camera pans to catch firefighters threading hoses through the chaos.

I lean forward, searching the screen for anything familiar, but they all just look like shapes moving in and out of the smoke.

Lucy's standing inches away from the screen, not blinking.

"They'll be okay," I try to assure her.

She nods, but her jaw is tight. "They always say that. Until they're not."

I don't argue. I've heard enough stories to know that she isn't wrong.

The news then cuts to a reporter on the ground. "We've received reports that two firefighters are trapped inside the building."

Lucy reaches back and grabs my hand. We don't say anything as we watch.

"The fire is proving difficult to contain, and with risk of collapse, we aren't sure the firefighters will make it out."

I'm not sure how long we wait, but I know I hold my breath the entire time. Then suddenly, the camera swings, and two firefighters emerge from the doorway, dragging a civilian between them. The man's face is streaked with soot, and his clothes are torn. The firefighters hold him until they reach the ambulance.

I hold my breath. So does Lucy.

Is that Hansen? Riggins? The shape is right, and the walk looks familiar, but the camera pulls away too fast, replaced by more shots of flames and shouting.

Lucy lets out a ragged sigh, her hand squeezing mine. "That was them," she says, though her voice is barely more than a whisper. "I saw Riggins's number. It was them."

She pulls me into her, and I sigh with relief, but my heart still races.

The anchor's voice fades into the background. They may be okay physically, but I can't shake the feeling of dread in my stomach.

The fire drags on for hours. First, it's only on the TV, then it's alive in my mind, looping images of flames and sirens and Hansen walking out of the building. Lucy finally turns off the TV when, gratefully, no fatalities are reported. I keep my phone attached to me, hoping to hear from Hansen even though I know it could be hours before I do.

I try my best to distract myself. Juniper finally comes home, and we make dinner and watch reruns of whatever '90s sitcom is on TV.

After dinner, I finally text him.

Me

> Hey. Saw the fire on the news. You guys okay?

He doesn't respond, causing the dread in my stomach to grow.

By midnight, the news has moved on. The fire's out, the street sealed off, the cause "under investigation." Lucy finally goes to bed after hearing from Riggins. He's okay, just shaken. I ask him how Hansen is. He says it's better if I talk to him myself.

I try to call. Nothing.

I don't even attempt to sleep. All I can do is pace. I text him again.

Me

> I'm really worried. Please answer me if you can.

Nothing.

Time slows the rest of the night. I make coffee, drink half, then pour the rest down the sink. I sit by the window, watching the city empty itself out. I see Hansen running. The marks on his hands. Him walking out of the building.

Then I see my brother. Sitting in a hospital bed. Lifeless in the funeral home.

I try and fight all the images away, but the mind is a powerful thing.

When morning comes, I can't wait anymore. I grab my keys and head to Hansen's. I knock on his front door, and like everything else, there's no answer. I knock again, louder, my whole body buzzing. Finally, the door clicks open.

He stands in the doorway, barefoot in sweatpants, with red eyes and exhaustion written in every line of his face. The relief of finally seeing him alive spreads through my body like a drug. "Thea," he says in a low voice.

I don't think, I just pull him into a hug. At first, he's stiff, but then his arms wrap around me, and he breathes out.

"Hey," he says, smoothing down my hair.

I step back, searching his face. "Are you okay?"

He nods. I don't believe it.

"You didn't answer my messages. I was worried."

"I'm sorry."

"How bad was it?"

He scrubs a hand over his face. "Bad."

"Can I come in?"

He nods and steps aside. All the curtains in his apartment are drawn, so the room is dark. The soft glow of TV is the only light. I head to the couch and take a seat. Hansen stands in front of me, his arms crossed tight against his chest. He doesn't talk, just stands with hollow eyes. It looks like a piece of him has been scraped out and replaced with fear.

"Hansen. Talk to me," I beg.

He shakes his head. "I'm fine, Thea. You didn't need to come."

"Bullshit." My voice is harsh, but I don't back down. "You're not fine, and I'm done pretending with you. You told me you wanted to be better. Then *try* Hansen."

He goes quiet, eyes fixed somewhere past me, and I can't help thinking he's slipping away again. Then, after a while, he finally speaks.

"I got in trouble with the captain. I didn't listen to orders, didn't get out when I was supposed to. And because of it, Riggins almost got hurt. They're giving me time off. Suspension. He thinks I should talk to someone." He lets out a bitter laugh. "Time off. Like that's supposed to fix anything."

He sinks into the chair next to me, hands covering his face. His shoulders start to shake.

"I don't know how to do this anymore," he says. "I keep screwing up."

He's breaking, so I leave the couch to kneel in front of him, placing my hands on his knees.

"Hansen. Listen to me." He lifts his head, his brown eyes meeting mine. "I get punishing yourself. Believe me, I do. But like you've taught me, it doesn't fix anything. It won't bring him back."

"I walked away that night. I left him. I left you. Maybe if I hadn't, he'd still be here."

"We can't know that."

"I see him everywhere. In everything I do, he's there. And when I was in that building, I couldn't leave. Not when I knew there might be someone else. Riggins wanted me to go, but I didn't listen. I was willing to risk his life, take Juniper's father away, just because I feel like I have to save everyone now."

He rubs his face, and his expression is so defeated. "It's my fault. My dad. Beck. Today. All of it. If I could just save enough people, maybe it would mean something. But nothing ever changes."

I cup his cheek. "I get it. The guilt, the questions. I know that pain. I've felt it. You keep thinking that if you could just suffer enough, it will bring him back. But it won't. And you can't carry that pain alone. You're not supposed to.

"You did what you had to do that night. I didn't see it then, or at least I didn't want to, but I do now. I realized a few months later that the way I was handling things wasn't working. That he had to want help before he would ever take it."

He nods, tears slipping down his cheeks.

"I tried to get in touch with him," Hansen admits. "More times than I can even remember. He never wanted anything to do with me again."

"I know. Just know that he cared about you. All the way until the end."

His eyes drift down, but I grab his face so he's looking at me again. "I've felt lost most of my life. Never really wanted, never really important. But you always made me feel like I was. You taught me it was okay to be happy." I lean in closer. "You make me want to be happy, Hansen."

He shakes his head. "I can't drag you down, Thea. Not when I'm like this."

"No. You made that choice for me once before, and I won't let you do it again. You're not dragging me down. You're the only thing keeping me up."

He looks at me, and I see him wrestling with the fear, the hope, the wanting.

"After my dad died," he says, touching my cheek, "it felt like my world ended. It didn't start again until the day I saw you on that track. The way you were running—"

"Hey," I interrupt.

"Let me finish," he says with a hint of a smile. "The way you were running was so adorable. So much so that I purposely ran into you."

"You didn't."

"I did. And even if it wasn't the smartest way to get your attention, I don't regret it. Not for a second. Every minute I got to spend with you, every letter you wrote me, every story you told me about the life you wanted—I fell harder. I loved hearing the way your mind worked, Thea. You see the world so differently than me, and it was beautiful.

"I love your kindness, your stubbornness, the way you make even ordinary days feel like something I'll miss when they're gone. I love how you argue with me, and how every time I'm with you it makes me want to be a better person. I love the way you look at the world, and the way you look at me."

It feels like all the air has left my lungs, but he keeps going. "I was scared when we were younger. Scared you'd resent me if I asked you to stay, so I let you go. Because that's what I've always done. But when you left, it was like my world stopped spinning, and nothing felt right until you came back. I'm in love with you, Thea. I always have been. Even through the mess. Even when I was trying not to be. Even now, when I'm still scared."

His attention settles fully on me. "You're it for me. You always have been."

My heart is pounding, and all I can do is stare. I want to say something, anything, but the words are tangled up inside of me.

All my thoughts of fear come rushing in at once.

What if it doesn't work? What if we only end up hurting each other more? What if I let myself believe in this, and then I lose him too?

But then there's a thought bigger than all the fear: What if loving him is the best thing I'll ever do?

What if this—right here, right now—is what makes it all worth it?

The world burns, and people make mistakes, and most of us are just trying to find someone to stand with in the middle of the mess.

And my someone is right in front of me.

I lean my forehead against Hansen and whisper, "If you're scared, be scared with me."

And then I kiss him.

Chapter Thirty

When our lips meet, everything we've left unsaid crashes between us. Hungry, urgent, impossibly messy. He pulls me closer, arms tight around me, like he's afraid I'll slip away. I slide onto his lap, pressing my body tightly against his, and his mouth moves against mine with a desperate heat that lights me from the inside out.

"Thea," he whispers in the dark, almost like a plea.

My hands scrabble at his shirt, fists tightening in the thin cotton, and I want his skin, all of it, now. I pull his shirt up, shoving it over his head so fast I hear the seam protest. I toss it to the side and smile down at him. He stares up at me, those dark brown eyes ablaze, and I shiver with want. He retaliates by yanking my tank top over my head in one swift motion, exposing me to the cold air. He explores my bare sides gently, as if memorizing every curve.

"Do you have any idea what you do to me?" he murmurs, and I answer by leaning forward to kiss him again, grinding my hips into his hardness.

I lean close enough to whisper, "Take me to your room."

Before I can blink, he's sliding me off his lap, gathering my legs around his waist, and lifting me as if I weigh nothing. "Hold on tight," he rasps against my skin, and we stumble into the hallway.

I smile as he kicks open his bedroom door and nearly trips over the rug before gently laying me on the bed. "Nice entrance."

He smiles, brushes a strand of hair from my face, and sinks down over me, hands trailing fire along my hips. "I've waited so long for this," he whispers, and I tug him back into another heated kiss.

His fingers slip beneath the waistband of my leggings, coaxing them down as I kick them off without care. In turn, I tug his pants and boxers down in one impatient yank, the world narrowing to the brush of skin on skin. I find him in the dim glow, and he moans my name into my shoulder, a sound that makes my heart pound and the pressure in my stomach build.

I want to feel him against me, so I move my hands to my hips but then he stops me. "Let me." So, I stop and watch his hands peel away my last barrier. My underwear slides down my legs with torturous slowness. When it's gone, I grab him again, pressing him flush against me. We're naked and trembling, every nerve alive.

"Do you have a condom?" I ask, breathless.

He nods, then reaches into his nightstand and pulls out a wrapper, rips it open with his teeth, and rolls it on.

"Are you okay?" he asks.

I nod.

Our lips meet once more as he settles above me. His first thrust is deliberate, and slow enough that my lungs forget to fill. "God," I moan, arching into him.

"I know," he whispers, and the sound sends a shiver through me.

"Don't go slow," I say against his throat. He obeys, finding a rhythm that hits every pulse point. We move together as if we've been learning each other's bodies for years.

He says my name like a secret prayer he's held onto for too long. I clutch his hand above my head, nails grazing his skin, as pleasure builds to a roar inside me.

"Tell me you love me again," I gasp.

"I love you."

I drag my nails down his back, pushing his hips closer to me, wanting all of him.

"Again."

He stills for a heartbeat, eyes locked on mine. That same strand of hair falls in his face, and I brush it aside. Our sex has felt urgent, desperate. But right now, in this moment, looking into the eyes of the man I've loved for fifteen years, it feels lighter. It feels powerful.

"I love you, Thea."

My stomach tightens, and I want to say it back, more than anything, but he doesn't let me. He just captures my lips again and starts moving. His fingers come between us until he finds the perfect spot.

"Don't stop," I beg.

"Never," he breathes.

Moments later, I feel him tense inside me, and that's when I give myself permission to let go. Pleasure spreads through me with a force I've never known before. He says my name over and over as his body comes undone.

When we come down, he collapses beside me, our fingers still entwined. Silence settles around us, broken only by our ragged breaths. In the calm, I trace patterns across his chest, memorizing the rise and fall.

He's the first to move, kissing my shoulder and whispering, "I'll be right back." Then he slips quietly from the bed to take care of the condom.

"Worth the wait?" I ask when he crawls back in beside me.

His eyes find mine. "More than you'll ever know." His fingers graze my hip, sending butterflies straight back to my stomach. "You're so beautiful."

I smile up at him, finally blurting out the words I've been holding in all night. "I love you."

At first, he just blinks, like he's making sure he heard me right. And then it hits, and his whole body goes still, and then he beams, this wide, dizzy smile that lights up his whole face. He lets out a shaky laugh of pure relief and happiness and pulls me into another kiss, deeper this time, like he can't help himself.

I kiss him back but then pull away a little, searching his eyes. "Do you think this is all too fast?"

He shakes his head, brushing his lips over mine. "No. It's us. It could never be too fast."

His answer makes me laugh, and I kiss him again. Our bodies quickly get tangled up in the sheets, but before things can heat up again, I break away and slip out from under his arms.

"Hey—" Hansen protests, trying to catch my hand. "Where are you going?"

I grin over my shoulder, already halfway off the bed. "If I don't pee right now, I'm going to get a UTI, and that would totally ruin this."

He chokes out a laugh and watches as I disappear into the bathroom. When I return, I crawl right back into bed, curling up against his side, my head on his shoulder.

Hansen yawns, and I meet his tired eyes. I've completely forgotten about the fire and the hard day he had.

"Do you want me to go so you can sleep?"

He brushes his thumb across my cheek. "Stay," is all he says.

So I do.

⁂

When I wake up, everything feels weirdly good. The bed is softer than mine and the blanket's heavy in a way that makes it hard to move. It takes a second before I realize where I am. Not my place—Hansen's. Because last night, I slept with Hansen. After he told me he loved me.

My heart picks up. I sit up, squinting at the morning light bleeding through the blinds. The other side of the bed is empty, which makes my chest tighten for a second, but I try to be reasonable. He's probably in the bathroom. People do that in the morning.

His shirt's on the floor, so I tug it on, then hunt down my underwear and do my best to look somewhat put together. My hair isn't cooperating, but I rake my fingers through it anyway and head for the kitchen.

I stop in the doorway. Hansen's at the stove, barefoot, hair still damp from a shower, humming to himself. He glances over, and his smile is slow and sort of ridiculous, and for a second I forget about everything except the way he's looking at me.

"Morning," I say, trying not to sound too pleased with myself.

He doesn't take his eyes off me. "I was hoping you'd steal that shirt."

I spin like an idiot just to make him laugh. He sets down the spoon and pulls me in, pinning me to the counter, kissing me like we don't have places to be. It's softer than last night, but somehow more intense, like he's trying to memorize it.

I run my fingers through his damp hair. "Did you shower already?"

He smiles. "Just wanted to be clean for you."

I roll my eyes. I know he went for a run. The thought stings, but I push it away. Not right now. Right now, he's making breakfast.

"What's cooking?" I ask, eyeing the bread.

"French toast."

"My favorite."

He glances back, playful. "Is it? That's wild. Total coincidence."

I nudge him. "Show off."

"You sleep okay?" he asks.

"Mmmhmm." My fingers trace his chest. "Though someone kept me up pretty late."

He laughs. "How weird. The same thing happened to me." His eyes meet mine, suddenly unguarded. "No regrets?"

I shake my head. "None. You?"

He just smiles, and it feels like something in the room settles.

"I love you," he says. Then he's kissing me again, deeper, and I lose myself in it. I can't help the sound that slips from my throat. It's a needy, desperate noise that I didn't know I could make.

"Jesus, Thea," he breathes against my lips. "Do that again."

"What?"

"That sound."

My mouth curves against his. "I think our breakfast is burning."

His eyes fly open. "Shit." He spins around, lunging for the stove, cursing as he flips the French toast that's gone dark around the edges.

"Smooth," I tease, leaning against the counter.

He glances back at me. "You're distracting."

"So, it's my fault?"

"Completely." He abandons breakfast, comes back to me, hands warm under his shirt on my skin. I rest my head against his chest, listening to his heartbeat.

He says, "Go on a date with me."

It catches me off guard. "Now?"

"Not now. But soon. Like, an actual date."

I laugh. "Don't you think it's a little late for that?"

"I don't care. Say yes."

I lift my gaze. "Yeah. Okay. Yes."

He shows his excitement by kissing me again, and suddenly breakfast is the last thing on my mind.

"French toast?" he asks.

I shake my head. "Forget it."

He laughs, and I let myself get lost in him for a little while longer.

Chapter Thirty-One

I can't remember the last time I felt this nervous. Not the "I hope I don't forget this math equation for the test" kind of nervous, not the "they're calling my name for the interview" nervous. This is deeper, the kind of anticipation that starts in your stomach and spreads out to your fingers and toes.

My heart is beating so fast I'm afraid Lucy might hear it from across the room.

She's helping the best she can. She's planted herself on my bed, scrolling through her phone and humming some song I'm sure she's made up. Every now and then she glances up, grins, and says, "You look gorgeous."

"This is ridiculous," I mutter, running a brush through my hair for the millionth time. "It's just a date. People go on dates every day."

Lucy snorts. "Yeah, but most people didn't get the dicking of a lifetime from their date the night before."

I throw a rubber band at her. She ducks, laughing.

When I told Lucy about my night with Hansen, she didn't bat an eye. In fact, I think her exact words were, "About fucking time." Then she wanted a play-by-play of each minute. Drawings included.

I stare at myself in the mirror. The black dress I finally settled on is simple, a little stretchy, and might not be as flattering as the other four I tried on but makes me feel the most comfortable.

I set down my brush, suddenly aware of just how much her spare room has started to feel like my room. I've known for a long time that I don't want to leave South Creek, but I haven't been able to say it out loud. After last night, I know it's time.

"Hey, Lucy?" I say. She looks up. "How would you feel if I . . . stayed in South Creek?"

She blinks at me, like she's not sure she heard right. "Stayed? Like, for real?"

I nod, biting my lip. "Yeah. I mean, I'd obviously get a job and my own apartment so I'm not mooching off you forever. But I don't know, Luce. I think I want to stay."

She just stares at me. Then her whole face lights up. "Are you serious? Thea, are you—oh my God, yes!" She practically launches herself off the bed and tackles me in a hug.

I start laughing. "You're not just saying that?"

She pulls back, eyes a little watery. "You could live in my closet and eat nothing but ramen, and I'd still want you here. Are you sure, though? I know this town has a lot of memories."

"I'm sure. I want to be here. With you and Juniper. With Hansen."

Lucy just sits there, grinning through happy tears. "You're gonna kill me."

I hug her again, and then the doorbell rings.

Lucy jumps away from me. "He's here!"

"You have to be nice."

She raises her hand in protest. "Me? I'm a perfect angel."

I give her a *yeah right* look. She simply smiles. Then, no doubt sensing my nerves, puts her hands on my shoulders. "Hey, you're going to be okay. You look amazing. And if he isn't speechless when he sees you, I have no problem knocking some sense into him."

"Didn't I just say you have to be nice?"

"Okay, fine. I'll *nicely* knock some sense into him."

I smile. "Thanks, Luce."

She gives me another squeeze. "Go get him, tiger."

We head for the door, only to discover it's already been answered by none other than the fourteen-year-old in the house.

Juniper stands tall, nearly blocking Hansen from our view.

"I promise I'll have her home by midnight," Hansen signs to her.

"Aw, she's interrogating him," Lucy says in a whisper. "I'm so proud."

I laugh before walking up to the door. Hansen looks almost cinematic. He's wearing a black sweater I've never seen before and jeans that I know will make his ass look great, and his hair is perfect, except for the one strand falling across his forehead.

His eyes find mine past Juniper, and my cheeks go hot.

Juniper must notice his sudden shift in attention and turns. Her smile widens. "Wow, Aunt Thea. You look amazing."

I break eye contact with Hansen and give her a smile. "Thank you, Junie."

"Don't worry, I was just asking him his intentions."

"I hope they were pure."

"The purest," Hansen responds, a hint of last night in his eyes.

"Come on, sweetie," Lucy says to her daughter. "Let's let these two be ridiculously adorable by themselves."

Juniper gives Hansen one last *I'm watching you* look before heading off. Lucy gives me an encouraging smile and a wink as they walk away.

Once they are gone, and it's just Hansen and me, he says, "You look beautiful."

I do a little spin to show off the dress. "You like it?"

"I really, really do."

I wrap my arms around his neck, breathing in his cologne. "You clean up pretty well yourself."

I'm just about to kiss him when Lucy's voice comes out of nowhere. "You crazy kids, don't stay out too late! Or do! I'm not your mom! Just remember condoms! Or don't! Juniper would love a cousin!" I groan, but Hansen is laughing.

"Ready?" he asks.

"Like you wouldn't believe."

❊❊❊❊❊~ ~❊❊❊❊❊

The car ride is torture, in the best, most maddening way. Hansen's got one hand on the steering wheel, but the other is planted firmly on my thigh, his thumb tracing slow circles that make it really hard to think straight. I keep trying not to squirm, but it's impossible. Every time I glance over, he's got that little smirk, like he knows exactly what he's doing to me.

It's not like I haven't been distracted all day. We spent hours at the cabin. Supposedly getting work done. But every time I tried to focus, I'd catch him looking at me, and suddenly I'd forget what I was even supposed to be doing. It was the kind of day that felt like it could go on forever, and I wouldn't mind.

But through all of it, Hansen's kept this one secret. Every time I ask where we're headed, he just shakes his head, acting all mysterious. He won't give me a single hint. I've tried everything—bribery, pouting, begging—but he's not budging. And now, with his hand on my bare skin and the road rolling out in front of us, I'm about to lose my mind. I want to know where we're going. I want to know everything. But all I can do is sit here, try to breathe, and watch him drive.

"You want to ask me where we're going, huh?" he says, glancing over at me.

I turn in my seat, facing him. "Oh my God, yes. I'm trying to be chill and go with the flow, but I'm not chill, and I've never liked a flow."

He laughs and taps my knee. "I'm proud of you for making it this long. Want to try a guess?"

I sigh dramatically. "Are we seeing a movie?"

He shakes his head.

"Bowling?"

Another shake.

"Vandalizing your archnemesis's house?"

He shakes his head again.

"Bummer. That's a riveting first date. Is it a firehouse event?"

"Nope."

"Going to your cousin's wedding where you've told everyone I'm your girlfriend?"

He looks genuinely horrified. "Tell me you haven't actually had that date before."

I shrug. "You'll be happy to know it ended with him proposing to me in front of the bride and groom."

His mouth drops open. "You're kidding."

"Moral of the story is, the bar for first dates is extremely low."

He snorts out a laugh. "Why don't you just sit back and wait, you impatient girl."

I huff, but I can't help grinning. I lean my head back against the seat and watch the city lights slide by. I steal a glance at him as often as I can, watching how the passing streetlights cut across his face, and the way his jaw flexes when he concentrates on driving. He's so careful, always checking the mirrors, always reaching over to adjust the heat when I shiver. When a song that I love comes on the radio, he turns up the volume without asking.

It's small, but it matters.

※※※※※ ※※※※※

We pull into a parking lot, and I sit up straighter, trying to see where we are. My heart skips when I spot the marquee.

No way.

"You're fucking kidding," I say, turning to him. "Hansen—"

He keeps his eyes on the attendant waving us forward. "Thea."

"We aren't going in there, are we?"

He just keeps driving, following the line of cars, and I feel my anticipation building until it's almost unbearable.

When we finally park, he turns to me, unbuckling his seatbelt. "Do you want to go inside with me?"

"How did you . . . how did you know about Kelly Lakeson?"

"You listen to her all the time. After hearing you sing along to her cover of 'The Wizard and I' for the thousandth time at the cabin, I looked her up."

I stare at him, trying not to feel embarrassed that he overheard me singing that many times. "I tried to get tickets for this show. They were sold out."

He just shrugs again, like this is no big deal.

"When did you get these?"

"That doesn't matter."

I narrow my eyes. "Hansen Reed, you are ridiculous."

He leans over, undoing my seatbelt for me, his fingers brushing my hip, sending a jolt up my spine. "Well, you coming? Or do I have to sing all the Broadway songs by myself?"

I arch an eyebrow. "You like Broadway songs?"

He smiles. "They're growing on me."

The outside of the venue is wrapped in string lights, soft and golden, and the night feels almost unreal. I don't let go of Hansen's hand as we walk in. It's an intimate room, covered in small tables, each one with a candle burning. The smell is enchanting, and I wish I could bottle it up for later. My eyes go wide as I see how close we are to the stage. "These aren't just regular tickets, are they?"

"Define *regular*."

I spot the VIP signs. "You got us VIP seats?"

He leads me to our table, front row and just off-center. It's the best spot in the house. "Wanted you to have the best view."

I sit, honestly stunned. "This is too much."

He looks at me. "It's not enough."

Everything else blurs. The noise, the small crowd, all of it fades. It's just his eyes, the way he looks at me like I'm the only one here. "I love you."

"I love you too."

The lights dim, and Kelly Lakeson walks out on stage. I can't breathe. She's right there. In real life. My whole body goes tense with excitement. Hansen squeezes my hand under the table.

She starts singing, and it's everything. I know every word, but I sing them softly under my breath, too shy to let anyone but Hansen hear. He never looks away from me.

When Kelly takes a break, I finally come back down to earth. "Sorry I'm such a nerd about this."

Hansen leans across the table. "Don't ever apologize for loving something. Not to me."

When the second half of the show starts, I lose myself in the music. But every few minutes, I catch Hansen watching me. And for the second time since Beck died, I feel like maybe I understand what Hansen was talking about. Maybe there is space for both the pain and the happiness.

The show ends way too soon. The crowd stands, clapping and whistling, and I'm on my feet, hands stinging as I applaud. Hansen's right next to me, his hand finding the small of my back. I can feel myself grinning like an idiot.

We drive home in comfortable silence. My head is spinning, but in a good way. The city lights blur past.

"So," he says finally, glancing over at me. "Was it okay?"

I let out a breathless laugh. "It was no marriage proposal at your cousin's wedding, but it'll do."

He grabs my hand and squeezes it. "Don't worry. There's always the second date."

When he pulls up outside Lucy's house, he kills the engine but doesn't move to open the door. And neither do I. Instead, I turn in my seat and reach for his face. My palm fits perfectly against his jaw, rough with stubble, and I kiss him. Hard. There's nothing tentative or polite about it. His mouth opens under mine, and the whole world tilts. My seatbelt is still holding me back, so I unclip it, toss it aside, and suddenly I'm straddling him, my knees pressed into the seat, and my hands in his hair.

He lets out a sound, almost a gasp, and his arms come around my waist, pulling me closer. His hands are everywhere. My back, my thighs, sliding up under the hem of my dress. We fit together like we've done this a thousand times, but it still feels new and electric. The windows are fogging, the steering wheel pressing awkwardly into my back, but I don't care. I can't get enough of him. Of his mouth, his hands, the little hitch in his breath every time I move.

He kisses me back like he's making up for every second we had to behave ourselves tonight. The kiss goes on and on, wild and desperate, until I'm dizzy. I break away only because I have to breathe, pressing my forehead to his.

"Come inside," I whisper.

He looks at the house, then back at me, and I can see him weighing it—the risk, the want, the way we can barely keep our hands off each other. "Not sure that's the best idea. Lucy and Juniper are inside."

I flop my head against his chest, groaning. "We should have gone to your place."

He laughs, low and rough, and his fingers draw slow, lazy circles on my spine. "I wanted to drop you off at your door like a gentleman."

I meet his eyes, my hand sliding down his chest, lower, until I'm cupping the evidence of just how un-gentlemanly he feels. "There's nothing gentlemanly about this."

He shudders, biting back a moan, and I can feel his heart racing under my palm. I kiss him again, and honestly consider dragging him inside anyway, Lucy and Juniper be damned.

But I force myself to slow down, to just breathe him in. I rest my forehead against his, my hands tangled in his hair. "I should get my own place. Once I get a job and can afford it, of course."

His dark eyes flicker with hope. "Does that mean you're staying in South Creek?"

"I've been looking into PhD programs at the university nearby. I'll have to get a job while I do, but it feels like the right thing to do."

His thumb traces my cheek. "Are you sure? You don't have to stay. We can do long distance. We can make it work."

I smile. "I'm sure."

He leans in, tucking a strand of hair behind my ear, his face so close I can feel each word against my lips. "I love existing in the silence with you, Thea Miller."

I close my eyes. "Then stay a little longer in it with me."

Chapter Thirty-Two

FIVE YEARS AGO

The drive took three hours, but it felt more like twenty. The radio murmured in the background, some old playlist shuffling through Beck's phone, but neither of us really listened. He stared out the window, hands in his lap, fidgeting with the rubber band on his wrist, twisting it until his knuckles went pale.

I kept sneaking glances at him, half-hoping he'd say something, half-hoping he wouldn't. There was a lump lodged in my throat that wouldn't leave. With every mile, I felt more exposed, like we were heading straight for the edge of something, and I couldn't turn the wheel.

Beck finally broke the silence as we passed a sign for the rehab center. "Looks quiet."

"Yeah." My voice barely made a sound. "Supposed to be peaceful. That's what the website said."

He nodded, still watching the landscape blur past. I gripped the steering wheel tighter. I wanted to say something wise, something to make things easier for him, some big-sister magic. But the words wouldn't come. All I could think about was how small he looked, even though he'd been taller than me for years. I still saw the kid who used to beg me to kill spiders for him.

I pulled into the parking lot, and the tires crunched softly on the freshly fallen leaves. The building was low and sprawling, half-hidden by large trees. Wind chimes hung by the door, catching the breeze.

I put the car in park. We just sat, listening to the engine tick as it cooled. Beck let out a long, slow breath. "You don't have to come in, you know. They said I could check myself in."

I shook my head. "I know. But I want to."

He smiled, just barely.

I blinked back tears. "You sure you want to do this?"

He reached over and squeezed my hand. "Yeah. I'm sure." He let go and looked at the trees. "It's time."

We climbed out, the sun already high and bright, burning off the last of the morning fog. Beck grabbed his duffel from the backseat and slung it over his shoulder. I saw his hand tremble as he zipped it up, but he didn't mention it. We walked together up the path, the wind chimes tinkling as we passed.

At the door, Beck stopped. "You okay?"

I tried to smile. "I'm fine. I just . . . I'm going to miss you."

He shrugged, trying to make it sound casual. "It's only ninety days."

I nodded, but it felt like forever. "Still. The apartment's going to be really quiet."

He bumped my shoulder. "You'll finally get some sleep, huh?"

I laughed, but it cracked in the middle.

"I'm going to be okay, Thea. I promise."

I wanted to believe him. I wanted to trust that this would work, that he'd come back whole. But I was scared, so scared he'd get lost in there, or come out a stranger, or not come out at all.

I reached up and hugged him tight, feeling every bone in his back. "I'll be here when you get out," I whispered, my voice breaking.

He hugged me back. "I know."

We stood like that for a while, neither of us ready to let go. Eventually, he pulled away and wiped his eyes with the back of his hand. "You should go. Before you start crying and embarrass us both."

I rolled my eyes, already crying. "Shut up."

He grinned and gave me that same lopsided smile I hadn't seen in years. Then he turned, duffel bouncing against his hip, and headed up the steps to the front desk. I watched him hand over his forms, and then the nurse led him inside.

He glanced back once, just before the door closed, and gave a small wave.

I waved back, unable to say anything. The door shut behind him, and the wind chimes rattled in the sudden silence.

When I finally got back in the car, I sat for a long time, staring at the trees, waiting for my chest to loosen. I drove home with the windows down, Beck's playlist still playing through the speakers. The road wound away behind me, and I kept telling myself he was going to be okay.

He was going to be okay.

When I got home, the apartment was cold and empty. The first thing I did was light the candle Beck left behind. It was Christmas Time at the Farm. Not my favorite for fall time, but the scent was growing on me. After a shower, I checked my emails, mostly just to distract myself from the silence. Eventually, I sat on my bed with my notebook in my lap.

It had been a while since I'd written a letter, but today felt like the right day. I turned the page over.

Dear Beck,

You went into rehab again today. Third time's the charm, maybe. I think it'll work this time. At least, I hope so. You seem like you really want this. And Beck, I want it for you too.

I'll miss you. Know that. These stretches are never easy for me, but I have to admit, it's a relief not to worry. It's good to know you're safe. That if something happens, you'll be around people who can help.

I'll talk to you soon, Beck.

With love,
Thea

After I folded the letter and put it away in my drawer, my phone buzzed. Mom.

Mom

Have you heard from Beck?

Thea, I swear to God if you know where he is and don't told us.

I ignored the messages and put my phone face down.

Then I flipped the notebook over again and wrote a different name at the top.

Dear Hansen,
It's been two years since I saw you. Two years. Feels like a lifetime and also like yesterday. I'm not really sure what to say except that I hate you. And yet, I don't. I'm so angry with you. And yet, all I want to do is call you. I want to tell you that Beck's in rehab again. That my life feels like it's falling apart a hundred different ways every day. I want to tell you about my job. My pervy boss. The cute guy who asked for my number at the coffee shop and how I said no. I hope you're doing okay. And miserable at the same time. Lucy says you're all right. I wish I could hate you for leaving, but the truth is, I think I just hate myself for missing you so much. If you ever think of

me, I hope it hurts. It does for me. Every day.
With love,
Thea

Chapter Thirty-Three

Now

The paintbrush glides along the trim, edging a line of paint right where the baseboard meets the wall. It's not the puke green color (thank God) but a deep blue. Beck's favorite blue. The moment I saw it, I knew it had to be the color of the cabin.

I keep my wrist loose, trying to make sure each edge comes out clean and sharp. Sunlight cuts through the window, catching on the flecks of paint on my forearm. The air upstairs smells like fresh paint and pine from the candle burning somewhere down in the kitchen.

Hansen whistles under his breath. It's a Kelly Lakeson song he's been obsessed with, and I can't help but smile. He's crouched at the other end of the room, tongue sticking out a little as he runs his brush along the baseboard. There's paint in his hair. A smudge on his jaw. He looks ridiculous. He looks perfect.

"Your line's crooked," he says, not even glancing up.

I roll my eyes at him. "My line's fine. Yours, however, looks like a one-year-old painted it."

He smiles, finally looking at me. "I'd like to see a one-year-old paint lines this straight." He winks. I snort. It's like the warmth of the sun itself is inside my chest. It's just us. Hansen and me and the cabin. I don't remember the last time I felt this . . . safe.

A tiny flicker of guilt sneaks into my happiness knowing that we're only here because of Beck. Together because my brother is gone. If he were here, would he resent this? Would he understand?

I just hope he would.

Hansen leans back, surveying his work. He wipes his forehead with the back of his wrist, leaving a streak of blue in his hair. "You missed a spot," he says, nodding at the corner.

I flick my brush at him, sending a splatter of blue across his arm. He gasps, clutching his chest as if wounded, then lunges at me, growling low.

"Don't you dare!" I shriek, but he's already got his brush and swipes a big streak down my bare thigh.

I grab my own brush and chase him across the room. He dodges, but I catch him, dragging my brush right across his back.

"Oh, you fight dirty," he says before swiping at me again.

Soon, we're both covered in paint, and we collapse on the floor, tangled and laughing. All I can say, is I'm glad the carpets are getting replaced next week.

I end up sprawled on top of him, my hand pressed against his chest, feeling his heart beating steadily under my palm.

He's looking at me, and I don't think, I just lean in and kiss him.

He wastes no time deepening the kiss, his hand cradling the back of my neck. "You're getting paint everywhere," I murmur, lips against his.

"You started it."

"Well, now you have to finish it." I arch against him, feeling his body under mine. He slides his hand up my shirt, fingers rough but careful, and I shiver. I want more. I want all of him.

He pulls my shirt off, tossing it somewhere behind us. I reach up, unhook my bra, and let it fall away. His eyes go dark, and he traces his fingers down my side. I slide my hands under his shirt, feeling the heat of his skin. Every part of me feels too alive.

He pulls me closer, his mouth finding my neck, my collarbone, my breasts. I gasp, digging my fingers into his shoulders. I tug at his pants, desperately fumbling with the zipper. He's already hard.

He kisses me again, hungrier this time, and I reach for his shirt, wanting his skin on mine. He stiffens suddenly. "Thea, wait. Don't."

But it's too late. I have his shirt halfway up and see it. There's a bruise, huge and purple, blooming on his hip.

I stop, and he jerks away from me, snatching the shirt back down.

"Hansen. What the hell is that?"

"It's nothing."

"Don't fucking say that. Tell me where that bruise is from."

He's standing now, putting back on his pants, and he won't look at me.

"I'm a firefighter, Thea. It happens."

I pull on my shirt as I stand up. "I know what you do, Hansen. But that's not from a call." I force our eyes to meet. "Don't lie to me."

His eyes soften. "It looks worse than it is."

"Are you getting in fights? Are you . . . are you doing it to yourself?"

He winces, and that's all the answer I need.

A wave of helplessness rises in me so big I can barely breathe. I love him. But I don't know how to do this. I don't know how to help him if he won't talk to me.

"You said you'd let me in."

He doesn't answer.

"Is this about Beck? Because if it is, you can talk to me. I want you to talk to me. I want to help like you've helped me."

He finally turns. There's a distance in his eyes I hate. "You can't fix this, Thea."

His words land like a slap. I swallow hard. "I know I can't. But you can't keep trying to fix it yourself. You can't keep hurting yourself and shutting me out. I'm right here, Hansen. I want to be here."

He sinks to the floor, rubbing his face with his hands. A suffocating silence stretches between us.

Then, he finally speaks. "There's this place. It's some busted-ass basement under a junkyard outside of South Creek. We don't use names, or weapons. Just fists." His eyes move up and meet mine. "I get in the ring and . . . I *let* them hit me. I get in fights on purpose. Or I run. I push myself until I can't feel anything. I do whatever it takes to hurt because pain is the only thing that makes me feel better. At least, it was. Until you. Now it's you. You make me feel better. And yet, every single day I wake up and still have this need to feel this pain. I try to be different, but I can't turn it off."

I resist the urge to hold him and tell him it'll be okay, because I'm honestly not sure if that would help or just make him shut down harder.

"Maybe your captain was right. Maybe you should talk to someone," I say. "Like, a professional. Maybe we both should."

He laughs, but there's no humor in it. "Maybe we're both too messed up for this to work."

The words are a punch to my gut, but I force myself to sit with them. To really hear them. Because I don't want to pretend everything is perfect and love is easy. I want the truth, even if it hurts.

"Yeah," I say softly. "Maybe we are too fucked up to make this work. But that doesn't mean it can't. Relationships are hard. *Life* is hard. But that doesn't mean you stop trying." I pause, swallowing tears. "I'm not walking away, Hansen. Not this time."

He looks at me. "Thea—"

I stand to grab my shoes and purse. "I'm going to go home and get cleaned up. You can sit here and think about whether you really want this. Whether you really want me. Think about if you want to keep choosing pain, or if you want to try choosing something else."

He gets to his feet as I reach the door.

"You know I love you, right?" he asks.

I nod, blinking back the tears forming in my eyes. "I know. I love you, too. That's why I'm not leaving. But I can't make you choose me. You have to do that yourself."

Chapter Thirty-Four

I barely remember driving home from the cabin. I just blink, and suddenly, I'm standing in my own bathroom. I peel off my clothes and step into the shower, turning the water as hot as I can stand. For a while, I just stand there and let it run over me, hoping it'll rinse away everything. It doesn't.

After, I find myself in town, walking on Main Street. The town feels empty and quiet, almost like it knows about the war waging inside me. I walk, not really sure where I'm going.

My mind is a mess of everything that happened at the cabin. Hansen's voice, my own words, all tangled up and replaying on a loop. I keep thinking if I just run through it one more time, I'll unlock some version where I said the right thing, or didn't say the wrong thing, and everything turns out different. But maybe it was always going to end up here.

I keep walking, passing the small gas station where Beck once made an older guy buy him cigarettes when I was a sophomore in high school. I then pass the bench where I watched him try that first cigarette. He coughed so hard I honestly thought he'd stop breathing. Instead, he just laughed. Then told me life was an adventure, and we should try it all.

I wish I could talk to him. I wonder what he'd say if he saw me now, fighting with Hansen, making a mess of things. Would he be disappointed? Would he understand? Would he hate me because I'm so mad at him for leaving me?

The pain settles into my chest, and tears well in my eyes. I don't want to cry. Not now, not in public. I swipe at my eyes, trying to force them away.

When I stop to try and regain myself, I look up and nearly laugh. The Bakery Bee stands tall, with bright yellow doors and little bees painted on the windows. The door opens and a customer exits, letting out a rush of warmth and the smell of sugar and cinnamon. Without thinking, I step inside, letting the bell over the door announce me.

Winnie is behind the counter, her hair up in a messy bun and a bee apron around her waist. She looks up, and her whole face lights up with surprise.

"Thea, honey. Oh my goodness, what a treat." She hurries around the counter and pulls me into a hug. It's quick, but it nearly makes me lose the fight against the tears I'm trying to hold back.

I try to smile. "Hi, Winnie."

"What brings you by? Coffee? Or something to eat? I just pulled a fresh batch of scones from the oven. They're blueberry lemon, my favorite."

I stare at the glass case filled with different baked goods, but everything blurs together. "I . . . I don't know. I can't decide."

Winnie's face softens. She glances at the young girl wiping down a table. "Maya, can you cover the front for a second?"

Maya nods, and Winnie gently touches my arm. "Come sit with me a minute."

I hesitate, suddenly feeling way too embarrassed that I came to her place of work a total mess. "You don't have to—I know you're busy—"

"I'm not too busy for you, Thea," she says, and there's something in her voice that makes me believe her.

I follow her to a little table in the back and sink into the chair. She sits across from me, folding her hands on the table.

"I'm sorry," I say, still trying to hold the tears back. "For just dropping in like this and being a mess."

She shakes her head. "Don't you dare apologize for feeling. And I'm glad you came by."

I stare down at my hands, twisting my fingers together. "I don't even know where to start."

"Is it Hansen?" she asks gently.

My head snaps up. "How did you . . . ?"

She smiles, and it's amazing how much it looks like Hansen's. "A mother just knows."

I let out a shaky breath. "I love him. I do."

"I know you do. But there's more, isn't there?" Her tone isn't judgmental or upset. She's just genuinely interested.

"I can't help him in the way he needs. I'm not sure I can . . . love him in the way he needs."

Winnie sighs, and leans forward, resting her hands on the table. "Hansen has always been stubborn with his emotions, and I take a lot of the blame for it. When his father died, I shut down. He was the love of my life, and losing him so young was a lot. I could barely eat, barely sleep. I was so engrossed in my own grief that I lost sight of Hansen's. By the time I realized what I had done, it was too late. He was already punishing himself for what happened to his father and keeping it all inside. He thought he had to be strong for me. I'll never forgive myself for that."

I remember the first time he talked to me about his dad. How vulnerable he seemed in that moment. How I fell a little bit in love with him because of it.

Winnie reaches across and squeezes my hand. "Then he met you. And you were the first person who ever got him to open up, Thea. The first one he let see the mess. You saved him, I think." She gets quieter. "But you don't have to carry him now. That's not fair to you."

"I just wish I knew what to do."

She shakes her head. "Sometimes, all someone needs is love. And other times, love isn't enough to fix everything. It's too messy, and no matter how hard you try, it just doesn't work. But you deserve to be happy, Thea. If that's with my son, then it can be beautiful. If it's not, that's okay too."

I nod, and I finally let the tears fall.

Winnie stands and brings me a warm scone, setting it in front of me. "Eat something, honey. It helps, I promise. And whatever you decide, I'm here. You're not alone."

I take a bite of the scone, and the sweetness nearly undoes me. "Thank you," I say, and I'm realizing just how different Winnie and my mother are. Growing up, I could tell Winnie had shut down emotionally. She wasn't around much, and when she was, she hardly said two words, but I can see the change in her. And it makes me wonder how different my life might be now if I had a mother like that.

It brings up an ache for my own mother.

But I'm not sure where to start with that.

Winnie sits back down, and we talk for a while. She tells me stories about Hansen's dad, how he wanted nothing more than to be a father, how he loved fixing things, how he used to write her little love notes and hide them around the house.

I lose track of time, and before I know it, it's been more than an hour.

"I should go," I say, standing. "Thank you, for everything."

She gets up and wraps up a couple of scones. "Take these with you. Share them with Lucy and Juniper."

I thank her again and walk out into the cooling evening.

Lucy's still at work when I get home, but Juniper is at the kitchen table with her head in her hands.

I gently touch her arm, and she looks up. "Hey," I sign, dropping the bag on the counter. "I brought scones."

Her eyes widen with delight. "Oh my God, are they from Winnie's?"

"Yes. They're blueberry lemon."

She doesn't hesitate to tear into the bag and grab a scone.

"So, what are you working on?" I ask, leaning against the counter.

"Math," she signs, rolling her eyes. "It might actually kill me."

"You know I'm actually pretty good at math, right?"

She pauses, then her eyes widen. "Of course. I totally forgot. Can you help me? Please?"

I laugh. "I'd love to."

But before I can sit, Juniper interrupts. "Oh! Wait. Before we do that, Hansen was here earlier."

My heart jumps. "He was?"

She nods. "Yeah. Maybe an hour ago. I told him you weren't here, but he dropped something off. I put it on your bed."

"Give me one second," I sign and then head to my room. There, sitting on my bed, is a small box. I instantly recognize it as the one I threw out months ago. The one filled with letters I wrote to Beck. The one I thought was gone forever.

The one Hansen must have kept.

On top is an envelope with my name in Hansen's handwriting.

My hands shake as I pick it up.

Dear Thea,

I'm not really sure where to start.

I'm so incredibly sorry for so many things. I'm sorry for everything that happened at the cabin. For shutting down and making you feel like you're alone in this. I've always had a hard time opening up, scared that my emotions would be too much and I'd push people away. Instead, I'm finding that I do the pushing people away thing all on my own.

You asked if I really wanted this—if I really wanted you. The answer is yes. I want you, Thea. I want us, even if we're both 'too messed up.' Which, for the record, I don't think we are. I want to try, even if it's hard, even if it hurts sometimes. I want to try, with you.

You were right about talking to someone. I'm going to do it. I want to be better.

I'll tell you all of this in person later, but I needed to get it out now. Also, you may notice that I kept the box of letters you threw out. I understand if you're mad that I kept them. But I thought maybe you'd want them someday.

I choose you, Thea. I love you. Messy or not, scared or not, I'm in it. I'll be at the cabin after my shift if you want to talk.

With love,

Hansen

Tears blur my vision, but this time, they're tears of relief. I clutch the letter to my chest and open the box. My fingers trace the edges of the worn envelopes.

And just for the briefest second, I swear I can hear Beck's voice whispering to me, *It's going to be okay, Thea.*

Chapter Thirty-Five

After helping Juniper with her homework, I make my way back to the cabin to meet Hansen. It will still be a few hours until he's off his shift, but I want to be waiting for him when he does. The irony that the cabin used to once be a hell for me and now feels like a lifeline isn't lost on me.

Beck was sneaky that way.

The sky is dark the entire drive, but when I round the last curve, I see the smoke. It's black, thick, and rolling over the treetops like a storm. My brain doesn't catch up until I see the flickering orange behind the trees. I just sit there, frozen. The world narrows to the sight of flames clawing out of the roof, licking up the porch, the sky above the cabin glowing.

"No. No, no, no, no—" I slam the car into park and run, stumbling. I can't breathe. My heart is hammering so hard I think I might actually die. The cabin is burning. My cabin. Beck's cabin. Everything we built, everything he left me.

Flashing red and blue lights strobe through the trees. There are fire trucks, hoses snaking across the lawn, and silhouettes moving in the chaos. I can hear shouting, the whoosh of water, the greedy roar of the fire.

I break through the line of onlookers, not caring who tries to stop me. "No! Please!" I'm screaming before I even reach the yard. "No, I have to go in! Beck's in there!"

A fireman stops me. "Ma'am, you have to step back and let us work."

I try and push past him. "You have to let me in! Please!"

Someone grabs me in a desperate, rough grip. "Thea! Stop!"

It's Hansen. He's in his turnout gear, with soot smeared across his face and his helmet pushed back. His eyes are wild with fear, but he's real, and he's here. He wraps his arms around me as I thrash, trying to get past him.

"Let me go!" I sob, fighting him. "I have to save it. I have to save him. Please—"

He holds me tighter. "It's too late, Thea. You can't go in. It's not safe."

The heat is a monster, pressing at my front. The flames devour the porch, the windows, everything. I can hear things collapsing inside. I keep screaming, trying to claw my way out of Hansen's grip.

"It's my fault. It's my fault." My voice breaks through all the noise.

Hansen's team is working in front of us, shouting orders, spraying water, but it's not enough. The cabin is already lost. The fire is greedy and wild and merciless.

I collapse against Hansen's chest, sobbing so hard I can barely breathe. "I'm sorry. I'm so sorry."

He pulls me away from the heat, his arms tight around me, holding me up when my knees buckle. "It's not your fault, baby. You're safe. That's all I care about."

But I can't hear him. I can only hear the crackling, the shattering glass, the flames roaring higher. I call out for Beck, again and again, as if my brother might somehow answer.

Someone brings a blanket and drapes it over my shoulders. Another firefighter tries to usher me away, but Hansen waves them off. "I've got her," he says, and I hear the sorrow in his voice, too.

I watch, helpless, as the last of the roof collapses. Ash floats up into the sky, glowing like dying stars. I sink to the ground and scream until my voice gives out.

The cabin is gone. Beck is gone. All of it—everything I tried to hold together, everything I thought I could fix—burned away in a single night.

Hansen kneels beside me, his hand on my back. "I'm here. I'm right here, Thea."

But I can't stop crying. I can't stop shaking. I can't stop wishing for things I'll never get back.

Somewhere behind us, the fire dies to embers. The crowd disperses. I don't remember how long we sit there, Hansen and me, but eventually the woods are silent. I lean into him and let myself fall apart.

Chapter Thirty-Six

NINE MONTHS AGO

B eck's train got in late, but Penn Station was still buzzing. People were dragging suitcases, couples were holding hands, and the air was thick with the cold of December.

I spotted him in the crowd and breathed a sigh of relief. He looked good. Healthier. Like he'd come back from some place dark and finally found the sun.

He smiled when he saw me, and I felt like a kid again, running to meet him at the elementary school gates. We hugged.

"Hey, city girl," he said into my hair.

"You made it."

He held me at arm's length. "You look older. Like, official accountant old."

I rolled my eyes, but it felt good to laugh. "You look like you finally got a good night's sleep."

He shrugged, and I saw the ghost of what he'd been. But it was just a shadow. "I'm working on it."

We took the subway back to my apartment. Beck pressed his nose to the window, watching the city slip past, his knee bouncing. He hadn't been here for years. Not sober, anyway. When we got upstairs, he dropped his bag and took in my tiny space.

"Still looks great," he said.

I smiled.

"Well, here. I have something to make this place a little more festive." He dug into his backpack and pulled out a scraggly pine tree wrapped in plastic, with a string of dollar store lights tangled around its branches. "Merry Christmas, Thea."

I stared. "You brought me a tree?"

"You can't have Christmas without a tree."

We set it up on the windowsill, laughing as we tried to get the lights untangled. Beck insisted on making hot chocolate while listening to Christmas music. The apartment filled with the smell of chocolate and cinnamon and the sound of two people not worried about anything.

We spent the evening walking through the city, watching people skate at Bryant Park, letting the cold bite at our faces. Beck told me stories about his recent travels. Some funny, some dark. He never shied away from the hard parts, but he didn't dwell on them either. I kept waiting for the other shoe to drop, but he was different. Not cured. Not perfect. But trying.

Back at my place, we ate a steak dinner then curled up on the floor with more mugs of cocoa, the little tree blinking behind us.

Beck was the one who broke the silence. "I'm not really sure how to tell you this, but I saw Hansen a few weeks ago at the grocery store."

I went still. My mug hovered halfway to my lips. "Oh."

He nodded, eyes on the tree. "He looked good. Better than I've seen him in years."

I bit down on a thousand questions and settled for an easy one. "Did you talk to him?"

"No. He didn't see me. I'm sure I could have said something, but it just didn't feel right."

I tried to keep my face blank, but Beck saw right through me. He always did. "Thea," he said quietly. "I know you still blame him for cutting ties, and I did too for a long time, but I'm realizing that I wasn't a good friend to him. I get why he walked away. Hell, I think I needed him to."

I shook my head. "You don't know what you're talking about."

He gave me a gentle but steady look. "I do. I treated him like a lifeline. Like he was supposed to save me. Just like I've done with you."

"That's not true, Beck."

"It is, and it's okay to admit that." He let out a shaky breath. "All the times I fell apart, and you had to pick up the pieces."

"It's okay. You're my brother."

He smiled, but I could see the sadness in his eyes. "Exactly. I'm your brother. Not your problem."

"Beck—"

"No, let me say this. You've been the best sister I could have ever asked for. You put up with things you never should have had to. You paid for my rehabs. You let me stay here when you were working long hours and barely making ends meet. I've made so many promises I couldn't keep. I just want you to know, I'm sorry. I'm doing better. I'm going to do better. I want you to be proud of me."

I blinked hard. "I am proud of you, Beck. I promise. And I'll always be here for you."

His face lit up, hopeful and fragile all at once. "I'm proud of you too. I want you to live the best life. I want you to get married and have kids, if you want them—" I laughed, and he smiled, "—and be a math nerd and do all the things that make you happy, whatever they are."

"I am happy," I said, hoping he believed it.

He smiled, but I could tell he was questioning me. "Then I'm happy too."

We left it at that, turning on a bad Christmas movie and spending the whole time tearing it apart, laughing so hard my stomach ached. For the first time, I let myself believe that maybe things could get better. That we could have more nights like this.

Much later, after Beck fell asleep on the couch, I stood in the doorway, watching him breathe, his hair falling into his eyes, his chest rising and falling slow and steady. I was proud of him. I hoped he knew it. But even as I watched him, I couldn't shake the gnawing thought that good things, for us, never seemed to last. Not for long.

Chapter Thirty-Seven

Now

I'm on Lucy's couch with her old plaid blanket pulled so tight around me I can hardly breathe. My hands are wrapped around a mug of tea that's gone cold. I can't even remember Lucy making it. She sits across from me, silent, her eyes swollen and worried, her whole body angled toward me like she wants to reach across the space and fix me.

The house is too quiet. The only sounds are the fridge and the distant rush of cars on the road. The ache in my chest spreads wider with each heartbeat.

Lucy waits. She doesn't push, just sits there with me while the weight of everything presses down. The flames are still dancing behind my eyes, the walls caving in, the air thick with smoke as Hansen's arms wrap around me and I fall apart. He drove me here. I barely noticed the drive. I barely noticed anything except the smell of smoke on my skin and the way my hands kept shaking.

Now I see the look in his eyes when Lucy opened the door. So worried. So desperate for help. He asked if I wanted him to stay. I almost begged him to, but instead I told him to go. I craved his comfort. I still do, but I had no words for him. I'm not sure I ever will.

When Lucy finally speaks, her voice is quiet and gentle. "Thea, do you want to talk?"

I shake my head. Talking feels impossible. I failed him. I failed Beck all over again. That cabin was the only piece of him I had left, and I killed it. My fault. It's all my fault.

There's a silence so long I almost forget Lucy's there. Then she walks into the kitchen and comes back with toast. The kind that's ridiculously buttery, just the way I like it. She sets it in front of me, her hands lingering, like she's thinking of reaching for mine but doesn't.

I stare at the toast. I can't eat. I can't move.

She sits beside me and waits.

I try to swallow the tears, but they rip out of me, anyway. They're fast, ugly, and unearthly loud. Lucy pulls me into her, and I sob so hard it hurts.

She rocks me, whispering, "You're okay. I've got you. It's okay."

But it's not. Not even close.

❧❧❧❧❧ ❦❦❦❦❦

Lucy finally fell asleep around six the next morning. I still haven't slept at all. The fire's gone, but the ache it left behind keeps burning deep.

It's hard to say how much time passes before there's a knock at the front door. I ignore it, hoping that if I stay perfectly still, whoever it is will go away. But the knock comes again, more rapid this time. I slide carefully from the bed, trying not to wake Lucy. Thankfully, she doesn't stir. I walk down the hallway and open the door.

To my shock, my parents are standing on the other side. My mom's eyes are puffy and stripped of her usual makeup. My dad looks like he hasn't slept in days.

"Thea," my mom breathes, reaching for me. She pulls me into a tight hug. "We were so scared." She pulls away, her hands fluttering to my hair, my cheeks, as if she's checking to see if I'm still real.

My dad manages a small nod before placing his hand on my shoulder. "We're so glad you're all right."

I'm not sure what to say, so I settle on, "What are you guys doing here?"

"We heard about the cabin," my mom says. "About the fire."

"It was all over the news," my dad adds.

My mom hesitates. "Can we come in?"

Can they come in? I mean, obviously they can if I let them, but do I want them to come in? I'm not really sure of anything right now, so I move aside, wordless.

The house shrinks with them inside, and the walls press in around me. In the living room, I curl up on the couch with the same plaid blanket Lucy placed on me yesterday. My mom sits close beside me, and my father takes the chair to my left.

"Why didn't you call us?" is my mother's first question.

"I'm sorry." My words dissolve into silence.

She puts her hand on my leg, and it's meant to be comforting, but it makes me want to crawl out of my skin. I think of all the times she wasn't there, how they've been ghosts in my life since Beck died, and now she's here, worried. Now she cares. Tears start to sting my eyes.

"I think you should come home with us, Thea," she says quietly. "Just for a while. Until you decide what's next."

I nearly laugh. "No."

My dad leans forward, elbows on his knees. "Thea, we could've lost you last night. After Beck . . . we just want you safe."

"We can't lose you too," my mother chokes out.

That's when something in me snaps. All the guilt and fear and anger swirl together. My voice comes out stronger than it's been in days. "Why now? Why do you care so much now?"

I look between them. "Where were you when I needed you? When everything fell apart? You spent years looking the other way. You missed my graduation, my competitions, everything. Now you—what, want to play parents?"

"Thea," my dad tries, but I shake my head.

"Just listen to me for once." The tears I thought I'd cried out start to fall again. "My whole life I wanted you to see me. I tried so hard to make you proud, to be enough. And now that Beck is gone, you act like you've been here all along."

My mom covers her mouth, crying openly. My dad moves to her side, his hand trembling on her back.

"You know how much Beck needed us," my dad says.

"I know. But I was there too. I needed you too. I was your daughter too."

Silence settles over us, thick as wet wool. Nobody moves.

When I can't take it anymore, I stand, feeling hollowed out. "I think you guys should go."

My mom nods, wiping her tears. "We're sorry, Thea. I hope . . . I hope you know that."

My father pauses at the door, his face a broken shell of the man I once knew, and I think I may shatter. But I stand strong, keeping what tears I have left inside me, and they leave without another word.

Once they're gone, I sit back down, letting the grief and anger wash over me. At first, it feels like being hollowed out and scraped raw, left with nothing but the ache. I stare at the wall, tracing the cracks in the paint, and think about every moment that led here. There's been so much pain. So much to be furious about. And I am still angry.

But as the house grows quiet again, something else flickers up from underneath it all. Something lighter. That I think might be relief. Maybe, for the first time, I don't have to pretend anymore. I don't have to keep hoping my parents will be different, or that Beck could have been fixed, or that anything I do could bring him back.

None of it can be changed. Beck is gone. My parents are who they are. There's no fixing it, and maybe there never was. I feel the truth of that settle in my chest.

But I'm still here. I'm the one left to carry it, and somehow, I am. I think of Lucy sleeping down the hall, Juniper's face when she saw those scones, of Hansen's love. The people who have shown up through all the mess. The love that's still there, under everything.

Maybe that's all life is, really. Not pretending things don't hurt, but learning to carry the hurt alongside everything else. Letting the pain and love exist right next to each other. There will be days when it's too much, when it feels like the weight could break me. But then there are moments like this, quiet and clear, where I know the love is still worth it.

Chapter Thirty-Eight

The next morning, the kitchen smells like fresh coffee and warm pancakes as I stand at the counter. Lucy sits at the table across from Juniper, the two of them deep in conversation. Juniper's hands move in quick motions, and her mother listens, just like she always does.

I let myself just stand there, soaking it all in. After everything, it's these quiet, ordinary mornings that feel the most precious. The pain and wreckage left behind by the fire will still be there tomorrow. For today, I can just be here.

I set a plate in front of Juniper, and she looks up at me, eyebrows raised. She signs, "You okay?" There's a warmth in her eyes that makes my throat tighten.

I nod, then sign back, "I will be."

Lucy smiles at me over her mug. "These are impressive pancakes," she signs, then adds aloud, "But don't let it go to your head."

Juniper rolls her eyes, but I laugh. "Don't worry, Luce. No one could ever replace yours."

Lucy arches an eyebrow, but she's pleased. "So, what should we do today? A hike? Movie marathon? Learn to Dutch braid each other's hair? Learn to Dutch braid while watching movies and then go on a hike? Actually, you know what, forget the hike and the learning something new, we should just watch movies all day in our pajamas."

The words are out before I can rethink them. "I think I'm going to talk to Hansen."

Both of the girls stare at me. I brace for their objections, their concern, but Lucy just sets her mug down and asks, "You sure?"

"I'm sure."

She smiles. "Then give him hell. But you know, in like a, loving, emotionally mature way, of course."

I lean over to kiss her on the top of her head.

Juniper smiles, signing, "Good luck, Aunt Thea."

I look at them both, all at once overwhelmed. "I love you guys. I wouldn't trade you for anything."

Lucy dabs at her eyes, pretending it's nothing, then waves me off. "Enough. Go talk to your man before I start crying again."

There's a round of hugs, and then I step out the front door. The air is crisp, and I can feel the autumn season starting to settle in. I'm halfway down the front steps when I see him.

Hansen, standing in the driveway, with that same backwards baseball hat. He looks like he hasn't slept, but his eyes—God, his eyes—are steady, and searching for me. I'm not sure how long he's been here, or what he's doing, but I don't care.

He takes a step forward, opening his mouth. "Thea, I'm so—"

I don't let him finish. I fly down the rest of the steps and close the space between us. Then, I'm kissing him with everything I have. It's not careful, not tentative. It's all the things I've been holding back, all the hope and fear and wanting. He kisses me back, and it's fierce and desperate, and everything in me breaks open.

When I finally pull away, I'm breathless. "I love you."

He laughs, the sound bursting out of him like he can't hold it in. "I love you too."

"I'm sorry. About the fire. About sending you away after. About all of it."

He shakes his head. "None of that matters now." He breaks off, looking away, and when he meets my eyes again, he's stripped bare. "I'm so sorry about our fight. About pushing you away. I thought if I punished myself enough, maybe I could fix things. Or pay for them. But I know that's not how it works. Bad things just . . . happen. I'm done running. I want to be here. With you."

It hits me all at once. The wild, impossible sense that maybe we get to want something more than just survival. "We're both a mess," I say, half-laughing, half-crying.

His dark eyes light up as he smiles. "We are. And that's okay. I don't know what the future looks like, but I know I want to spend every minute of it loving you."

I rest my forehead against his, closing my eyes. "Me too."

He lifts my head, kissing me again, softer now. It's the kind of kiss I know I'll think about until the end of time.

When we break apart, I glance at the house, where Lucy's face is pressed dramatically against the window. Hansen laughs. "They're watching us."

"We should really give them something to talk about, then."

Chapter Thirty-Nine

I'm not even halfway up the walkway when I start to regret this. The trees surrounding my parent's house have lost all their leaves, reminding me just how much time has passed. It's been months since I set foot here. Not since the funeral.

My palms are sweating, but I know I'm ready for this. I can't keep hiding. I can't keep pretending Beck's things aren't sitting in this house, waiting for me to come home.

I force myself up the steps and knock, even though it feels ridiculous considering this was my childhood home. I wait in agony and almost give in to the voice that's telling me to leave, but then the door opens.

My mom stands in the entryway, and I almost don't recognize her. There's a tiredness in her expression I've never seen before. She looks . . . broken.

She doesn't say anything. She just reaches for me and pulls me in. Her arms are thin but strong, and she buries her face in my shoulder. She smells exactly the same as I remember, and it brings up such conflicting feelings. I've spent my whole life wishing for this, for her to love me like I needed, and now that she's trying, I don't know how to react.

I nearly start crying—not for what's happening now, but for the little girl I used to be who needed her mother so badly. For all those nights I tried to be braver than I was, wondering if she'd ever notice how much I wanted her.

Then my dad appears behind her and wraps his arms around us both.

It's only been a few weeks since the fire. Since I told them to leave. I wish I could say things got better overnight, that they became the parents I always needed, but that's not how life works.

I started therapy a few days after the fire, and it was my fourth session when I felt ready enough to talk to my parents. They reached out first, and have many times since, and my therapist is helping me navigate it all. We've talked about what forgiveness and boundaries would look like. I don't know if we'll ever get there. But if they're trying, I can try, too.

My mom brushes a strand of hair behind my ear the way she used to when I was a kid. Back then, she did it because she hated when my hair was in front of my face, but this time it feels different.

"I'm so sorry," she whispers, tears already tracking down her cheeks. "I'm so, so sorry."

"I know, Mom."

We stand awkwardly in the entryway, not sure what comes next, until she finally clears her throat. "Why don't we go upstairs?"

I agree, and my legs feel heavy as I follow them both upstairs. Everything in the house feels smaller now, faded by time and grief. The runner on the steps is worn thin, and the paint on the walls is chipped and fading. Nothing's changed, and yet everything has.

We stop in front of Beck's room. The door is half open, and I can see the edge of his bedspread. It's blue, rumpled, and exactly where he left it. My mom hesitates at the door, pressing a tissue to her mouth.

"There's not much left, as you know," she says softly. "Just a few boxes. Your father's looked through most of them, but—" Her voice catches. She pushes the door open and steps inside.

I follow, and for a moment, the three of us just stand there in the room, surrounded by Beck's things. My mom kneels beside one of the boxes and brushes the cardboard, but she doesn't open it. Instead, her shoulders start to shake. She tries to stifle a sob, but it's no use.

My dad crouches beside her and rests his hand on her back. "It's okay," he whispers. "Let's go downstairs for a minute."

My mom looks up at me with red eyes. "I'm sorry, honey. I thought I could."

I shake my head. "It's okay, Mom. I've got it."

She squeezes my hand, then lets go. My dad nods at me before giving my shoulder a squeeze. "Let us know if you need anything," he says before gently steering my mother out of the room. I watch them go, my mom's quiet crying trailing down the hall and out of sight.

Suddenly, I'm alone. With Beck's room waiting for me.

The air is stale, all traces of Beck's smell gone with time. Sunlight falls in thin stripes through the blinds, showing off the dust that has started to collect. On the nightstand is a stack of books and a chipped mug I recognize from my childhood. The desk is cleared, but there are a couple of shirts folded neatly on the desk chair.

On the floor, there are three cardboard boxes taped shut and each labeled with just one word: Room.

I sit on the edge of the bed. The mattress sags under my weight. I run my fingers over the blanket, tracing the threadbare pattern. My mom's muffled crying drifts down the hallway, but I can't move. I just sit, staring at the boxes, willing myself to open them.

Finally, I reach for the first box. Inside is an array of clothes, a pair of battered headphones, and a notebook with a cracked spine. At the bottom is a photo album filled with childhood pictures. I flip through the pages, my sudden tears dripping onto the plastic sleeves.

The second box is mostly papers. Old report cards, receipts, a few letters in my mom's slanted handwriting. There's a hospital bracelet, a crumpled pack of cigarettes, a half-empty bottle of cologne. Relics of a life stopped too early.

The third box is heavier. I drag it closer and kneel on the floor. Right on top is another notebook. This one seems worn and soft. The corners are bent, and the cover is nearly falling off. I pick it up, thumbing through the pages. Most are blank, but a few have some half-finished lists. In the middle, I find a sheet of paper. It's folded and stuck to the lined paper.

I peel it off carefully and open it. Beck's handwriting is steadier here, and the date at the top makes my breath catch. December 18th, 2024. Five months before he died. My hands shake so badly I almost drop it.

I grip it tighter and start reading.

Dear Thea,

It's Christmas, and I'm at your apartment in New York. You're at work right now, and I just felt like I needed someone to talk to. This trip has been amazing. It feels different. But I can tell that every time you look at me, you think I'm going to break, and I guess I can't blame you. I'm waiting for me to break too.

I've been sober for nearly a year. Can you believe it? Sometimes I can't. I want it to stick so badly this time, Thea. I want to be different. For you. For Mom and Dad. For myself. I don't know what's wrong with me. Every day feels like such a battle. Drinking makes it better. It makes the chaos in my head feel so much better. My therapist would say that I need to learn healthy coping skills, ones that aren't drinking, and I've tried. Jesus, I've tried. I guess that's what I want you to know more than anything. That I've tried.

Maybe when you get home, I'll convince you to move back to South Creek with me. We can fix up Grandpa's cabin like I've always wanted. We can start over. Maybe change our names and pretend like the last thirty years haven't happened. Be the sitcom siblings we were meant to be. I hope you're happy, Thea. You deserve to be. More than anyone I know.

I love you more than I can ever say.
Beck

I clutch the letter to my chest, letting sobs escape me that feel like they might tear me open. The guilt is a living thing, curling in my stomach, twisting around my ribs. I know I'll feel it forever. But after reading the letter, I can almost see Beck sitting here with me. He's smiling, and I know he's okay.

The grief washes over me, and I let it. I allow myself to feel every emotion. Then I cry for my parents, for Beck, and most of all, for myself.

Chapter Forty

Fall comes and goes until suddenly it's November. Somewhere in the middle of it all, after the fire department clears it, I finally work up the nerve to go back to the cabin.

Hansen and I drive out on a warm afternoon. The closer I get, the more my heart pounds, the grief and dread all tangled together. Even though I knew it was gone, even though I saw it burn with my own eyes, when we get there, it's surreal. There's nothing left. Just blackened beams and a few warped pieces of metal sticking out of the ground where the kitchen used to be. I walk around the wreckage, looking for something, anything, but there's nothing left to take, nothing to save.

It's hard, harder than I expected. But Hansen and I are together.

Thanksgiving rolls around and looks a bit different. Less like a tradition, more like something we're all learning how to do again. Winnie invites my parents to her place, and to everyone's surprise, they actually show up. The dinner is huge, and the house is noisy with friends and relatives. Hansen is there, and when our eyes meet across the table, he smiles at me. And I smile back.

December arrives, and I keep going to therapy every week. Some days it's a battle just to walk through the door, but I can feel the difference it's making in my life. I'm learning that I can be angry, or sad, and still be okay.

I notice the changes in Hansen, too. He's softer with himself now. We talk about everything. Our darkest thoughts, our biggest fears, all the things he used to keep hidden. When he feels that old urge to punish himself, he talks to me instead. He's not perfect at it, and neither am I. We both have our hard days, but we're both getting better.

We spend as much time together as we can. We talk, we laugh, and at night, when it's just us in the darkness, we find comfort in each other.

So when the last two weeks pass without seeing each other once, it's torture. My schedule has been overloaded with work and school, and he's been taking extra shifts at the station.

Then one particularly cold night, while I'm hunched over textbooks, there's a tapping against my window. I wait for a second, thinking it must have been a bird or something, but then it comes again. I go to the window and laugh when I spot Hansen outside all bundled in his coat and tossing pebbles up at the glass. I grab my phone and dial his number.

He answers before the first ring even finishes.

"What are you doing?" I ask.

His face lights up. "Open your window and find out."

"It's snowing. And freezing."

There's a sparkle in his dark eyes. "Are you scared of a little snow, Thea?"

I hang up and crank the window open. "Are you seriously throwing rocks at my window?"

He smiles up at me. "Yes."

I roll my eyes. "Get in here."

It takes him only a few seconds to run to the front door where I'm already waiting. When he steps inside, he shakes the snow from his hair, and the room is filled with his familiar scent and warmth. He pulls me into his arms, and we just hold each other.

"I've missed you," I murmur.

"I've missed you too."

He kisses me, and it's so slow and perfect that it sends shivers down my arms. I deepen the kiss, moving my arms around his neck.

"I didn't come here for this," he says, smiling against my lips.

"Why not? Lucy's working. Juniper's at her dad's. Seems like the perfect time."

He laughs, pulling his lips away from mine. "I came because I just got word that Cap is getting married. Tomorrow night."

I give him a surprised look.

"Yeah, we were all surprised too. Apparently, they eloped last week and decided to have an intimate reception at the firehouse," he explains.

"That's kind of adorable."

"Incredibly, and I want you to come with me."

I press a soft kiss to his lips. "And be your date?"

He slides his hands slowly down my back. "And be my date."

"In front of all your coworkers?"

He stops at my waist, pulling me closer. "You've already met most of them."

"Yeah, but this time it's serious."

"It's always been serious, Thea."

There's a fluttering in my stomach. "I'd love to go with you."

He tightens his grip on me. "And I love you."

I step out of his hold and raise an eyebrow. "Prove it."

He doesn't hesitate, just scoops me up and slings me over his shoulder. I let out a startled laugh as he heads for my bedroom. "With pleasure."

———— ❦❦❦❦ ————

The night of the reception, I'm still fussing with my dress when the doorbell rings. My hands are shaking as I smooth down the deep green fabric, checking my reflection for the tenth time.

"You look incredible," Lucy says from the doorway, leaning against the frame. "Hansen's not going to know what hit him."

"You think?" I ask, nervously biting my lip. It may be freezing outside, but the room feels about a thousand degrees. "Man, is it hot in here or just me?"

Lucy comes over and sets her hands on my shoulders. "Thea, deep breath."

I breathe in. Then out.

"Good. Now repeat after me: I'm a smoke show badass with the confidence of every white man the second they sit in front of a microphone."

I give her a look, but she just waits. "Say it."

With a sigh, I repeat it: "I'm a smoke show badass with the confidence of every white man the second they sit in front of a microphone."

Lucy beams. "That's my girl."

"You look gorgeous too, Lucy," I say. She's wearing a deep blue dress that sparkles when it catches the perfect light. Her curly hair is pinned up with just a few loose, dark curls falling around her face.

She puts her hands on her hips, smirking. "I know."

"You sure you want to go?"

It was technically Riggins who asked her to come in the first place. And to my surprise, she said yes.

We haven't spoken much about Lucy's feelings toward Riggins since the night of her date with Archie. Every time I try and bring it up, she tells me she's okay. I don't believe her, but I know she'll tell me when she's ready.

"I'm sure," she says. "It's an excuse to wear this dress. Plus, I know Captain Martinez loves shrimp, so, ex-husband or not, if there's free shrimp, I'm going."

"You don't have to pretend like it doesn't hurt to see him."

She fiddles with the neckline of her dress. "I know. But it's time I move on from him, and hiding won't make it go away."

"If you want to bail, I'll get you out of there. No questions asked."

"I know you will." Lucy steps forward and wraps me in a hug. "Thank you, Thea."

"Always," I say, squeezing her tight.

Lucy finally pulls back. "We should probably get the door. It's been, like, five minutes."

We laugh again before heading downstairs. The cold air rushes in as I open the door. Hansen is dressed in his uniform, with his hair combed back perfectly. My mouth goes dry.

"Wow," he says, eyes flicking from my face to my heels and back up, lingering in all the right places. "You look beautiful."

"Thank you." I wrap my arms around his neck so I can whisper, "And you look devastatingly handsome."

He smirks before closing the gap between us and kissing me. The world shrinks down to just the two of us, and suddenly my dress feels too tight and my skin too warm.

"Maybe going is a bad idea," he says against my lips.

"Yeah? And what's a better one?"

"I could think of a few."

"If you two are done being disgustingly cute," Lucy calls from behind us, "some of us have a wedding and endless shrimp to get to."

Hansen laughs, and I reluctantly drop my arms from his neck. Thankfully, he fills the void by putting his hand on my back.

"Hey, Lucy," he says. "You look wonderful."

Lucy beams. "Why thank you, Reed. You're looking especially good tonight yourself."

"You ready to go?"

She shakes her head. "Oh, don't worry. I called a ride. There's no way I wanted to interrupt this."

"You aren't interrupting us, Lucy," I say.

She squeezes my arm. "Don't worry about me, honey. Just enjoy your alone time." She grabs her coat. "Now, you two can take your time making out in my entryway like two teenagers, but just don't let the actual teenager see you, okay?"

Lucy blows us both a kiss, then leans in to whisper in my ear. "I'm so happy for you, Thea."

We choose not to stay and make out in the entryway on account of how cold it is outside. Instead, we drive to the station in near quiet, stealing glances and half-smiles at each other. His thumb traces circles on my skin the entire time, and I worry that my cheeks will be so red when we get there, everyone will know what I'm thinking.

When we arrive at the venue, I'm stunned. There are string lights hung from the ceiling, turning the space into a sparkling wonderland. The tables around the room are draped with white tablecloths, contrasting against the red flowers in the centerpieces.

Riggins finds us as soon as we walk in. "Miller! You look amazing." He turns to Hansen next to me. "And you," he grabs his shoulders and nearly shakes him. "I should have known you'd show up looking like a god." He looks behind us. "Where's Lucy?"

"She took a separate car," I say.

Riggins barely hears me since he's already scanning the room looking for her. "Yeah? Hope she—" His words cut off as the doors open and Lucy steps inside. I think he may actually stop breathing for a second. "Well, damn. Talk about making an entrance."

Lucy crosses the room, oozing confidence in every step, her dress catching the light. Riggins straightens as she approaches, suddenly looking way less cocky than he did a minute ago.

"Luce," he says, his eyes not leaving hers for a second.

"Riggins."

"Thanks for being my date tonight."

Lucy arches a brow, smiling. "Oh, don't get it confused, I just wanted an excuse to wear this dress."

"And get free shrimp," I remind her.

"Yes, that too."

Riggins smiles while offering her his arm. "Well, in that case, can I escort you to the shrimp? And maybe a drink?"

Lucy hesitates briefly, and I can tell she's weighing everything. I watch and wait for any signs that she wants to bail, but ultimately, she slips her hand through his arm.

"Lead the way," she says.

"Those two are either going to kill each other or hook up before the night is over," Hansen says quietly enough that only I can hear it.

I look up at him. "Do you think Riggins is still in love with her?" I wouldn't call Hansen and Riggins best friends, but they do work together. And Riggins loves to talk.

Hansen meets my gaze. "Of course he is."

We wait in line to greet the newly married couple, and they're glowing so brightly it's contagious.

"Thea, it's great to see you again," Martinez says. "This is my new bride, Susan."

"It's lovely to meet you," I say to her. "This reception is beautiful, and so is your dress."

She beams. "Thank you. It's nice to finally put a face to the name I've heard Hansen mention so many times."

I raise an eyebrow at Hansen, who only shrugs, unashamed. "Not even going to deny it."

"Thank you for including me," I say.

"Anyone in Hansen's life is family," Susan responds warmly.

Captain Martinez gives Hansen a fatherly pat on the shoulder. "I'm happy for you, son. For both of you."

"Thanks, Cap."

As we walk away, Hansen puts his hand on the small of my back and whispers, "Dance with me?"

I nod, and he leads me onto the floor. My hand fits perfectly in his, and I press the other to his chest while he rests his on my waist.

"What are you thinking?" I ask him after one song turns into another.

He leans in, his lips brushing my ear. "That I really want to kiss you right now."

"What's stopping you?"

He nods toward the crowd. "About fifty pairs of eyes, including my captain's."

I glance around. He's right. Everyone is watching. Even Riggins, who's openly gawking from the sidelines. Lucy is the only one standing at the table, ignoring us and actively shoveling shrimp into her mouth. "You'd think they've never seen you with someone before."

"Because they haven't," Hansen says quietly.

My heart does a flip as he guides me across the floor.

"Do you think we would have found each other again?" I ask suddenly. "If Beck hadn't died and left us the cabin?"

Hansen pulls me closer. "It might have taken me too long, but I would have found my way back to you. Always."

Warmth spreads through me, and the butterflies I've been feeling all night in my stomach are too intense to ignore. "We should sneak out. Go somewhere with fewer spectators."

He raises a playful eyebrow. "Yeah?"

"Yeah. I mean, only if we can slip out without being noticed. I don't want to be rude."

Hansen's eyes light up. "I'm sure they won't miss us for a second."

"Well, I hope it's more than a second."

Hansen smirks and, instead of answering, dips his head and presses a quick kiss to my shoulder, right where the dress leaves my skin bare. It's soft, barely there, but it speaks more than anything he could have said. "Always with the jokes," he whispers against my skin.

The song ends, and I pull away. Hansen then grabs my hand and starts guiding me through the crowd and toward the door.

"Thea!" Lucy calls out from the food table, causing us to stop. "You have to come try this shrimp. It's mouthwatering."

I laugh and turn to Hansen. He rolls his eyes, but there's a smile on his face, too. "Let's go."

At the food table, Riggins greets us with a proud smile. "Man, watching you two out there got me hotter than my high school prom night."

Hansen flips him off.

Riggins only winks. "Your rejection only makes me stronger, baby."

I consider trying the shrimp and then dragging Hansen home, but then Riggins says something, and Lucy laughs so hard she nearly spits out her drink. Then Captain Martinez and Susan join us, and soon everyone is at the table talking.

So, we stay. We eat, we dance some more, and we let ourselves just be part of it. And for the rest of the night, I'm happy.

Epilogue

After the new year, Dr. Fisher, my therapist, recommends that I write a letter to Beck. Tell him all the things I didn't get a chance to say when he was alive. Hansen joins me, and when we finish, we seal them and place them in the same box as the letters my brother and I once shared.

It's now been a year since the cabin burned to the ground, and I can honestly say, each day, things feel a little . . . less. My heart still aches—God, does it ache sometimes—but neither Hansen nor I are running from it anymore. When I'm angry at Beck, I scream at nothing. When grief pins me to my bed, I let myself cry. And sometimes, I eat ice cream in the bathtub while watching *How I Met Your Mother* reruns because that's what I need that day. There are good days when I can think of Beck and only feel light. Days when I'm excited to get up and face what comes next. Days when a year ago felt like the farthest possible thing. And there are ones filled with darkness.

The grief isn't going anywhere, and I don't want it to. Healing isn't a straight line, and sometimes when I think I'm going the right way, something will trip me up and make me fall again. And that's okay, because I know how to get back up.

For now, the plot of land where the cabin once stood remains empty. We've had our fair share of ideas of what to do with it, but none have felt right quite yet. But that's okay. Once a week, we go out there and have a picnic on the grass. We tell stories about Beck, look at pictures, just try and remember him. My parents have even joined a time or two. It's not perfect with them, but it's something.

Last night, Hansen got off his twenty-four-hour shift, and I was waiting for him the second he walked in the door. He wasted no time picking me up and dragging me to his bedroom, where we spent the next few hours making up for all the time we've lost.

There's some slight movement in the bed, and it pulls me out of sleep. When I open my eyes, the sun is just starting to slip through the white curtains. I'm on my stomach, my face pressed into the pillow. Hansen's just a few inches away, propped up on his elbow, watching me. It's not unusual to wake up to Hansen staring at me, but today there's something different in his eyes. He's smiling, but there's a flicker of nerves there too.

"Good morning," I mumble, burrowing deeper into the pillow.

He just looks at me for a moment, then reaches over and tucks a stray piece of hair behind my ear.

"I want to ask you something," he says, and his tone is unsettling.

I move my head up. "You're being weird."

He laughs. "I mean it. I was thinking—"

"You're not proposing, are you?" My heart picks up. "Not that I'd say no if you did, I just—I thought we wanted to wait until I graduated and—"

He covers my mouth gently with his hand. "Thea. Let me finish."

I roll my eyes and nudge his hand away. He just smiles.

"I was just thinking, since you're already here ninety percent of the time anyway, and your lease is up soon, maybe you should just move in with me. Officially."

I blink, completely caught off guard. Not by the question itself—we'd talked about moving in together a million times—but because of how suddenly possible it feels.

"Yes," I say. "I'd like that."

He leans over and kisses me. Then he raises an eyebrow. "So, you'd say yes if I proposed?"

I groan and lunge at him, rolling us both into a tangle of sheets. He laughs, pulling me close.

"I guess you'll have to wait and see."

"I guess we will."

He kisses me again, and the morning dissolves around us.

If I've learned anything in my thirty-one years of living, it's that life can be a real bitch. Grief doesn't end, it just takes new shape, becoming something you carry instead of something that carries you. The sharp edges soften, but the missing stays. And maybe that's how it should be, this quiet ache that reminds me how deeply I loved Beck. These days, I can laugh without feeling guilty. I can make plans for tomorrow without thinking I'm betraying what happened yesterday. I can love without pretending that it's ever perfect or painless, but always knowing it's worth it.

I've learned that the world keeps spinning in its stubbornly beautiful way, and I can keep finding ways to be in it—not without Beck, but because of him.

The End

Dear Beck,

Thea and I decided to write you letters. She says it's supposed to help, and honestly, I think it will. We're supposed to say all the things we would if you were still here. So, I'm going to try.

First off, I'm sorry. God, Beck, I am so fucking sorry. Sorry that I wasn't there when you needed me most. Sorry I walked away that day. The truth is, watching you destroy yourself was killing me too. I know you wanted to stop; I know you tried. But I was angry. Angry at you for pushing everyone away, for hurting Thea, for hurting me. And then I'd feel guilty for being angry, because I knew you were struggling. I'm only now realizing that sometimes, two things can be true at once. And that love isn't always enough to save someone. I hope you knew I loved you anyway. I wish I'd reached out again, fought harder, done something, anything, to keep you here.

Your friendship meant everything to me. My biggest regret is that you ever felt so alone. If I could've taken even a piece of your pain, I would've. Every damn day.

I hope you're at peace now. You deserve that. Thea and I, we miss you. There's not a day that goes by that we don't.

Speaking of Thea, and I know this won't come as a shock to you in the slightest, but I'm in love with your sister. Like, really, truly in love. She's sitting across from me right now, writing her own letter to you, and it just feels right. I think you knew—hell, maybe that's why you left us both the cabin. (You can stop smirking now, you smug bastard.) She makes me better, Beck. She's taught me it's okay to hold on to something good, to stop running from pain. I'll take care of her, I promise. For as long as I have the privilege of living, I'll love her enough for the both of us.

I miss you, man. Promise me you'll be waiting for me with open arms.
With Love,
Hansen

Dear Beck,

Shit. This is so much harder than I thought. I guess I should start out by explaining myself. My therapist said that we should write a letter to you for some kind of closure. That I should say all the things I would say if you were standing in front of me one last time. At first, I thought I would just scream at you. Tell you how angry I am that you're gone. That I'm so mad at you for giving up. For not fighting harder. For leaving me after everything I did. But there's another side. A side that wants to say just how sorry I am. Sorry that we weren't closer. Sorry that you got handed the life you did. Life wasn't always easy for either of us, Beck, and I don't think that was very fair.

I thought I owed it to you to fix this cabin. That it would somehow bring you back. Or bring you peace wherever you are, but I don't think that's why you left it to me. I think you left it to me so that I could come home. So that I could finally choose myself.

I miss you, Beck. Every single day. I know we weren't perfect, but I know you tried as hard as you could. There are still days I don't understand why you had to go. I don't think I will ever fully understand, and that's okay. If you were here now, I would tell you just how much I love you.

Also, I wanted to let you know that your plan worked. I'm in love with Hansen. Even when you aren't here, you're trying to play little matchmaker. I'll spare you the details (for now), but just know that he loves me in a way that would make you proud.

Mom and Dad are okay. It's not easy. There is a lot of hurt there, a lot of years to make up for, but they're trying. Also, I know you kept my letters, you sneaky little bastard.

which I think is what you wanted me to find. Some nights, I stay up and read them for hours, imagining what you might have been thinking while you were reading them. It's the closest thing I have to seeing you again.

I hope wherever you are, Beck, you're happy. This world is hard, and I understand how you couldn't live in it anymore.

I love you. And the second I get to see you again, you better be ready to hear ALL about Hansen and me. It's what you deserve.

I'll write to you soon.

with all of my love,

Thea

P.S. The cabin burned down. I'll explain later.

Acknowledgements

Wow. As I'm sitting here writing this at nearly midnight, I can't believe it's actually going in the back of my debut novel. This feels like it's been a long time coming, and I'm so grateful Thea and Hansen's story gets to be the first one I share with the world. Ever since I could read, I knew I wanted to be a writer. In middle school, I started writing on Wattpad (lol), and it was honestly the best time of my life. I'd write stories with my friends or for my friends, and I truly learned how much writing meant to me. I knew I wanted to do this forever. (Madi knew who she was at a young age. iykyk.)

As an adult, I've written several full-length novels, but it didn't take me long to know this would be the first one I'd share with the world. Fifteen years ago, I was talking with my brother-in-law Dan about reading and writing, and I told him I wanted to write a book someday and be someone's favorite author. I thought maybe he'd make fun of me (the curse of being the youngest of a lot of siblings), but he didn't. Instead, he said, "I think you'll be a great author someday." I'll never forget that.

I stopped writing when I was nineteen, letting that piece of me a die a little, but I found it again later, and I'm so thankful I did. I'll always be grateful for those early drafts of books I forced all my friends to read. (Sorry, guys.)

When deciding what I wanted my debut novel to be, I knew I wanted to write about grief. Fourteen years ago, that same brother-in-law I mentioned took his own life, and it changed the way my own life looked forever. Since then, I've been no stranger to grief or suicide. It's such a complicated and complex topic, and I wanted to share how truly difficult it is—especially when you bring love into the story.

Now, in no particular order, I want to thank all the amazing people in my life.

First, my cousin Ellen and soul sister. There's so much to say to you and not nearly enough paper to print it all. I wouldn't be anything without your support and love. Thanks for listening to me talk about books and book ideas until the cows come home. I'm sorry for always changing up the storyline after letting you read it. I wish I could say that will change, but no promises. Thanks for never giving up on yourself or on me. Also, thanks for always catching the times when I write "expect" instead of "except."

My bestie since day one (and editor), Haley. She spent hours on the phone with me while I crashed out, working through so many things about this book (for free), and then helped me make sure there were no typos (so if there are, blame her—lol). I can't thank her enough. (See you for book 2?? lol)

Catherine Jones. Our endless yap sessions about writing and reading are a huge part of why this book exists, and why I exist. You are truly such a light in my life, and I'm so grateful we found each other all those years ago. Let's keep killing it. (Also, please write that book. You know which one I'm talking about.)

Lisa. I can't forget you, girl. Thanks for always being there, even when you had a stroke lol. Thanks for always listening and never judging. Even when I talk your ears off about politics for hours. Keep being the kind, wonderful friend that you are.

A huge thank you to Kathryn, my developmental editor, who saw a book that needed a lot of work and gave me the exact guidance I needed to turn it into one I'm so proud of. I don't know how you do it, but your words will forever be with me.

Even though it'll be a LONG time (or never) until my kids read this book, I want to thank them for being so patient during all this. Having their mom locked away to write is never easy, and I hope they see me following my dreams and do the same one day.

To all my beta readers and writing friends I've met online during this process (and my writing group at the library!), thank you for your friendship, encouragement, and support. I can't wait to see where the world takes us.

Sam (the girl I met at Emily Rath's book signing), you're fucking awesome, girl. Thanks for following me on Instagram, and I hope you've enjoyed learning what "why choose" and "sword crossing" are.

Thank you to my parents. I'm one hundred percent sure I don't want them to read this book (especially not chapter 30), but I also feel like I can't stop you, ha. Thank you for always supporting me in my dreams. I know I haven't always been the easiest daughter (I come with A LOT of opinions), but you have never made me feel bad for wanting something big for myself. Mom, you've taught me to keep going, even when it's the hardest thing in the world. I owe so much of my passion for life to you. Thank you. Dad, any good grammar skills that I have come from you. And any of my good writing comes from after you fed me on Wednesdays.

To my sister Jess, who was dealt the hard hand of losing someone she loved far too young. I'm not sure how you'll feel about this book, but I hope you know that I love you.

To the rest of my siblings and family members who have supported me in this and so many other things, thank you.

I'd like to also acknowledge the back problems I've developed from sitting like a deflated balloon in my bed for hours on end to write this thing—I know you'll be with me forever. Also, Dr. Pepper. Where would the world be without you?

Thank you to my husband Jason. I could write an entire 100,000-word novel on how supportive you've been, but this will just have to do. Thank you for listening to eight million different storylines and helping me make sense of them all. Thank you for being a therapist so you can tell me exactly why a character would do what they do. You are my number one fan, and I hope you know that I could never do this without your love and support.

I'd also like to thank myself. Because writing a book is really fucking hard. You did it, girl. Be proud.

And also a huge thank you to you, my reader (did you make this far? Geez, someone take this keyboard away from me). I hope this is the start of a beautiful friendship, one that lasts forever. I'm so grateful that you're here and willing to listen to Thea and Hansen's story.

If you liked Lucy and Riggins (yes, his name is a tribute to Tim Riggins. Clear eyes, full hearts, can't lose), then stay tuned for their story. Coming 2026!

Find me on TikTok or Instagram if you want to be friends! I hope to see you there!

About the Author

Madi J. Anderson has always been a hopeless romantic, devouring and secretly writing romance stories long before she was technically old enough. Now, she brings her love of happily-ever-afters (with some hardships along the way) to life as an author. When she's not being a mom to her three kids, or talking with her husband, she's tucked away somewhere, writing swoon-worthy stories for anyone who believes in love.

www.ingramcontent.com/pod-product-compliance
Lightning Source LLC
Chambersburg PA
CBHW010736130726
47899CB00015B/3286